Quicksands

by

B. M. Croker

Double 9
BOOKS

Quicksands
by B. M. Croker

ISBN: 978-93-64288-63-7

Published by

DOUBLE 9 BOOKS

2/13-B, Ansari Road
Daryaganj, New Delhi – 110002
info@double9books.com
www.double9books.com
Tel. 011-40042856

ABOUT THE AUTHOR

Bithia Croker born on November 6, 1849, Mary Croker, s(
known as B. M. Croker, was a British author who died on October
During the late 19th and early 20th centuries, she was a well-kr
prolific writer who was well-known for her captivating novels
stories. Croker lived a significant portion of her life in India, '
husband was a British Army soldier. Her experiences there had a
effect on her work. Her paintings frequently portrayed the life
expatriates in India, providing realistic depictions of the peopl(
and natural surroundings of the area. Croker's writing was dis
by its intricate character development, captivating narratives,
descriptions. Croker was a prolific writer whose works we
during her lifetime. She wrote over 50 novels and numerous sl
contributing significantly to the genre of popular fiction in the l;
early 20th centuries. B.M. Croker's legacy is marked by her c(
to popular fiction, her exploration of social themes, and her im
contemporary readers and future writers. Her works remain a
her talent and the significant role she played in 19th and early
literature.

CONTENTS

CHAPTER I
THE BRIDGE OF DREAMS

One sultry September afternoon, some years ago, my brother Ronald and I, being tired and dusty, found a temporary resting-place on the parapet of a little old bridge that spanned a sleepy stream. Through a thin silk blouse a comforting sun beat upon my back, and I was serenely conscious of an unusual sense of happiness and well-being—though I owed little to my surroundings. In all England it would have been difficult to find a more featureless and monotonous outlook than the prospect that lay stretched before us. A series of flat, marshy fields, exhibiting here a space of willowy green, and there a patch of black soil, enclosed by ragged hedges or deep, dark dykes. Occasionally a few lonely and distorted trees, or a humped-up cluster of red roofs, varied the scene, which gradually faded until sky and horizon seemed to melt away into one pale blur.

"What a region!" exclaimed Ronnie, as he tossed away the stump of a cigarette. "The back of beyond, the Land of Never Never! Never again, so far as I am concerned! Who discovered it?"

"It was discovered by the Danes, I believe," I answered; "they say it was once under the sea."

"A pity it did not stay there!"

"It's rather cheerful now, and the air is splendid; but you should see it in winter, when it has a grey, weird, starving sort of look, and the face of the country is like a dead thing."

"Well, thank goodness, I am spared that," rejoined Ronnie. "I shall be out in the nice sultry East, sunning myself among the big red boulders that are scattered round Secunderabad."

"And you start on Friday? Oh, Ronnie, I believe you are *glad* to go back!"

"Yes; I am jolly glad, only for leaving you, old girl—and in such a hole as Beke. My leave has gone like a flash; just a month at home. I must say it is a beastly shame they did not ask you to Torrington when I was there."

"Aunt Mina sees as little of me as possible—she does not like me, and is at no pains to conceal the fact. The girls and I have never what you call 'got on'; we have nothing in common. You see I am much younger than they are."

"And so much better looking," supplemented my brother.

Waving aside his compliment, I continued:

"You know, when I first went to Torrington I was a small child, and by all accounts dreadfully spoiled; later on, in the holidays, I was too young to appear in company, and was generally hustled out of sight. My goodness, but it was dull, all alone, in the old nursery! Coming down to lunch as a treat, cross-examined and snubbed by the girls, and overawed by Aunt Mina—she had a way of looking at me that made me feel as if I had no clothes on!"

"My dear Eva, don't be improper!"

"You see," I resumed—now comfortably embarked on a flowing tide of talk, and eager to impart my confidence to a sympathetic ear—"I can realise what a nuisance I was in those days. The house was full of grown-ups and smart people, and I was just a lanky girl who slunk in to lunch or was met roaming about the grounds! Then twice I brought home infection, and gave most of the establishment mumps and chicken-pox—so you can't wonder that I was not popular! After all, I am only Aunt Mina's niece by marriage; Uncle is nice to me in his cheery, vague, irresponsible way, but he has no *say*. Living in the nursery, I naturally heard a good deal of backstairs talk, and gathered that Aunt manages everything—even to evicting tenants and arranging the shoots."

"Oh, come! I don't think it is as bad as all that," protested Ronnie; "though of course a man who marries half a million must pay *some* sort of interest. The family were in very deep water, when potted meat came along and hauled them out. When were you last at Torrington?"

"Two years ago this Christmas."

Ronnie was about to exclaim, but I put my hand over his mouth.

"Do let *me* talk," I pleaded. "I want to tell you things I can't write. It was the Christmas before last. I was in long frocks with my hair up, and had just left Cheltenham. I caught a slight cold on the journey, but was nevertheless in the wildest spirits, full of anticipation of the delights that awaited me now that I was officially fledged."

"Yes, yes," interrupted Ronnie impatiently; "that is all stale news."

"The evening after I arrived there was a dinner party, and I happened by good luck to sit next to a charming man, who was very agreeable, and no doubt drew me out. A lively girl sat opposite to us; she had a loud voice, and talked the most ridiculous nonsense, much appreciated by Beverley, her neighbour.

"'What is your family disease?' she asked him; 'ours is softening of the bones.' And Bev replied:

"'Our hereditary disease is gambling.'

"'Which leads,' said the girl, 'to softening of the *brain*!'"

I paused, turned to my brother, and said:

"Did you ever hear that there was gambling in the Lingard family?"

"There's a taste for gambling in every family," he answered evasively. "Well, go on about your dinner party. What happened?"

"I am afraid I allowed my spirits to get the better of me, for I laughed and chattered incessantly. I know I always talk too much."

"No doubt of that—when you get the chance," corroborated my listener.

"I pulled crackers, put on paper caps, exchanged mottoes and poetry, and in short enjoyed myself enormously. Afterwards, when the men came into the drawing-room, my dinner friend found me out at once, and at his suggestion we retired into an obscure corner, in order to cement our acquaintance. All at once I began to notice that the surrounding atmosphere was chilly: I saw my cousins whispering together, and I believe Clara summoned her mother, for presently Aunt Mina swooped upon us, and told my companion that she had something she particularly wished to show him, and, in spite of his obvious reluctance, she took him in charge, and marched him off. A significant glance assured me that I was in deep disgrace, and when people had settled down to music or bridge I stole away to bed."

"Best place for you," interposed Ronnie.

"I was woke out of my first sleep by Clara, who came into my room, candle in hand, wearing her most venomous expression; the visit was on purpose to inform me that she 'was really *sorry* I had made such a dreadful exhibition of myself at dinner, laughing and screaming at the top of my voice, pulling crackers, sticking things in my hair, altogether behaving like a shop girl'! I heard no more beyond a murmur, as I covered up my head with the bed clothes. When at last I was compelled to emerge from want of air, the room was in darkness, and my cousin had disappeared. As my cold was pretty bad I was confined to my old quarters, the nursery, and there I remained for several days. Beverley, just home from Eton, used to come and sit with me, and bring me the news. He informed me that Major Halliday, my charming friend, had been making tender inquiries after me, adding:

'I suppose you didn't happen to know that he is by way of being Clara's young man—she had all but landed him!'

"Bev befriended me—supplied me with magazines and chocolates, but when he began to make love to me—that was another pair of shoes!"

"So I should think—the moon-faced idiot!" commented Ronnie.

"Well, one afternoon he tried to kiss me, and was actually chasing me round the table, when Aunt Mina entered. She was furious. Bev fled headlong, and on me she poured all the vials of her wrath. She said I was a bold, designing minx, a disgrace to the family. For once I protested, and protested with fury—assured her that I loathed the sight of Bev, and never wished to see him again—no, nor anyone at Torrington! Naturally I was soon squashed. Aunt was too strong for me, and the scene ended in humiliation and tears. Possibly my prolonged weeping increased my cold, which presently developed alarmingly. The local doctor (Aunt Mina's slave) was summoned. He talked gravely about pneumonia, and my lungs, and announced that I had a delicate chest, and must on *no* account remain at Torrington—the place was too low and enervating—so I was promptly packed off to Beke, where I have been ever since!"

"Great Scott!" exclaimed Ronnie. "Why, it is a sort of countrified Bastille. How on earth did Aunt Mina discover it?"

"Quite easily," I replied. "Miss Puckle was the girls' governess when I was small. I remember her well; so trim and punctual, and authoritative, with a trick of pulling down her belt if she was going to be disagreeable, but always indulgent to me. When I was in trouble I used to sit on her lap and just sob and sob."

"I wonder you don't do it now," said Ronnie.

"I am afraid I am a size too large. As for Beke, some years ago an old relation died and left a fine legacy and 'The Roost' between Lizzie and her uncle the professor, so they retired together, and are now in what is called 'easy circumstances.' I contribute a hundred a year."

"You are humbugging! Why, they ought to pay *you* as companion—and lady help."

"Aunt arranged everything; she declared I could not be better off than at 'The Roost.' The doctor particularly recommended this marshy air, with a dash of sea, she said, and I might continue my music and sketching with Lizzie—who would finish me properly."

"Finish you indeed!" cried Ronnie, "I wonder Beke has not finished you long ago. Hallo, I say, who are the riders coming down the road? Shall I put my arm round your neck and pretend I am your sweetheart, and give the poor natives a fresh piece of gossip?"

"Put your arm round my neck if you like, but all the village knows that you are my brother, my only near relation. Clarice has a cousin at 'The Beetle,' which is our newsagency."

"Clarice," repeated Ronnie, "is that the shuffling parlour-maid with the cock eye?"

"She is a capital servant," I replied, "and sees as much as three. Here come the Soadys."

"Who are they?—tell me quickly," urged Ronnie.

"Sam Soady and his daughter. She is the only girl I know in these parts, and has been my great stand-by. He is a rich farmer, sells cattle and horses, and lives in an old manor house the other side of Beke."

Almost before I concluded, the Soadys were upon us, a fine, solid, up-sitting pair, with the same open countenances, ruddy cheeks and blue eyes. As they halted, Tossie cried out:

"Hallo, Eva, fancy seeing you roosting beside the road!"

"Yes, my brother says I have walked him off his legs. Let me introduce him to you. Mr. Lingard, Miss Soady, and Mr. Soady."

The latter touched his cap and said in his loud, hoarse voice:

"Not much to see in these parts, sir!"

"No, I have not come across anything to touch your two gees; fine weight-carriers," walking over to his side as he spoke—horses always attracted Ronnie.

"Aye, they are good 'uns," assented the farmer, "and rarely bred. My girl and I have been giving them a bit of a gallop in the fields yonder now the crops are in, getting them fit for the cub-hunting. I will be pleased to do a deal, sir," he added jocosely.

"Thanks, awfully, but I ride ten stone, and I'm off to India on Friday. I should have thought you would only have had otter hunting in this part of the country."

"Round here there is naught but water rats, but on our side of Beke there is rare fine going, and two good packs within reach."

During this conversation Tossie was considering Ronnie with an air of fascinated attention; her eyes resembled two blue glass balls, and her gaze expressed undisguised approval. Ronnie and I were the same height—that is to say, five-foot-eight. He was slight, well set up, and remarkably good looking. From his earliest childhood he had been excessively particular about his personal appearance, had never objected to having his hair brushed and his hands washed, and, as he stood on the road before Miss Soady, he presented a picture of a thoroughly well turned out and admirably groomed young man. Tweed suit, boots and shirt, were precisely what they should be; his glossy hair was delicately scented; socks, tie and handkerchief were all in sympathy; and yet there was nothing remarkable in his get-up—it was subdued, simple, and absolutely "the right thing." What a contrast to my own countrified appearance in a home-made serge skirt, a baggy blouse, sunburnt sailor hat, and bare hands—we rarely wore gloves at Beke.

Ronnie now turned to Tossie's horse, patted its damp neck, and looking up at the rider, said:

"So I hear you and my sister are great pals; she tells me you have been awfully kind to her."

"Not a little bit of it, it's the other way on," she protested in her loud, far-reaching contralto.

"Eva keeps us all alive, she plays tennis like a professional, and her singing is just a treat. Are you making a stay?"

"No, I am off to-morrow."

"A little of the professor goes a long way?" she suggested archly.

"I did not come to see him, but my sister," he answered stiffly.

"Aye, I expect you came home to look up missie," put in Sam. "There be only the two of you."

"Partly, and partly business; it is bad luck I can't wait on and have a shot at the partridge."

"Aye, and I could give you a rare day's sport. Well, maybe another time," said the farmer. "Now Tossie, these horses be too warm to be kept standing. Good-day, sir, and good luck. Good-day, missie—see you soon," and he moved off.

Tossie, I observed, was not disposed to follow, but inclined to linger and improve her acquaintance with Ronnie.

"I think your sister *might* have brought you up to see us, Mr. Lingard; I do, indeed," she said emphatically.

"We have only had a short time together, Miss Soady, and Eva had such a lot of talking to get through," he replied with his charming smile; "better luck next time."

"I hope so," agreed Tossie, as she wrung his hand, and, with obvious reluctance, followed her parent. As they departed at a walking pace Ronnie declaimed:

"'I saw them go: one horse was blind,
The tails of both hung down behind,
Their shoes were on their feet.'

"All the same, those are fine weight carriers, and have lots of bone. That girl must ride thirteen stone, if she weighs an ounce. I think she seemed a little sniffy because you did not take me there to pay a visit of ceremony."

"Oh, Ronnie, I have only had you for two days, and the day we spent together in London."

"Well then, let's make the most of our time," he said, seating himself once more on the bridge, "and continue to talk of our joys and sorrows."

"*Your* joys and *my* sorrows," I corrected.

"Yes, there is something in that. I have, ten to one, the best of it. Here am I at six-and-twenty, on the point of getting my company, returning to a life that suits me down to the ground, strong and healthy, with lots of pals, and a fat balance at Cox's. Oh, Sis, I tell you, it's jolly to be alive!" and he thumped me violently on the back. "This old world is a grand place; I have a feeling in my bones that in some way my name will ring through it—my subconscious what-you-may-call-it tells me that I am going to have a ripping career—I shall make the race of Lingard famous!"

"I hope you will, with all my heart," I answered with enthusiasm. "And I shall play the part of proud sister to the manner born."

"Yes, you have always been my backer," said Ronnie, "and no end of a brick."

"What happens to you in a way affects me; your good luck will be my good luck. Perhaps this old bridge may be uncanny, for I too have my premonitions, and I believe that in some unexpected way our fortunes will be bound together."

"I'm afraid there's not much chance of that," said Ronnie, "but who knows?" Then, starting to his feet, "Oh, Lord, here are the professor and Lizzie coming to look for us! We can finish our jaw in the garden, after our so-called dinner. Let us advance to meet them, it saves time, and looks *empressé*. Call up that dog, he is hunting water rats. Well, good-bye, old bridge," he went on, slapping the grey stone parapet as he spoke, "I don't expect we shall ever meet again, but I jolly well hope those visions will come true!"

CHAPTER II
BEKE

Professor Septimus Puckle must have been considerably over sixty years of age, a burly, slouching figure, moving with a ponderous and pompous gait; he had a grey beard, two shallow little brown eyes, and a dome-shaped head covered by a soft cap—he also wore a roomy suit of creased black-and-white flannel, and elastic-side boots. In these days, Lizzie, his niece, seemed elderly to me—possibly she may have been about forty. Her figure was remarkably pretty, and her sharp, clever face was illuminated by a pair of bright eyes which shone steadily behind a pince-nez. Perhaps her manner was somewhat abrupt and authoritative, but Lizzie was a capable and cultivated woman, with a level head and warm heart.

"So here you are!" began the professor; "we have come out to look for you."

"Thanks awfully," replied my brother, "but there's not much fear of being lost in these parts, as apparently there is only one road."

"Oh, we have others—several others," protested Lizzie. "Where is Kipper?" now looking about. "We must be getting back to tea, as I have a choir practice at half-past five," and she screamed "Kipper! Kipper! Kipper!"

After a momentary delay, Kipper emerged from under the bridge a deplorable object, dripping with muddy water, and immediately proceeded to shake himself in our vicinity.

"Get away! get away!" shouted the professor, making a drive at him with his stick.

"Oh, poor boy!" I interposed, "he has been hunting rats, and having such a happy time."

"Yes, that's all he thinks of, the horrid brute. I hate the sight of him," declared his master.

"Uncle Sep loved him till you came, Eva, and cut him out in Kipper's affections."

We had now turned homewards, that is to say, in the direction from where the dagger-like spire of Beke church rose from the plain, and were walking four abreast, adapting our pace to the professor's self-conscious waddle, with the humbled Kipper skulking in our wake.

"Yes," continued Uncle Sep in his deep, scholastic voice, "I don't mind telling you, when the fellow was a pup I tolerated him, took him round the garden, suffered him to lie at my fire, and even gave him milk; and for thanks, he tore up my new slippers and several most important papers. I even forgave him that!" emphasising such generosity with a large, fat hand. "But when Eva arrived he simply turned me down, ignored my existence, never answered when I called him, no, no more than if I was a piece of furniture; to be dropped by a dog makes one rather small!"

"I am sure you could never feel that!" protested Ronnie with dangerous frivolity.

"Well, but, Uncle Sep," hastily interposed Lizzie, "you know Eva takes Kip for long runs over the marshes, she brushes him, makes up his dinner— *your* friendship was merely passive."

"He was glad enough of it once," rejoined the injured patron; "but two can play at that game. Now I never open a door for him—on principle."

"So you have your innings!" exclaimed my irrepressible brother, "and I am sure you have something else to do than wait on a cold-hearted terrier. By the way, how do you put in your time? Do you play golf?"

"Golf? No—do I look like golf?" The professor halted, and leaning both hands on his stick, challenged an opinion.

"Well, no," admitted Ronnie. "You look more like fishing—lots of sitting—eh?"

"I sit at my desk, my good sir, I fish for ideas. I write poetry, articles, reviews. 'My mind to me a kingdom is'—I require no outside interests."

"No; but what about outside exercise?"

"Exercise!" repeated the professor; "the world is crazy on that subject. I was brought up to a sedentary life; even at school I never went in for games, but was always keen on brain work. For years I was Lecturer and Professor of Classics and English Literature. Now I have retired my time is my own. I am enjoying the luxury of leisure, and I don't mind telling you that in my lighter mood I write plays."

"Plays!" echoed Ronnie, staring at the professor with blank incredulity. "By George, do you?"

"Yes, I have one now, a four-act comedy, under consideration at the Metropolitan Theatre. Just at present I am hard at work on the history of Slacklands and our local folk-lore."

The mere mention of the subject loosened the professor's tongue, and all the way home—and almost without drawing breath—he held forth on this topic in a full, monotonous voice, and with a fierce determination that would brook no interruption. Ronnie, poor victim, was helpless, so to speak, benumbed, by such an unusual experience; and I could not help smiling to myself as I glanced at his face of furious boredom. Our arrival at the village of Beke put an end to the lecture. The professor could not well continue declaiming and ranting in public—as was his custom in his own garden—and the sight of the first cottage was the signal for our release. Beke, a dreary old village, which had seen better days, consisted of one long, clean street, lined with irregular red-roofed houses, some of a great age. Half-way up the thoroughfare stood the church, a notable edifice, with flying buttresses, surrounded by the tombstones of its dead parishioners. Facing the church was the "Beetle Inn," a crooked black-and-white hostelry, which kept the only fly in the country; farther on, the Parsonage and "The Roost" confronted one another; the latter, a trim, red, Georgian residence, was approached by a brick path across a small enclosure, at present gay with a multitude of pink and lilac phlox.

Outwardly "The Roost" was insignificant, within both roomy and comfortable. The walls were wainscoted, the fireplaces of generous space. The doors of the principal rooms were of rich South American mahogany, and most of the furniture was quaint and old-fashioned: in former days "The Roost" had been the abode of taste and leisure. Now, alas! times were sadly changed.

The professor had ample leisure but no taste; his niece had a cultivated taste but no leisure—all her spare hours were dedicated to the parson and the parish.

Undoubtedly these changes had been anticipated, for a deeply cut carving on a panel in the passage said:

"All terrene things by turns we see

Become another's property.

Mine now must be another's soon,

I know not whose, when I am gone;

An earthly house is bound to none."

A glass door at the back of the hall opened upon an unexpectedly large garden, gently sloping to the sluggish river; here there were long gravel walks—worn bare by the professor's pacing—bordered with box and old standard roses. Here was also a notable mulberry tree, several rustic seats, and a sundial on which was inscribed, "Time will tell."

That evening a full white moon illuminated the land, and after dinner Ronnie and I effected our escape, and strolled to and fro arm in arm along the professor's pet walk; this would be our last hour together.

"I cannot stand that slovenly old bore," said Ronnie. "Did you notice the ink on his fingers and the crumbs in his beard? I don't know which is the worst—his drivelling talk or his appearance. I wonder he hasn't driven you mad long ago. I've only been here two days, and already my reason is tottering. Does he *never* stop talking?"

"Sometimes," I replied, "when he is not pleased and sulks."

"Is it really true that he writes plays?"

"Yes, for his own entertainment. They are never accepted. He spends lots of money on dramatic agents, typewriting, and so on, and, as a great favour, he generally reads the plays to me."

"You long-suffering martyr! I should certainly kick at that."

"They are not so bad; it is his poetry that I cannot endure—so sickeningly sweet, it makes me feel positively squeamish! Sometimes he brings it to meals and reads it between the courses, and says, 'Lizzie and Eva, you must really hear this, it is *delicious.*'"

"What lunacy!" cried Ronnie. "It seems to me you would be just as well off in an asylum for idiots."

"By no means," I objected; "the professor is as dull as a wet Sunday, but Lizzie is immensely clever, a thorough musician, speaks French like a native, and has no end of certificates. She was governess in the family of a Russian Grand Duke before she went to Torrington. Besides, I am really fond of her; I think she finds Uncle Sep trying at times, and after he has read me a play she will say, 'Now don't pretend you liked it, Eva—speak the truth. Tell him it is just wordy *rubbish*! I implore you not to encourage him; as long as he writes letters and poetry for the *Slacklands Post* it is all right, but the plays burn a hole in his pocket.' He is really not a bad old boy—rather simple and weak, in spite of his fierce eyebrows—anyone, even a child, can lead him by flattery."

"I wish I saw my way to leading you out of this hole," said Ronnie; "my visit has been a shocker; if they would only have you at Torrington—but I suppose that as long as those girls are unmarried you will be what I may call 'reserved.'"

"I have no wish to go to Torrington," I replied. "Beke may be dull, but here I don't live in fear and trembling of anyone. I wonder why Aunt Mina, who detests me, is so friendly to you?"

"I think I can answer that," rejoined Ronnie. "I am a Lingard—quite the family type—ears and all. I am self-supporting, I have four hundred a year, I have done pretty well for myself so far, and I am in a crack regiment. Also I can shoot and dance, make myself useful in a house party, and do not—like my pretty sister—extinguish the girls or fascinate Bev—quite the contrary, so far as he is concerned; moreover, should anything happen to that long-necked young pup, I am the next heir. When I told Aunt Mina I was coming here she was inclined to be apologetic, and said she was so sorry that Torrington did not agree with you, and that she had settled you at Beke solely on account of your health and education, as they had found you extraordinarily young and unformed for your age. Tell me, Sis, how do you put in your time when you are not doing lessons?"

"Oh, I dust the china, practise, go for long walks with Kipper, poke round the village among my friends, and play tennis with the Soadys, who sometimes give me a mount. On wet days I help Clarice to clean the silver, and besides all this I read a lot. I've unearthed no end of old books in a closet, some horribly musty, and printed with those long S's. I've just been devouring a fearsome tale, called 'Sir Lancelot Graves'—it's all about a ghost in armour."

"Oh, bother ghosts and books!" interrupted Ronnie impatiently. "Have you no people of your own class around here?"

"There are one or two big places," I answered, "but the Darlingfords and the De Veres would not dream of visiting at 'The Roost.' Lizzie was only a finishing governess, and Uncle Sep was never a real professor; he is called that hereabouts, and he likes it, and has come to believe in it himself."

"And have you no variety at all?" Ronnie's tone was despairing.

"Yes, twice a year we spend a riotous fortnight in London. We stay at a Bayswater boarding-house that calls itself a private hotel, which the Puckles always patronise. Lizzie and I stare into windows and compare opinions, do a little shopping and go to concerts. Sep spends most of his time in theatres and worries managers with his plays."

For some moments after this announcement Ronnie sat beside me in dead silence, then suddenly he sprang to his feet and began to walk to and fro along the professor's well-beaten track; at last he came to a halt and said:

"Eva, I had no idea of all this! You always write such cheery letters— even that time in London you were mum. It is thundering bad luck that

I'm obliged to be off so soon. However *something* has got to be done. Uncle Horace must find you a more suitable home. Look here, I have just hit on an idea! I shall suggest your going out to India as a P.G.—paying guest, you know—lots of girls do that, and Anglo-Indians are glad enough of the coin now that everything is so expensive. Of course the people you go to must be top hole—that is understood. Aunt Mina is a wonderful woman for references and position, and I believe you will get along famously; you can dance and sing and ride, and chatter nineteen to the dozen. You and I will be on the same continent, which will be a change. I shall offer to pay your passage, and I expect Aunt Mina will be so glad to be rid of you that she will give you a ripping outfit—what do you think of my idea?"

"Oh, Ronnie," I exclaimed, "it is too splendid for words. How did it enter your head?"

"It came into my head just now as I walked up and down and saw you crouched here on the garden seat, and thought of you cooped up in that gloomy old house, with the sham professor, the clerical governess, and the great empty, ugly country that cuts you off from all the world—and you only nineteen! Before I go to sleep this very night I shall write Uncle Horace a letter that will make things move."

"I doubt if your letter will move Aunt Mina or remove me! Ronnie, wouldn't it be lovely if I could go out and keep house for you—I am such a clever manager?"

"My dear, crazy child, if the colonel were to hear you he would have fits. He bars married officers and——-"

"Is married himself," I interrupted impatiently.

"Well, the fact is, *she* married him. Away from the regiment, he fell a prey, like Samson minus his hair. She was an old maid, a squiress, with a long pedigree and a large fortune. She was sick of her village and schools, and of unflinching determination to see the world; she met 'James' at a dinner party, and, so to speak, nailed him! She's a rattling good sort I must confess, entertains a lot, mothers what she calls 'her boys,' and keeps us as well as she can under her own eye."

"And he?"

"Is wrapped up in the regiment, its past glories, its present fitness, and its future exploits. 'James,' as we call him, is as hard as flint, and as tough as boot leather; the orderly room and parade ground are his real home; he looks black on married couples and, if possible, hurls them to the depot. If a subaltern were to adventure on matrimony, all I can say is, that I would be sorry for him—and if I were to turn up with a pretty sister I expect it would be a case of a court-martial!"

"What a narrow-minded, detestable tyrant!" I exclaimed.

"Yes, but very civil in civil life; he plays a good game of billiards, and is prominent in square dances with 'Burra mems.' Apart from soldiering he is delightfully tame, and will, so to speak, eat out of your hand."

"What is a Burra mem?" I inquired.

"You will know soon enough when you get east of Suez."

"Ah, if I ever do, perhaps you will see that my presentiment will come true, and that we shall be together always."

"No such luck," rejoined Ronnie. "Even if I do succeed in transplanting you I am afraid it will be a case of 'so near and yet so far,' though, of course, wherever you may be I shall fly to see you. Now I am off to write a scorcher to Uncle Horace."

"It is awfully good of you, Ronnie, but I am afraid you will find you have only wasted your time and a penny stamp," I replied as I followed him into "The Roost." Nevertheless, in spite of my dismal forebodings, that night I lay awake for hours thinking over Ronnie's plan, and when at last I fell asleep I dreamt of India.

CHAPTER III
A MEETING ON THE MARSHES

Trains from the station nearest to Beke ran at inconceivably inconvenient hours; for instance, a quarter to eight in the morning, and half-past four in the afternoon, the latter wandering into London about midnight. Ronnie, of course, departed by the first, and I took leave of him in the front hall with copious tears (the professor, in a plaid dressing-gown, and with dishevelled locks, peering over the banisters).

"Buck up, old girl!" he said; "it will be all right; within six months you will be hugging me in India. Mind you write every mail, take great care of yourself—and—er—good-bye." Then he tore himself away, and ran down the tiled footpath to where an aged fly—once the equipage of a countess—and a sprightly young horse were waiting to transport him to the junction.

As I watched the light-hearted animal plunging and straining at the shafts I was conscious of a guilty hope that he and the venerable vehicle would part company, and thus spare me Ronnie for a few hours; but no, tottering and swaying, the ancient landau rolled away intact.

Then I went upstairs to my own room, locked the door, and huddled down in the deep window seat, there to mourn and meditate. I seemed to have come to the end of my hopes and had now nothing to look forward to. A painful conviction for a young and sanguine soul!

For one whole year Ronnie's return had been my lodestar; my first thought in the morning, my last at night; now he had come and gone—it was all so soon over. Surveying the future, what a bleak, monotonous outlook lay before me. It appeared to me that I might almost as well have been born a cabbage or a thistle! So far as the result of Ronnie's letter was concerned, I had not been foolishly sanguine; I knew Aunt Mina, from what might be called her "wrong side," and how she disliked anyone to interfere with her settled plans; her plan with respect to me was that I should remain harmlessly at Beke, and I had frequently heard her express a horror of India—a country that, in her opinion, was full of second-rate people, fast, disreputable women and impecunious gambling men; no, there would be no gorgeous East for me, and I could not reasonably expect to see Ronnie for three long years.

I must confess that for some days after my brother's departure I was a moping, undesirable house-mate; even a letter from Marseilles, a gold wristlet watch, and Tossie's enthusiastic admiration for my beloved, scarcely helped to raise the clouds. Still, it comforted me to talk about him to Lizzie and Tossie, who were both sincerely sympathetic—not so the professor, who became portentously glum whenever Ronnie's name was mentioned, and sat silently aloof with an air of Olympian detachment. Apparently their antipathy had been mutual, for he imparted to the parson, who told Tossie, who told me, that "young Lingard was a conceited, empty-headed dandy, just a good-for-nothing, impudent jackanapes!"

It was about this time, I imagine, that he began to work with arduous enthusiasm upon a new play, in which the ne'er-do-well and scapegrace was a full-sized portrait of my brother—so far as his personal appearance was concerned; particulars dealing with his dress were given in microscopic detail. For once there was much mystery concerning this effort. Naturally the professor never read it to me, and for this "let off" I was profoundly thankful, for it was something of an ordeal to sit in a stuffy study, which reeked of stale tobacco, dust, and worm-eaten furniture, whilst Uncle Sep read aloud with sonorous complacency, occasionally pausing to look over his glasses and say, "That is a fine speech, eh? How does it strike you?"

Lizzie, who was not a fellow sufferer, warmly approved of these readings. "It was better," she declared, "not to disturb the amiable delusions of our fellows, but to encourage such friends to believe in themselves!" The result was that I was immured in the study, administering to Uncle Sep's vanity, whilst she bustled about the village, doing parish work or conferring with the rector.

The rector, a distinguished looking white-haired old widower, had contrived to appropriate Lizzie as lay worker and curate. Beke was a large and scattered parish, and she visited various outlying hamlets on her bike, controlled the Sunday school, undertook mothers' meetings, the Red Cross, the village nurse, Girls' Friendly Society and the choir, whilst the Reverend Clement Chesterfield enjoyed an amount of spacious ease, and had ample leisure to read the *Guardian*, the *Spectator*, the heavier monthlies and the particular class of literature which appealed to him. When the rectory had guests or entertained the bishop, Miss Puckle managed the housekeeping; when the rector was sick, she made poultices and beef tea, and nursed him most efficiently. All the village believed it would be "a match," although Mr. Chesterfield was seventy. The rumour went further, and one of his married nieces had lately invaded Beke; her manner to Miss Puckle had been pointedly disagreeable, and she was reported to have "said things."

Lizzie's time, as may be supposed, was fully occupied, but I had many empty hours in spite of practising and readings. Some of these hours I filled in with visits to my intimates in the villages, to the Soadys, or by long tramps over the country, accompanied by Kipper. To Myson's Dyke was his favourite excursion; here were rabbits, rabbits, and rabbits—oh, such good hunting! Our path lay over a series of ugly flat fields, ending in the palings and outlying plantations of one of the big places.

On this particular occasion, although it happened to be my birthday, my reflections were by no means cheerful. The morning's post had brought me the gift of a lace pocket-handkerchief from my cousin Dora and a note in which she said, "Father had a letter from Ronald; he said that you are looking splendid—so much for Beke!"

So much for Beke indeed! Apparently Ronnie's appeal had fallen flat; there was not a word about India. Alas! that door of escape was closed. As I turned my face towards the village, and contemplated the hateful, too familiar and forbidding path across the dried-up marshes, a memory suddenly flashed into my mind:

"Over the meadows that blossom and wither

Rings but the note of a sea-bird's song;

Only the sun and the rain come hither.

All year long."

I asked myself impatiently how long was I to lead this empty, dull existence? A life given over to the monotonous duties of an alien household and to pandering to the vanity of a garrulous old man! My school-fellows wrote to me from time to time. Several had asked me to visit them, but Aunt Mina vetoed all such hospitalities. "These people," she said, "were not in our set. You must remember that your grandmother was a duke's daughter and only associate with your own class, not with second-rate acquaintances." It was evident that she liked to play dog-in-the-manger, and would neither suffer me to stay with others nor offer me an invitation herself!

As I strolled along in a melancholy mood, musing on the misery of my virtual internment, an acute sense of homelessness overcame me. My eyes were dim with tears of self-pity, when, through these tears, I discerned a distant speck on the pathway; it approached, gradually grew larger, and presently materialised into the figure of a man, tall, square-shouldered, and carrying a gun under his arm. Nearer and nearer he strode, and when within ten yards I saw that he was a well set-up, soldierly individual, in orthodox shooting garb, with dark, rather sleepy eyes and a masterful chin.

He looked me straight in the face, as we passed almost touching—the sole human beings within sight over miles of space. Kipper, with his hackles on end, sniffed suspiciously at the man's leggings, and then, so to speak, "accepted him," and I proceeded homewards, listening to the steady tramp of a pair of heavy shooting boots till the sound had ceased. I had advanced a certain distance, when an imperative curiosity impelled me to halt and look back—I am well aware that this was a most unladylike action; nevertheless I fell! To my horror and embarrassment, I discovered that the stranger was doing precisely the same thing, standing apparently immovable as a milestone. Undoubtedly our curiosity and, I think I may say, interest, had been mutual! I was sincerely thankful that the distance was too great for us to distinguish one another's features, and felt deeply ashamed, exquisitely flattered, and painfully shy. Before I could turn he had snatched off his cap and waved it to me! What audacious impertinence! My heart beat unusually fast, and my face flamed. Here was an adventure at last, and although its form was highly indiscreet—nevertheless I liked it!

Possibly it may not be surprising when I state that I thought of the stranger all the way home; my mind was so full of him that the monotonous miles seemed as yards. I recalled his upright bearing, his handsome eyes, his kindly word to Kipper. Was this the hero that every girl of nineteen sees in her dreams? It is a remarkable fact that at dinner I, who usually poured out my budget of small news—such as, how someone had broken Mrs. Hogg's window, the postman's baby had croup, or a party of motorists had stopped to tea at "The Beetle"—never once mentioned my experience, but kept it locked up in my heart; yes, even from Tossie, who brought all her joys and sorrows to me. Behold my first secret! After all how puny and insignificant; nevertheless, I hugged it like a child with her first doll! On Slacklands Flats I had encountered a good-looking stranger—no doubt one of the guns at Myson—who had stared hard, looked after me, and signalled a gay greeting. "Ships that pass in the night"—"a couple who pass at sundown." I must confess that I allowed my mind to dwell on the adventure as I sewed, as I listened to the professor's plays, yes, even in church, when naturally I ought to have been engrossed in holy thoughts and the rector's short, crisp sermon.

CHAPTER IV
A DANCE AT "THE PLOUGH"

Before Christmas my relations departed to Nice. Aunt Mina, who suffered from bronchitis, went in search of a little sun, my cousins in quest of amusement. The Riviera was gay, and they were by all accounts a large and congenial party. Perhaps their consciences may have troubled them with regard to me, for they sent me unusually nice presents—a large box of chocolate, a fan, and a gay parasol. There was not much occasion for these latter at Beke in winter time, but one must not look a gift-horse in the mouth! Our Christmas was profoundly dull, not to say depressing; it was cold work decorating the bleak old church—assisted by Lizzie, the schoolmistress, the landlady of "The Beetle," and many others, including Tossie and her most recent admirer, a smart young "vet" from Newmarket.

As we pricked our frozen hands and made a great holly wreath for the font she said,

"You look awfully down, dear, and I suppose there is no fun going on at 'The Roost' on Christmas Day—no party, eh?"

"Need you ask?" I retorted derisively. "We are to have early dinner, as Clarice has a holiday, and the professor indigestion."

"You will be getting a letter from your brother to cheer you. My! he is the best-looking fellow I ever saw, although he *is* on the small side; I admire his whole style, his neat little moustache, and the lovely scent on his hair. Only that the others are so pressing I would wait for him, I declare I would." And Tossie burst into a loud laugh. "See now, listen, Evie, I have a splendid plan for you."

"A plan?" I echoed.

"Yes, give me over that ball of twine, and I will tell you all about it. On New Year's Eve there is to be a grand kick-up at 'The Plough and Harrow' in Mirfield village; it is an hotel that was a fine place in old times, and has a great big room at the back, where they used to have routs, and soirées—whatever they were. The inn is getting up a dance; tickets half a crown for ladies, and I have got yours."

"As if Lizzie would allow me to go!"

"Wait now," urged Tossie impressively; "the company will be extra respectable, just farmer folk; there will be a piano and a fiddle, and a bit of supper, tea, and coffee and sandwiches. Mother is sending the soup, and she will chaperon us. We will have the top put on the old wagonette, which will hold six inside, and you must come and dine and sleep at the Manor, as you have done before of a wet night. I know you are mad keen on dancing. They say the floor is splendid, and you won't mind with whom you dance, so long as he is sober and a good partner—so say you will come?"

"Yes, you may be sure I shall, if Lizzie will let me."

"Oh, bother Lizzie! You must assert yourself, Evie, and not allow people to walk over you. It is all very well for *her* to be living in Beke; she is forty and has all she wants, and enjoys playing about the parish with the rector. You just talk up to her and say you intend to have a little fling. I am sure she will see it. Liz has been young herself, and she is awfully fond of you."

"Who are your party?" I inquired.

"Freddy Block the vet, and I am sure *he* looks good enough for any society; my cousin Bob from Leeds, he is in a big outfitter's; Annie Green, Dr. Mercer, Mother, brother Sam, and ourselves. It will be rather a crowd, but Sam can go outside."

"Tossie, it is too kind of you, and I should love to go. I have not been to a dance since I left school, and I will fall on my knees to Lizzie—but what about my frock?"

"Oh, your black will do elegantly, and stick a bit of mistletoe in your hair! Now mind you don't disappoint me, but try to get hold of Liz when she feels Christmassy and soft."

I believe Lizzie was a little sorry for me on Christmas Day; my letters and cards had been so few and there was nothing from India. The drawing-room fire smoked, the turkey was nearly raw, the groaning professor had retired upstairs; on the whole we had a miserable festival.

The village itself wore a convivial air, and from my post in a deep-seated window I commanded a view of the street, and enviously noted the many cheery couples and families passing to and fro. From my niche I was summoned by Lizzie; according to immemorial custom the school-children were to have a treat on Boxing Day, and I was bound to lend a hand with the preparations. Accordingly, I spent the remainder of the holiday helping to ticket presents—taking care to see that there was no cause for jealousy or rivalry in their distribution; for instance, that the Cobbs received nothing that might outshine the Bolters, that little Tommy Ware was *not* endowed with a knife, or the "Beetle" baby with a box of paints. With unscrupulous subtlety I seized upon this exceptional opportunity, as my confederate had advised, to "talk up to Lizzie."

"Lizzie," I began, "I am still legally what is called an infant, and *I* should like a treat, too!"

"I only wish I could see my way to your having one, my poor child," she replied, "I know this is a deadly existence for you, and I realise that you do have a *very* poor time, but what is the alternative?"

"We need not discuss that now, Liz, but the treat is to hand; the Plough and Harrow Inn, at Mirfield, is giving a dance on New Year's Eve, it will be quite a respectable affair, with a piano, a fiddle and sandwiches. Mrs. Soady will chaperon me. Do let me go, my dear Lizzie," and I seized her by the arm, "let me just have one dance, to circulate my blood, and try to feel like other girls!" I paused, and hung almost breathless on her answer. It was a long time in coming, but at last she said,

"Well, of course, the Soadys are all right, but they are not in your class, nor are their friends."

"Now you are talking exactly like Aunt Mina! Never mind the classes—I should like to dance with the masses."

"Oh Eva," and as she spoke her face seemed to lengthen by inches, "what *would* your aunt say?"

"She will never know," I rejoined with easy confidence, "and you might not have known either. If I had just gone to dine and sleep at the Manor, you would not dream in your wildest moments that I was dancing the New Year in at the Plough and Harrow, in Mirfield. You see, it is five miles from here, and quite out of our beat; not a soul will recognise me. But I could not play you such a trick, Liz—whatever I am, I am not sly!"

"Well, I really do not know what to say," declared Lizzie sitting down with a Noah's Ark in her lap. "I halt between two opinions. On the one hand, I should like you to enjoy yourself and have a little bit of amusement for once; on the other, I must say I rather shrink from the idea of your making your debut, chaperoned by old Mother Soady, and dancing with such partners as Sam and Bob Tate. If you do go——"

Here I broke in,

"Oh, you dear good Lizzie, and I shall have no end of funny things to tell you afterwards."

"If you do go," she reiterated, "the whole thing must be a dead secret; above all, not a word to Uncle Sep; he *talks*—and when he went over to 'The Beetle' for tobacco he would tell the village all about it; it is also to be a dead secret from *me*. Understand, that I give you permission to dine and sleep at the Manor; however they may entertain you there is no longer my affair."

"Oh, Liz, what a nice Jesuitical way of looking at it! But whatever happens I have your official consent." Then I fell upon her and kissed her.

We certainly were a tight fit, and a noisy party, in the old wagonette, which was somewhat severely tried by the weight of the company and the slap-dash pace of a fine pair of young horses. Nevertheless, we arrived safely at the "Plough and Harrow," and in capital time. The old inn was all lit up, spectators were crowding round the door, gigs, phaetons and even milk carts were depositing happy guests. The ladies' cloakroom was crammed; here we unpinned, uncloaked and reported upon one another's appearance, as there was not the smallest chance of approaching the one looking-glass. Tossie looked blooming in blue and white. Annie Green was in flowered muslin of a bold and lurid design—somewhat resembling a perambulating wall-paper. The style, she informed us, "was the very latest thing in Paris."

Mrs. Soady, chiefly remarkable for her kind heart and her circumference, was dressed in her best black satin, which was many inches too short in front, a large plaid bow crowned her good-looking smiling face, and an enormous cameo brooch fastened under her chin imparted the effect of a martingale.

As soon as we had emerged from the struggling mass of women in the cloakroom we were joined by our cavaliers; thus supported, as we entered the ballroom in a body, I was sensible of an atmosphere of delicious adventure! The ballroom was long, narrow, and wainscoted, and held a powerful atmosphere of potatoes—no wonder, since, as Sam informed me, several tons of this useful root had been but recently removed.

It was illuminated by wall lamps, and profusely garlanded with Christmas greenery. At one end was the band (piano, flute and violin), and the first set of lancers was promptly arranged. There were few forms for sitting out, as most of the company were young and meant business; in other words, they had come to dance—and dance they did! I found myself as a partner in flattering demand. I waltzed with Doctor Mercer, who bore me round in a series of leaps and bounds; the next waltz was with the "vet," a most creditable performer; then I danced with young Sam, who gambolled about like a clumsy colt, talking all the time at the top of his voice.

I was resting after my second waltz with Mr. Block, the vet, when he drew my attention to two men who were contemplating the scene from an opposite doorway. They were in shooting dress; one I had never seen before, but instantly I recognised his companion as "the stranger." The couple had evidently just looked in casually, to see what was going on, and had happened upon a most animated gathering. There could be no possible doubt of the company's enjoyment.

"You see those two fellows over there?" said my partner, "they are officers stopping here for the duck shooting."

Almost before he had ceased speaking, I beheld the stranger dodging about among the dancers. He came straight up to me, bowed, and said,

"May I have the honour of a dance?"

In for a penny in for a pound! Without a moment's hesitation I replied,

"Yes, with pleasure."

"The next?"

I was engaged to the local telegraph clerk for the next. Should I throw him over? No.

"I can give you number twelve," I said looking at my card.

"I say, and what about *me*?" clamoured the stranger's companion, who had now joined us, clicking his heels together and bowing before me with exaggerated respect.

Somehow I did not feel favourably disposed towards this would-be partner; he had not, like his friend, an arresting personality. I disliked his prominent nose and teeth and bold goggling eyes, and fixed him with my best imitation of Aunt Mina's glare.

"But why should I be left out?" he argued, totally unabashed; "you have given him one, and you dance like an angel."

"This lady and I have met before," coolly interposed the stranger. Then to me, "I shall look forward to number twelve"; and taking the other forcibly by the arm, he removed him from my vicinity. Subsequently, as I swam round the room in the charge of the telegraph clerk, I noticed the two watching us closely from the doorway, and as soon as the waltz was over I was promptly claimed.

My new partner danced admirably, our step suited, the floor was in first-rate condition, and the old "Amoureuse" was one of my favourites.

"Why do you try to steer?" inquired my partner, when we halted.

"I am sorry," I replied, "but I suppose it is because, being one of the tall girls, I always danced gentleman at school."

"And since?"

"This is my first dance—elsewhere."

"Then I am afraid your people must live in a desperately dull neighbourhood?"

"I do not live with my people," I replied, "in fact, I may tell you, I have no people to live with. My parents died when I was quite small, and my only brother is in India." I paused abruptly, and felt myself growing red with self-consciousness. Why should I offer all this autobiography to an absolute stranger? What were my affairs to him? As usual my tongue had run away with me, and I felt stricken with confusion and remorse.

After a short silence, he said,

"Possibly you may not remember me, but we passed one another on the marshes some time ago. I was so astonished to see a young lady walking alone in that dreary side of the country, I might have thought you were an apparition but for the dog. Do you live in that part of the world?"

"Yes," I replied, "within a few miles."

Mrs. Soady, passing by on the arm of the doctor, patted me on the arm and said,

"Come along and get some soup before it's all gone. I hope you are enjoying yourself, dearie?"

I nodded an emphatic assent, and as she disappeared in the direction of refreshments my companion looked at me interrogatively.

"My chaperon," I briefly explained.

"I see," he assented, nevertheless it was evident that he was greatly puzzled. He surveyed my neat black frock, my well-fitting gloves, my beautiful French fan—also perhaps my smart satin shoes and silk stockings, which were crossed in front of me, for I never made any secret of the fact that I had remarkably pretty feet.

After this we talked perfunctorily of the weather and of dogs; presently he conducted me to the buffet in the hotel dining-room, where, as I stood sipping coffee, I noticed that many eyes were upon us, including those of the landlady. To this attention I was serenely indifferent; beyond our own party not a soul in the room, or among the company, had the least idea as to who I was, or that they were honoured by the presence of the great granddaughter of a duke! After a very short "interval for refreshments," we returned to the ballroom and danced two delightful waltzes; as the last sad strain sobbed itself to an end, my companion said:

"I am aware that we have become acquainted in rather an unusual fashion. Would you think me awfully presumptuous if I were to ask you to tell me your name?" I nodded my head with, I fear, ungracious emphasis. "I see," he exclaimed. "Well, all right—then I shall call you Miss Incognita. Mine is Captain Falkland—Brian Falkland."

"I see," I echoed. I cannot imagine what possessed me to mimic him to his face. I felt "fey," the dancing had exhilarated me, and had gone to my head like champagne.

"This is a queer old inn," he went on. "The landlady told me that ages ago all the county came here, and in winter had routs in this room. I should say it had routs within the last week," and he sniffed fastidiously.

At this moment Sam, breathless from his exertions, mopping his big, red face, accosted me.

"Sorry to interrupt, Miss Eva," he panted; "Mother sent me to look for you. It is after one o'clock and we ought to be getting home," and turning apologetically to my partner he added: "You see, sir, we farmers are bound to be early folk."

"So sorry," said my companion; "I suppose there is no help for it; you must go, but I will only say au revoir, Miss Eva," and he bowed.

Still possessed by the spirit of giddiness, I made him a profound court curtsy, such as had possibly been executed in the adjacent ballroom a hundred and fifty years previously, and then I walked off attended by Sam. Ten minutes later, when our loud and hilarious party had all been packed into the "Black Maria," I noticed Captain Falkland and his friend standing on the steps of the "Plough and Harrow," watching our proceedings with unaffected interest, until our high-spirited horses whirled us away into the darkness of the January night.

On our arrival at the Manor, Tossie followed me into my room for "a talk"; as we unhooked one another, and so to speak disarmed, naturally we discussed the dance.

"I need not ask you if you enjoyed yourself," she said, "you were quite the beauty. And it was a real treat to see you and that officer dancing together; a good partner, wasn't he?"

"Yes," I replied, "he holds you so comfortably, and always seems to know where he is going."

"And you did have what they call a 'success,' my dear; everyone was asking who you were, and I told them, a friend from London, who is stopping with me; one may as well tell a good lie when one goes about it. Did you not feel for all the world like a swan in a duck pond?"

"No, but a goose—and very much a goose."

Before Tossie retired to her own apartment she became most confidential and interesting, and informed me that Fred Block had been on the verge of a proposal, but she had headed him off as she could not yet make up her mind.

"As for you," she added, "I was very 'mum' when they were chaffing you in the bus about your best partner—I believe you gave him five waltzes. I know all about him, and they don't; shall I tell you?"

"If you like," I answered with affected nonchalance.

"Don't drawl," protested Tossie, "be interested or you shan't hear a word."

"Well, go on, I am all ears."

"Then listen. Captain Falkland is in some cavalry regiment. He has been staying at Landmere for Christmas with the Earl and Countess of Runnymede, his cousins; it is said they want him to marry Lady Amelia, a plain, washed-out thing with weak eyes. He is the only son of General and Lady Louisa Falkland—awfully proud people—and is very good-looking, as you may see; I do love the nice way his hair grows down over his square forehead—I should like to see you married to him, so I would!" and Tossie gave me a playful push.

"I never heard such nonsense!" I exclaimed. "It is not the least likely we shall ever meet again."

"Then you did not give him a little clue, or tell him your name?" and Tossie thrust her red-and-white face close to mine, and stared into my eyes with her unflinching blue orbs.

"Of course not," I answered impatiently. "Why should I?"

"If it had been *me*, I'd have done it! Well now, there is three striking and I must go to my bed. The meet is at Harper's Cross at eleven—but you can sleep it out!"

On my return from the Manor to "The Roost," I related to Lizzie the history of my illegitimate outing. With more than usual glibness my tongue wagged freely, as I described the dance, the supper, the music, the most notable costumes, and my various partners—all except one; and she, kind and unsuspicious creature, declared that she was delighted to hear I had enjoyed myself so thoroughly, but added:

"If the tidings of this little escapade were ever to reach the ears of Mrs. Lingard, I believe I should be compelled to *emigrate*!"

CHAPTER V
THE GREAT INVASION

It is strange but true that my future lot was profoundly affected by the microbe of influenza. Influenza accomplishes various evils; this obnoxious germ carries weakness, depression and death, but it is rare to find it a medium that launches a young woman into the great wide world.

An excursion to London every January was one of the hard-and-fast rules of "The Roost"; about the middle of the month, when Christmas festivities had waned, the professor and his niece journeyed together to a boarding-house in Bayswater, and there enjoyed—each in their own way—a fortnight of the Metropolis. She, in attending sales and classical concerts, looking up old friends and going to "teas" arrayed in her best clothes. He, in personally worrying managers and dramatic agents, patronising theatres, telephoning incessantly, and giving expensive entertainments to needy professionals, who fed his insatiable vanity with enormous helpings of the sweetest flattery, and sent him back to his dull old den with a swollen head and a somewhat empty pocket.

Just before this half-yearly expedition, when rooms had been engaged, luggage packed, and our arrival formally notified, Lizzie suddenly collapsed under a violent attack of "flu." As her temperature was found to be 103, a journey was out of the question. The doctor who was summoned ordered bed and nursing, and declared the ailment to be of a particularly virulent type. Lizzie, painfully distressed and apologetic, endeavoured to assert herself and talked of "being all right in a couple of days," but when the doctor uttered the word "pneumonia" she succumbed.

At first the attitude of the professor was sympathetic, then by degrees he became silent, sullen, and finally morose; as vexed at his postponed holidays as any spoilt child.

"But I thought you hated London," I said, not sorry to tease him a little. "You have always said you were so thankful to live outside the noise and clamour of the world."

My remarks irritated the professor to such a degree that I believe he could have thrown a book at me had one been handy, but they had merely the effect of inflaming his passion for the great city with its vast opportunities.

"Why not let him go alone?" I suggested to the invalid. "He says the rooms will have to be paid for, and he is miserable about all the important appointments he is missing. If you could look out of the window, you would see him raging up and down the garden."

"Oh yes, I know," said Lizzie impatiently, "he always does that when he's put out. Somehow I am reluctant to let Uncle Sep out of my sight, especially in London; he does crazy, impulsive things and is so easily talked into follies, such as spending and lending, and I act as a sort of brake; then those chattering elderly women at Number 20 make no end of him and imply that he is quite a lady-killer and irresistibly attractive. Poor Uncle Sep never was either; clever enough, but not very wise, especially since he slipped on a banana and fell on the back of his head. You say he is dull and disappointed?"

"'Dull and disappointed' but feebly conveys the case! He is like Kipper when he sees me with my hat on, frantic to go out. He ate no dinner last night."

"Then, indeed, he is in a bad way! Well, ask him to saturate himself with eucalyptus, and to come and talk it all over with me after lunch."

The result of this talk was the departure of the professor the very next morning. He made an almost imposing figure in his London clothes, tall hat, frock coat, neat umbrella, and modern boots. As I escorted him to the little gate he remarked:

"Well, Evie, *this* time I shall do something with the managers. I have a presentiment that I shall bring back a huge success."

"Only it's so cold I'd throw my shoe after you," I replied, "but I wish you the best of luck."

Without any further remark, or even the formality of a farewell, he climbed into the creaking fly and was presently lumbering away. Lizzie's illness lasted longer than we anticipated; she kept her room for nearly three weeks; meanwhile, village and parochial business was more or less dislocated. Mr. Chesterfield the rector called daily and sent flowers, newspapers, and notes, but never approached the infected premises nearer than a hundred yards.

At last the ruler of "The Roost" crawled downstairs, a weak and shattered remnant of her keen and energetic self. However, the "sofa," and "feeding up" were duly prescribed, with excellent results. Letters from the professor—once so copious—had lately degenerated into picture postcards, and these chiefly conveyed bulletins of the weather. He had been absent nearly a month, and to me this was a happy relief. Lizzie was now convalescent, and once more managing Beke with her accustomed capability.

One afternoon we were returning from a long and muddy walk, when a boy darted out of the post office, and handed her a telegram. It came from Uncle Sep, and said, "Arrive to-night, send fly to the seven; have good fires and dinner."

"What a funny telegram!" she exclaimed handing it to me; "as if we don't always have fires and a good dinner. As it happens, there is a goose to-night. I will tell Eliza to make a roly-poly and Welsh rarebit—Uncle Sep loves them—and also to put a big fire in his bedroom. I expect he's had a play accepted, and wishes to commemorate his return with a feast."

It was nearly eight o'clock when I heard the fly stop at the front gate. I had been listening expectantly; even the return of the tiresome professor made a change in my monotonous existence. He would bring, if not news, at least some illustrated papers. I went into the hall and looked out; it was a cold, dark night, with drifting showers of sleet; nevertheless, I stood bravely at the open door, whilst Clarice, with the skirt of her dress flung over her head, pattered down to the cab. The professor descended heavily backwards, and instead of as usual hurrying indoors, he turned about, apparently in order to assist another to alight—a woman! In a second I divined the truth. Uncle Sep had brought home a wife!

Naturally a desperate moral coward, he had shrunk from announcing the marriage to his niece, and left it to the bride to break the intelligence in person. I dashed into the dining-room, where Lizzie was deliberately lighting candles on the mantelpiece, and gasped out:

"Your uncle has brought someone back with him—I think it is Mrs. Bickers!"

Lizzie turned about, and stood staring at me stupidly, her mouth half open—a lighted taper in her unconscious hand. I remembered Mrs. Bickers at the boarding-house, a plump widow of fifty with a strongly corseted figure, black eyes like boot buttons, a high colour, and a long chin.

Yes, I was right, it *was* Mrs. Bickers! Already she was standing in the doorway, clad in a black waterproof and an aggressive-looking hat covered with pointed wings. The cowardly professor pushed her into the room before him, saying in a loud, would-be jovial voice:

"Hallo, Liz, I have brought you a present from London. Here is your new aunt and old friend, Mrs. Bickers—now Mrs. Puckle. We were married ten days ago!"

The announcement was succeeded by a prolonged and dramatic silence. For my part, my nerves were throbbing with excitement, and it may appear callous and hard-hearted, but personally I felt as if I were witnessing a powerful scene in some play. The atmosphere seemed to be charged with animosity and fear; fear being well represented by Uncle Sep, who was breathing audibly in quick short gasps; animosity had sprung to arms within the eyes of the two ladies.

"My dear Lizzie," said Mrs. Puckle; then suddenly advancing upon her and seizing her unawares she attacked her with a vigorous embrace.

"Well, Uncle," said Lizzie, releasing herself as vigorously, and straightening her back; "you *have* indeed given us a surprise!"

I knew that Lizzie was furious, wild with indignation and consternation, but years of governessing had taught her extraordinary self-control.

"Yes, my dear, life is full of surprises," said the professor, to whom things seemed to be going unexpectedly well. "I hope there is a good fire in my room," he added bumptiously. "Jessie," to the bride, "you will like to take your things off, and we will have dinner at once."

"All right," she answered obediently. "Dear me, how warm and cosy it all looks!" and the bride's quick eyes travelled round the room, and noted the solid mahogany furniture, the massive table appointments, and the whole appearance of unostentatious comfort. On her way towards the door she halted and addressed herself particularly to Lizzie.

"Your uncle and I were always friendly you remember, and a fortnight's propinquity was too much for us both!"

"Was it really?" rejoined Lizzie, speaking with set lips, and a bright red spot on either cheek.

"Yes," replied the bride, "we have so much in common, and are both old enough to know our own minds." And then she turned her broad back on her new niece, and passed into the hall.

"This I suppose is the drawing-room?" And the bride threw open the door and stood in a "monarch of all I survey" attitude on the threshold. Within, it looked black and aggressively forbidding; it was as if the spirit of the old house distrusted this stranger.

"Oh dear me, what a horrible smell of damp and dry rot! I shall have a fire in here every day."

Having made this announcement, Mrs. Puckle closed the door with emphasis, and mounted the stairs.

The landing was already piled with luggage—bags, baskets, battered cardboard boxes, and shabby trunks. Lizzie conducted her supplanter to her quarters with exaggerated ceremony—even dissembling her feelings so far as to get out fresh towels and the best scented soap—and having been told to order dinner to be ready in ten minutes' time, she flew down to me.

As the craven and base professor was a refugee in his den, Lizzie and I had the dining-room to ourselves.

"So for once he *did* mind telling!" I began.

"Eva, how can you joke?" she interrupted indignantly; "I was wrong to let him go alone, but influenza makes one such a worm, not only weak in body but in mind, otherwise I never would have consented to this trip to London—a most fatal excursion for him. Mrs. Bickers is the worst, most catty, and pushing of all the widows. I believe she is penniless and has just flattered herself into this comfortable home." Then to Clarice who had entered gaping, "Clarice, your master was married ten days ago; let Eliza know."

"Eliza, she do know," was the prompt reply. "She says the master be daft!"

A stealthy rustle on the stairs interrupted Clarice, who hurried out, only to return almost immediately with the soup tureen and evidently prepared to enjoy a good leisurely stare at the stranger—a sleek, complacent matron, wearing a pink satin blouse and a large lace collar, fastened by a new-looking diamond brooch.

Seating herself at the head of the table and seizing the soup ladle, Mrs. Puckle said:

"I'll just sit here, Lizzie dear, I know you won't mind, and begin to take over at once—it saves trouble."

Lizzie's answer was a bow as she placed herself opposite to me; the professor now appeared and, with assumed geniality, announced that he was "starving."

I noticed that his appearance was considerably improved. He wore a glossy white shirt, his hair and beard had been trimmed—also his nails.

"Well, Lizzie," he began, blinking his eyelids—sure sign of nervousness—"I thought I'd do something to get out of the rut. Beke is such a stick-in-the-mud sort of place, eh? I suppose *this* is the surprise of your life?"

"Well, Uncle, I confess it is—so far——"

"'Happy the wooing that's not long a doing,' and you know we had no one to consult. We shall all shake down together, eh? The more the merrier. It's a fine big house. I remember hearing that old Elias Puckle, who lived here eighty years ago, had a family of fifteen children!"

"How many bedrooms?" inquired the bride in her brusquest manner.

"About eight," I replied, now thrusting myself into the conversation, as Lizzie seemed to be temporarily dumb. "Not counting the servants' rooms, garrets, and cellars."

"You are not thinking of taking P.G.'s?" put in the professor jocosely.

"No, no, darling, of course not."

To hear the professor addressed as "darling" was altogether too much for my gravity. I choked, and then stooped for an imaginary handkerchief to hide my smiles.

"Have you done anything about your plays?" I asked as soon as I had recovered my usual composure.

"Oh yes, I have everything in capital train now; the missis there has interest, she has relations on the boards. We expect great things from 'The Termagant,' don't we, ducky?"

"Of course we do; it will be an enormous success," she answered, speaking as it were in capital letters. "Recognition has been a long time in coming to the dear professor, has it not?"

As she spoke, Mrs. Puckle fastened her eyes on me; undoubtedly she had heard of "the readings."

"Most geniuses have had the same painful experiences. Shakespeare, by all accounts, had little honour in his own day, and think of poor dear Chatterton! It's my belief—and I know what I'm talking about—that the professor's plays will be acclaimed by packed houses yet—his name and fame will be world-wide."

As Mrs. Puckle's manner was distinctly challenging, I meekly murmured:

"I hope so, I'm sure."

The lady now proceeded to criticise, dissect, and destroy the reputations of the leading dramatic authors of the day. She talked ceaselessly; evidently she was talking for talking's sake, in order to counteract Lizzie's gloomy silence.

After the professor had swallowed a second strong tumbler of whisky and water, he ventured to draw his niece into the conversation; under the circumstances her composure was extraordinary. I sat amazed, as she unfolded parish happenings and domestic news, as if totally unconscious that a stranger had suddenly descended on her home and usurped her position. Meanwhile, I observed the new aunt carefully examining the forks and spoons and turning them about to discover the hall-mark. Satisfied that they were mostly old Georgian silver, she proceeded to cross-examine me.

"So you live at 'The Roost' altogether, Miss Lingard?"

"For the present—yes."

"And are you *really* related to the Lingards of Torrington?" she inquired condescendingly.

"Yes, Mr. Lingard is my uncle."

"And Miss Lingard who is to marry Sir Beaufort Finsbury is your cousin?"

I nodded assent.

"Torrington Park is quite a large place, is it not?"

"Yes," I admitted, "it is rather large."

"How many servants do they keep?"

"I really do not know."

"Doesn't it seem rather a pity that you cannot live with your own relations?"

This was a nasty one for me, and for the moment I could not think of any effective reply.

"And you," firing a shot at Lizzie, "were the governess at Torrington—nursery, or otherwise?"

To this impertinent question there was no rejoinder.

By this time the goose, pudding, savoury and cheese had been disposed of, and having dined satisfactorily, and figuratively shown her teeth, Mrs. Puckle made a move. Addressing the professor, she said:

"As I am rather tired, darling, I'll go up early and unpack. Don't be long, and don't smoke more than one pipe."

"All right, ducky," he assented, then rising with remarkable agility and pushing back his chair, he retired to the security afforded by his den. It amused me to see how desperately he was afraid of being left alone with us; possibly he was troubled by an uneasy conscience.

As soon as the happy pair had departed, Lizzie rang the bell for Clarice, but for once the bell was answered by Eliza, who came to inform us that "Clarice was upstairs with the mistress, unpacking her boxes." Having made this announcement she began to collect the dinner things as if she bore them a vicious personal spite. Eliza, like Lizzie, was in moments of emotional stress a woman of few words, and whilst she crashed crockery Lizzie was busy scribbling a note at the bureau, which, when finished and folded, she handed to our retainer and said:

"Just run over with this to the rectory, Eliza; there is no answer."

"And how would I run that am bent in two with the rheumatics?" demanded Eliza in a querulous tone. "One run I'll make, and it's out of this house—I know the class of that one, so I do."

"That is enough, Eliza," said Lizzie with dignity. "Come, Eva, there is a good fire in my room."

As soon as I was seated in a comfortable easy chair I flung out my arms and exclaimed: "What a dinner! I declare there was a smell of gunpowder in the air! Tell me, Liz, what you are going to do? I know you have some plan—I see it in your eye."

"We leave here to-morrow," she announced with curt decision.

"Oh! Not really?"

"Yes," she proceeded, "to stay at the rectory as a sort of *pied-à-terre*. I made up my mind about everything before that woman had been in the house five minutes. You shall go to Torrington."

"No, no, Lizzie," I protested, "anywhere but Torrington. Do you know it is a fact, that when I was last there I used to lie awake at night for *hours* hating Aunt Mina? Besides, they won't have me," I concluded triumphantly.

"But they must," she answered, with an air of serene resolution. "I no longer have a suitable home to offer you. I intend to move up to London and take a small flat."

"And leave Mrs. Puckle monarch of all she surveys?"

"By no means," deliberately turning up her skirt and placing a pair of neat black velvet shoes upon the fender. "Uncle Sep has misled her. She believes that the house and money are exclusively his, and is not aware that the half of everything belongs to me. I shall consult my solicitor, value, remove and store my portion of the furniture, let half 'The Roost,' and take my share of *all*—yes, to the ultimate egg spoon!"

"Will you?" I ejaculated. "What fun!"

"I'm afraid Mrs. Puckle will not see the humour of the situation, but find herself bitterly disappointed. With our united incomes, and your hundred a year, Uncle Sep and I were almost rich. Now he will be obliged to economise. I am sorry for Uncle Sep. I have always understood that Mrs. Puckle, who was penniless, contrived to make herself so agreeable to Mrs. Williams at Number 20 that she kept her on as useful help, advertiser and toady! I believe she has two ne'er-do-well sons and a married daughter, and no doubt will accommodate them all at 'The Roost.' Poor Uncle!"

To which adjuration I added a fervent "Amen."

"I shall be sorry to part with you, dear child," continued Lizzie, "but you are sensible for your age and have your wits about you, and it is time you put out from the shore; your aunt cannot refuse a harbour, and, with a favouring breeze, I believe your little skiff will go far. As for me, I shall have my freedom; I have saved, and in London I shall breathe freely among people of my own tastes. Well, we can do the rest of our talking at the rectory, for now I must pack. I intend to make an early flitting. Jones will cart over our boxes in the wheelbarrow, and, as I have a great deal to gather and sort, I expect to be up all night. You, my dear child, have only your clothes and books, so it will not be a long business, but go and set about it at once, and good night."

The next morning we found ourselves comfortably installed at the rectory, Lizzie encompassed with the results of many trips by wheelbarrow; and here, when her flight was discovered, she received the visit and onslaught of her aunt and uncle. But they found the fugitive firmly entrenched behind facts and will power; no alluring invitations would induce her to return to "The Roost" and "go shares." She was excessively polite but immovable, and her visitors were compelled to retreat in obvious confusion—the professor dazed and pallid, his bride on the contrary with a beetroot complexion, and seething over with suppressed passion.

Soon after their departure the dog Kipper arrived; formally dispatched in charge of the gardener, accompanied by his luggage so to speak—bowl, basket, coat and lead; to intimate that he was absolutely expelled from "The Roost."

And now the question arose, what was to be done with him? The rector—most selfish of men—flatly refused him a home, declaring that he was too old for a dog, and that his personal cat was elderly and a fixture. It was clear that Lizzie could not have Kipper in her flat on possibly a fifth floor, although there *was* a legend that, once upon a time, a lady had maintained a duck in similar quarters!

"You shall take him, Evie," she announced, with an air of cool decision. "He was always your friend, and in a big place like Torrington one dog more or less will never be noticed."

"But I am confident that Aunt Mina won't have me," I protested, "much less the dog."

"Oh yes she will," rejoined Lizzie with conviction; "I know your aunt. I ought to, after living under her roof for eight years. Whatever her feelings are she studies appearances, and now that Dora is going to be married there will be room for you in the landau."

My aunt's invitation was somewhat tardy. Before its arrival I made many farewell calls and spent a whole day with the Soadys, where I received (in confidence) the news of Tossie's engagement to Fred Block. She had made up her mind at last! I was much interested, so also was the village, in beholding great vans loading up in front of "The Roost," and subsequently carrying away Lizzie's share of the furniture. I also observed a large painted board, stoutly planted in the front garden, on which was announced "The Half of this House to be Let, Eight Good Rooms. Apply at the Post Office." The vans and the advertisement gave our little community plenty of topics for discussion.

Ultimately the "Beetle" fly transported Lizzie and myself to the junction station, and the curtain fell on Beke.

CHAPTER VI
IN AUNT MINA'S SHOES

In the creaking, rumbling fly conversation had been somewhat difficult, but when in a smooth-running first-class carriage—which luckily we had to ourselves—Lizzie and I enjoyed at last a heart-to-heart talk. My aunt's letter, so tardy in making its appearance, had been cordial and even affectionate. She no longer addressed me as if I were a naughty child, but a full-grown human being, and even an intelligent member of society! I drew her epistle from my hand bag and glanced over it once more.

It was written from Claridge's Hotel, and said:

"My dear Eva,—Do excuse my delay in writing to you with respect to your future plans, but I have been so busy, and so *rushed*, I've had scarcely a moment to myself. I have heard from Lizzie of her uncle's most *disgraceful* and *insane* behaviour; how she has been driven out of her comfortable home by a penniless adventuress. Silly, irresponsible old men such as the professor, should, in my opinion, be placed under proper restraint. As 'The Roost' is closed you will, of course, come to us and be one of the family—at least, for a time. Lizzie has reminded me that you are nearly twenty, and it is certainly desirable that you should come out and be presented, but somehow you have always seemed younger than your age. Girls shoot up so quickly and one forgets how years fly.

"Professor Puckle's aberration happens at a most awkward moment. You have heard from Dora of her engagement to Sir Beaumont Finsbury? We are all *so* pleased. He is quite charming, and has a lovely place in Sussex. A widower with one son, and that is the worst that can be said of him! The girls and myself are now in town getting the trousseau, making arrangements for the wedding, and have such hundreds of engagements, and so much to do, that I am afraid we shall not be at Torrington for another fortnight. However, your uncle is at home, and you and he will have to entertain one another. Unfortunately it is the dull time of the year (being Lent), but I dare say you will find a steady animal to ride, and you can always go and see dearest Mrs. Paget-Taylor, she is so cheery and sociable. The wedding will take place at Torrington early in April, and of course you will be one of the bridemaids. Post me a pattern, and I will order your dress at once. Your cousins send their love,

"Your affectionate aunt,
"Wilhelmina Lingard."

"P.S.—I hope you have good news from Ronnie?"

"Quite a nice letter," remarked Lizzie, as she watched me folding it up. I noticed that her colour had increased, and her eyes, like her uncle's, were blinking—invariably a sign that she had something unpleasant to disclose. She gave a little cough, and said, "Now that all is so amicably arranged, I feel that I am bound to tell you that at first your aunt was anxious that you and I should not part company."

I met her glance steadily and said:

"Then I presume that was the subject of all those letters and sheets of telegrams?"

"It was," admitted Lizzie; "she wished you to share the flat, and urged that we were so accustomed to one another, and so attached, etc. But I absolutely declined, and said that the time had come when you should take your place in society. In short, my dear, I refused to be a party to shutting you up in a flat with a middle-aged person like myself—you must have your place in the sun."

"Do you think I shall enjoy a place in the sun at Torrington?" I asked sarcastically.

With my mind's eye I read the whole correspondence between Aunt Mina and my companion. My aunt's urgent desire to foist me upon Lizzie Puckle; Lizzie's equally firm determination to establish me with my aunt. Possibly—nay probably—she had been offered a handsome bribe; but both the bribe and I had been declined. No doubt Lizzie had acted in what she believed to be my best interests, but the result left me rather sore. Apparently I was wanted neither at Torrington nor in the flat!

"Well, at least a few gleams must fall on you when Dora has become the Lady Finsbury; you will fill the gap in the family! Your aunt will no doubt move heaven and earth to transfer you to a home of your own. Perhaps you will be disposed of next season, and I hope— —"

Here I broke in angrily,

"If Aunt Mina attempts to make a match for me I warn you that I shall run away. I can always find a home with the Soadys."

"My dear Eva, you shall never arrive at that strait! Should you find Torrington unbearable you must come and live with me. I shall take a flat with a spare bedroom, and that will be, if the worst comes to the worst, your haven of refuge. But I can't help thinking that you will settle down comfortably at Torrington; you are a grown-up young woman now and must be treated as such; and for your part you will no longer give way to screaming fits of passion, or to biting saucers! You must be sure to write to me often, and tell me all your joys and sorrows. And remember, my dear child, that in any trouble or difficulty you may always look to *me*."

At a great junction sixty miles from London I was obliged to change, and as we steamed into the station, with a few words, many kisses and two or three tears, I took leave of Lizzie. Here our life's pathway also parted; she, to lead at last a free existence, and I, to enter once more my aunt's house of bondage.

I was met at our local station by a brougham and a luggage cart, and was soon bowling along the frosty country road. Torrington had splendid iron gates, flanked by imposing lodges. The avenue was long, and, so to speak, made the most of itself! About a quarter of a mile from the entrance the house came into view, but I felt no glow of joyful recognition; in spite of a park, delightful gardens and clipped yew hedges, I had little affection for the home of my ancestors. With its blank white façade it gave me the impression of some ghastly sinister face, peering out from among the surrounding woods.

The modern Torrington consisted of a vast domed entrance hall with suites of cold lofty rooms to right and left. To the rear was the old Tudor building and chapel; here were narrow dark passages, unexpected steps and low ceilings. It was in this part of the house that I had previously had my quarters; it was also in this region that the family ghost was reported to reside.

On my arrival I was ceremoniously received by Baker, the butler. Baker had been many years at Torrington and was a most trustworthy retainer. There was a legend that *he* was the butler who, when master said, "This champagne is corked," breathed in his ear, "Never mind, sir, it'll do for the ladies!"

Baker, who had grown portly with years, and had known me as a child, was rather inclined to be paternal in his manner. He had witnessed my fits of fury and been privy to my terms of punishment and disgrace. After a word or two of greeting, he added:

"We have put you in the pink room, Miss Eva."

"Yes, Baker, I am beyond the nursery now, am I not?" I said as I stood beside him in the hall and looked over his head, now bald and shiny.

"That's true, miss, a grown-up young lady. I should say you'd shot up a couple of inches since you were here last. Tea is laid in the library. I expect the squire will be in directly."

A pause of horror as he noticed Kip.

"I say, Miss Eva, this will never do; what about the dog?"

"Oh, the dog will be all right," I replied in my most offhand style, "and no trouble to anyone."

Baker gave a dubious cough and said:

"You know Mrs. Lingard don't allow visiting dogs. I can't see how we shall manage."

I made no reply, but turned to ascend to my room. Baker accompanied me, still muttering to himself and shaking his head. More than once he had carried me, kicking and screaming, up these very stairs! On the first landing I was met and taken charge of by a smart maid, who ushered me into one of the second best rooms—a pretty apartment, facing south—and asked me for my keys. I endeavoured diplomatically and with some success to interest her with respect to Kip, released my best hat from durance vile, bathed my face, got into a new blouse, and hurried down to meet my uncle in the library. He had just returned from hunting and brought with him a bracing whiff of keen fresh air and new leather.

For a moment he stared at me, as if I were an utter stranger, then exclaimed:

"Hallo, Evie! I scarcely knew you! Glad to see you!" kissing me on the cheek. "It's ages since you were here. How is that, eh?"

Impossible to tell him the bare naked truth, so I replied, "Don't you remember, the doctors thought this place too relaxing for me. But now I am perfectly well."

"Eh, that's good news! Now come along and pour out tea and give me a big cup. Your aunt and the girls are detained in London with all these wedding bothers. She sent me Miss Puckle's letter, that told all about that blithering old fool her uncle. Rather a smash up for Miss Puckle and you! Still it's an ill wind that blows nobody good, and I am very glad to have you here. I say, where did that dog come from?" as Kipper trotted in with the footman, escort to poached eggs and hot buttered toast.

"He was Miss Puckle's property," I explained, "and she gave him to me; he really is a very good fellow." (Yes, the days of slipper-eating were no more!)

"I'm afraid your aunt won't stand him!" said my uncle, looking unexpectedly grave. "You see she keeps griffons herself—she has them with her now—and these fox-terriers are the devil for fighting, and besides that he is bound to disturb the game. However, I suppose he can stay till she comes back, and then maybe we shall be able to find him a good home."

Uncle was a handsome dapper little man, with clean-cut features and a remarkably neat figure. Ronnie resembled him, and uncle reminded me of Ronnie in some ways. He and I, being *tête à tête*, got on famously: we went for long walks about the place, over the Home farm and round the coverts. Our tastes agreed; we both liked the country. We visited the gardens, the stables, and once or twice I rode to a meet in one of my cousin's habits—which was a decidedly easy fit. After dinner we played piquet and talked politics; in short, we became great friends. Uncle imparted to me in confidence that he was not much in favour of the brilliant match. Finsbury was a fellow of his own age and something of a *vieux marcheur*. I think—as he smoked an excellent cigar by the fire in the library—uncle forgot that his listener was only a girl, and talked to me as freely as one man to another. "Finsbury's lawyer had been very stiff over the settlements." I also gathered that "Bev was terribly wild and extravagant, but could do no wrong in his mother's eyes."

"By Jove, she even jokes at his bills! There is nothing of the Lingard in him, not like Ronnie, who is a Lingard to the bone. I sometimes feel as if he were my own son. I am proud of Ronnie. As for you, my dear," and he patted my arm affectionately, "you must make yourself at home here, now and always."

"I should like to, uncle, if I may."

"What is to hinder you?" he inquired.

I knew, but I could not tell him. Possibly he guessed, for he added:

"You know your aunt is a good sort, if you take her the right way. Having pots of money in her own hands is a handicap for any woman"—he heaved a tell-tale sigh, then pulled himself up and said, "Now come along, and let us play piquet."

It was rather startling to find myself temporary mistress of this great household, to enter rooms I had never seen, to examine things I had never ventured to touch, to play on the grand Steinway piano undisturbed for hours, to give orders, to ring bells, and to sit at the head of the table in the place sacred to my masterful relative. Once I ventured to open the door of her boudoir, and went in on tiptoe, but I did not remain long; the whole room seemed to be imbued with the personality of its mistress.

On hunting days I was alone. Uncle breakfasted, booted and spurred, fussed off to some distant meet, and rarely reappeared before five or six o'clock. I occupied my spare hours in reading, practising, and writing letters—seated at Aunt Mina's bureau in the morning room, and using the best paper headed "Torrington Park." As the family were known to be from home, there were no visitors except the rector, and the wife of uncle's agent, Mrs. Paget-Taylor, who had made a delightful home for herself in the old Dower House across the park.

It was an ideal hunting day, damp and cloudy. In the afternoon, Kipper and I, who had been for a long tramp through the bare wet woods, sat together on a big buffalo rug before the fire in the library. I think I must have been dozing, when I heard the door open and a sonorous voice announce:

"Captain Falkland."

I sprang to my feet, and so did Kipper. Captain Falkland looked astonished as he advanced, then halted and said:

"The butler told me I would find Miss Lingard here."

"Miss Eva Lingard," I corrected. "My aunt and cousins are in London. Uncle is out hunting, but he may be in at any moment."

"Ah, I doubt that," said the visitor. "The hounds met at Grantley, and it is a capital scenting day; if they find, he will have a long ride home."

"Won't you sit down?" I said, pointing to a chair near the fire.

"It's odd," he remarked, looking at me as he seated himself, "but I have never seen you here, and I have often been over for shoots. My people are only ten miles away."

"That is easily explained," I replied, "most of my time has been spent at school, and since I left Cheltenham I have been living with my old governess at Beke. At least"—correcting myself—"she is not *very* old, but she was with my cousins here for a long time."

"But Beke—why Beke? What a dismal hole! I have been there to buy tobacco, and rank bad stuff it was!"

"They say Beke is healthy, and the doctors thought Torrington didn't suit me."

"But surely you are all right now?" he remarked briskly. "I've come over to say good-bye, as I'm off to India on Friday. I am sorry to miss the squire, but, on the other hand, am awfully glad to find *you* here. You have been such a most distracting puzzle to me."

"A puzzle," I echoed, as I rang for tea and lights. "Why?"

"Why did you go to that beanfeast at Mirfield? You must allow that it was surprising to see a girl of your class among that crowd."

"I went to that dance just to break the deadly monotony of Beke. I worried Lizzie—that is to say, Miss Puckle—I made her life such a burden that she gave me leave to go for once. It was to be a dead secret, and I never dreamt that anyone I met there would ever see me again."

"I say, what a crew!" he exclaimed, "That fellow with the red tie and yellow boots, and the one in the white sweater!"

"Yes, they were unconventional, I admit, but good kind souls, and I was not in the least ashamed of being in their society. I enjoyed myself immensely—my first ball!"

"Your first ball!" he repeated scornfully. "Well, you had a festive time going home in that shandrydan, I should say!"

As I did not wish to pursue the subject, I asked:

"Do you take sugar?"

"If you please; and so I see you have brought your dog?"

"Yes, but only for a short stay. Dogs are not admitted here. I must find him a home somewhere. They won't have him at the rectory, and the gamekeeper says no, too—though he admires Kip."

"So Mrs. Lingard bars dogs?"

"All but her own griffons. And you are starting for India on Friday? How I envy you! I wonder if you will be anywhere near my brother?"

"I am going to Secunderabad in the Deccan."

"How extraordinary! That is where Ronnie is quartered."

"Then he is in the Service?"

"Yes, the 'Lighthearts,' and has just got his company. He came to see me last September, when he was home on leave. He was not favourably impressed by Beke, and suggested my going to India as a paying guest with nice people. There are only the two of us, and at least we should be in the same country. He wrote to Uncle Horace on the subject, but nothing happened."

"The squire is your uncle?"

"Yes; my father was his only brother."

Captain Falkland stared into his teacup, as if he saw something there of engrossing interest, then raising his eyes to mine, he said:

"I see; and so you have been released from Beke, and have come to live here? Are the Lingards your nearest relations?"

"My only ones, except Ronnie—and he is much more than a mere relation." I cannot imagine what folly possessed me, but I added, "He is very popular here—but I am not."

"Impossible!" exclaimed my companion with ready politeness, "How could that be?"

"Oh, it's a long story—much too long."

"Do tell it to me," he urged, "I shall wait for your uncle; there's nothing to do but talk this gloomy afternoon, and as you are deputy hostess, I expect to be entertained!"

"But it's merely a family prejudice," I objected, "and not the least amusing."

"Your family and mine are old friends and even connections, so why not share the little 'jars' with me?"

"Well, in that case you shall hear all there is to tell," I replied. (Alas! it never required much persuasion to encourage me to talk.) "Ronnie and I arrived here as orphans, when he was ten and I was four. Aunt Mina took to him at once, he has such a dear open face and charming manners; but I— well, we had come from France—and I missed my *bonne*. I loathed porridge and lots of things. I had been spoiled. I gave way to furies, and there is a legend that in one of my rages I bit a piece out of a saucer! In fact, I was always in disgrace, so I was sent to school at Cheltenham, where Ronnie was at college, and we saw one another every week. Then in the holidays I generally brought back something—measles, chicken pox or mumps—so you won't be surprised to hear that I was left at school altogether, and only for missing Ronnie, I much preferred it."

"The family black lamb!" he ejaculated with a laugh, then added, "Is that all?"

"Yes, my past career has been tame—and my future is uncertain."

"It lies in the lap of the gods?" suggested Captain Falkland.

"No indeed, but in the hands of Aunt Wilhelmina. Uncle and I get on together splendidly, but I don't know how it will be when she returns. You see my aunt has not seen me for two years, and she, I am afraid, can only think of me as a detestable, ill-tempered, sickly child. My fate, like that of Kipper, is trembling in the balance."

"Kipper's fate need no longer tremble," declared Captain Falkland. "With your permission, I will undertake his future."

"Ah, but you are going to India?"

"Yes, and I shall be rather glad of a dog. They are great company, and these fox-terriers are the only breed that really thrive in a hot place, and I believe Secunderabad is fairly warm."

"If you will really take Kipper," I said, "I shall be most grateful, and he will see an old friend out there—my brother. If Kip is tiresome, you must pass him on."

"I have never met your brother, as I am only recently appointed as A.D.C. to the general, but I shall look him up, and carry him any messages or parcels from you."

"Tell him not to be so lazy about writing, and that you found me happily established here."

"But still, so to speak, 'on approval?'"

"I suppose it amounts to that!" Then suddenly, overwhelmed with qualms at my indiscreet outpourings, I added, "But please, Captain Falkland, forget *everything* I have told you. You know you made me talk, and I am afraid I am only too ready to chatter, and let my tongue run away with me."

"There I envy you, for I can't talk, or ever get out half I want to say. When I was a boy I had a hesitation in my speech; it was cured, but the memory has always tied my tongue. My family call me 'Dummy.' I suppose Miss Puckle kept you in great order?"

"No indeed, she merely pointed out my faults."

"And these are——"

"Having told you so much I may as well confess that I like to talk when I get the chance. Since leaving school I have led rather a solitary sort of life. Miss Puckle was busy all day in the parish, or flying over the country on her bike. At night she was generally dead tired, and would lie on the sofa while I played to her, and the professor was buried in his books. Here, my uncle has been away since eight o'clock this morning, and I have had no one to speak to except Baker the butler, and of course we cannot advance beyond the weather, so when I get hold of listeners, I don't spare them!"

"But your faults?" he persisted.

"Talking too much—being unguarded and impulsive, proud, and they say, hot-tempered! Turn about is fair play. What about your weaknesses?"

"Silence is best," he answered with a laugh.

"And I have confessed everything! Just like me. Well, even so, it might have been worse. As you are going to India we are not likely to meet again, and you will soon forget my chatter and myself."

"I have a tenacious memory, Miss Lingard. In fact, I may say, that I am tenacious about most things and I shall not forget you. You never expected to come across me after that night of the dance, when you were so mysterious, and, may I add—so saucy? Yet here I am, and actually in possession of your dog. I shall keep you posted up in his career. I may write to you, may I not?"

"Write," I ejaculated, my breath taken completely away, "I should like to hear——" then I hesitated. "Of course I know that lots of girls write to men—my cousins do—but I've never corresponded with anyone but Ronnie; my aunt would ask questions, and wonder how I made your acquaintance."

"You made my acquaintance at Torrington. Our official acquaintance only began to-day. I shall certainly drop you a line."

"Oh no, no, please do not write," I protested with energy. Then, aware of the presence of a soft-footed manservant, who had entered to remove the tea things, I broke off abruptly and hastily changed the conversation. I believe Charles was deeply interested in our talk, for he lingered over his task, and rearranged the saucers on the tray with very deliberate exactitude. Just after he left the room a little tinkling clock chimed six and my companion sprang to his feet.

"I say," he exclaimed, "it is later than I thought! Awfully sorry I can't wait to see the squire; give him all sorts of messages for me. Well," stooping, "come along, Kip, say good-bye to your missis," suddenly raising the drowsy and astonished animal and holding him towards me.

"Must he go now, so soon?" I faltered.

Captain Falkland nodded, and as I kissed Kipper between his eyes I felt a great lump in my throat. I was parting with one of my very few friends, but I instinctively realised that I had bestowed him on a kind master.

With the struggling dog hoisted under his arm, his new owner wrung my hand, and said,

"Good-bye, I promise to take jolly good care of Kip." He paused as if about to add something, then evidently changed his mind, hastily opened the door, and went forth. For my part, I resisted an almost overpowering impulse to follow him into the hall, but I was aware that such a proceeding would be outrageously improper. What would Baker think and say? As I stood half-hearted and uncertain in the middle of the room, I heard a motor buzzing down the avenue. He was gone! Then I went and sat on the rug before the fire, now entirely alone, and was aware of a curious sense of personal desolation. I dared not trust my heart to answer the question, which of the two I most regretted—the man or the dog?

By and by uncle arrived in exuberant spirits, talking himself into the library at the top of his clear, well-bred voice. It had been as Captain Falkland predicted, "the run of the season." I was not a sportswoman, and I listened with politely assumed interest to a vivid description of the desperate going over Hippersly, the amount of grief that ensued, and the astonishing exploits of two hunters. At last, after having blown off sufficient steam, he said:

"So I'm told Falkland has been here?"

"Yes, he came to say good-bye to you. He starts for India on Friday. He waited ages."

"What do you call ages?"

"Over an hour."

After a pause of astonishment:

"You must have made yourself mighty agreeable, eh? Falkland hasn't much to say for himself. He is a rattling good sort and a keen soldier, but not a ladies' man."

"On the contrary, he made himself very agreeable to *me*, for he has taken Kipper off my hands."

"What, the dog! Well, well, that's all right! He would be a bit of a nuisance when your aunt came home. I hope he won't get into trouble with Lady Louisa's prize cats."

"Oh, there is no fear of that," I answered eagerly, "for Captain Falkland is taking Kip with him to India."

Uncle stared at me, and gave a loud whistle.

"I say, Eva, keep that dark! If your aunt were to hear of this dog-giving, and taking, she'd—anyway, there'd be wigs on the green!"

CHAPTER VII
THE FAMILY SKELETON

Mrs. Paget-Taylor, whose society had been so urgently recommended by my aunt, was the wife of uncle's agent, Captain Paget-Taylor, a broad-shouldered, long-headed, active man of fifty, a first-rate farmer and a celebrated shot. His consort was a little dark woman endowed with extraordinary animation, tact and capability. Her house was comfortable and well appointed, her cook a treasure, her delightful drawing-room furnished with most inviting sofas and chairs, delicious cushions, stacks of flowers, and softly shaded lamps. This apartment was the council chamber and scene of many important conferences, for Mrs. Paget-Taylor was a power in the neighbourhood. From her kidney-shaped writing table she pulled many strings and was credited with an ample supply of what is known as "interest." Her activities, although of the same genre, were on a different scale to those of Lizzie Puckle. Whilst Lizzie harangued school children, took the chair at meetings, got up rummage sales, and shepherded outlying hamlets, Mrs. Paget-Taylor merely held interviews and confidential conversations. She was known to be exceedingly insidious and persuasive, and I may say at once that she was my aunt's right hand! My relative referred to Mrs. Paget-Taylor on every question and in every crisis—whether it was the matter of a new kitchen range or a prospective son-in-law; and, as the agent's wife had no family and ample leisure, she was in a position to throw herself heart and soul into other people's affairs.

No one in the whole neighbourhood was so popular as Mrs. Paget-Taylor; she was always agreeable, well dressed, helpful, and sympathetic. Half the girls and the young married women laid their miseries before her, and she might almost be said to have kept a high-class registry office for marriages and situations!

When I arrived at Torrington the lady happened to be away from home. A week later I received a note from the Dower House, inviting me down to tea. Naturally I accepted with pleasure, although I impressed upon myself as I walked across the park that I must be very cautious and not give myself away, or burst into impulsive confidences, as had been the case in my last *tête-à-tête*.

Mrs. Paget-Taylor invited me partly from good nature, and partly in order to hold an inspection, on which to report on me elsewhere. As I entered, the atmosphere of the place seemed to exude warmth and comfort; the flagged entrance hall was covered with a thick carpet, heated by a great log fire, and furnished with old oak chests and chairs. Somehow I liked the feel of the place!

I found the mistress of the house in the drawing-room, hastily stamping letters for the evening post. As she rose and offered me an affectionate embrace, her keen dark eyes swept me with one swift glance and she said:

"So glad to see you, Eva! I am sorry I have been away until to-day. You must have found it terribly dull, I'm afraid."

"Oh no," I answered mendaciously. "Uncle is very kind, and takes me about with him. He lends me 'Old Soldier,' and on the days he doesn't hunt we go for long rides."

"You are grown up now," she said, drawing me towards the sofa, "and not a Lingard, like your brother! You look such a vivid, youthful, happy creature, you must be a Mostyn. I remember hearing that your mother had masses of wonderful hair and such smiling grey eyes."

"Are my eyes smiling?" I inquired.

"Yes," she assented. "I noticed them when you were here two years ago—sunny eyes, I would call them. Now come and let us have a nice talk and tell me all about yourself."

"There's so little to tell. If you knew Beke, you would understand."

"You are quite strong, I can see—the picture of health. I am sure you are glad of the change and looking for a little excitement, and things to happen, are you not?"

After we had talked about the family and the forthcoming marriage, my aunt's bronchitis and the professor's enormities, there was a slight pause, and I was surprised to hear myself saying:

"Mrs. Paget-Taylor, you know everybody and everything. I should be so grateful if you would tell me a little about my parents. Whenever I ask my aunt her answers are vague. I have my mother's picture, and I know she died in France, and that my father was so broken-hearted that he threw up his commission and disappeared to America, where he died."

"I never saw your mother," said Mrs. Paget-Taylor, now looking at the fire with an immovable face. "She was seldom in England. Your father's regiment was quartered in the Mediterranean, but I have always heard that she was most attractive, well born, and an orphan. Your father met her on board ship, coming home from Egypt. She had a moderate fortune—which luckily was settled on the children."

"But why do you say luckily?" I inquired eagerly.

"Because, my dear girl, your father was hopeless in that respect. He had no conscience where money was concerned. He was a confirmed gambler. I am sorry to say it is in the Lingard blood—and just let me give you one little friendly hint: do not ask questions or talk about him at the Park?"

"But why not?" I asked.

Mrs. Paget-Taylor made no reply, but again turned away her face and stared steadily at the fire.

"He is dead, is he not?" I persisted.

"Yes," she answered slowly, "dead, this many years, but I would rather not say any more except this: he is the family skeleton in the cupboard—best leave him there."

For a moment, indeed for much longer, I sat beside my hostess in stunned silence, then with a great effort I began to put on my gloves, and prepared to take my departure.

Mrs. Paget-Taylor noticed my emotion, and instantly became motherly and sympathetic.

"I know exactly how you feel, my dear," putting her hand on my shoulder, and looking into my face, "completely unhinged, of course; what I have told you must be a most painful shock, but it was better—yes, and kinder—to put you on your guard. It is all such an old story now; thank goodness, most people have short memories. It is said that nothing which is in the blood dies. The Torringtons have always been afraid that the family curse might reappear in you or Ronnie—especially Ronnie, but he is as steady as Old Time—such a relief! My dear, whenever you feel inclined, I shall be too glad if you will come down to see me, and I do hope you will find yourself *very* happy at the Park."

Here, as the door opened to admit some belated visitors, I effected my escape.

All the way home in the dark, although I might still be "youthful and vivid," I was no longer a "happy" creature; my mind was tormented with the problem of my parents' story, and it exercised my thoughts for many a day.

I struggled to recall what I could from misty memories of long ago. There was an impression of a great deal of bright sunshine, of being carried up long streets with steps, of a tall lady in white, and a dark man with gold buttons on his coat—and that was all!

CHAPTER VIII
"AN OPEN DOOR"

Two days after my visit to the Dower House, Aunt Mina arrived home. Her return occasioned an extraordinary commotion; what conscientious dusting, what airing of rooms, and what extravagant fires! She was accompanied by my cousins, her future son-in-law, and various guests, also by several maids—including her kennel-maid and four tiny griffons. We had not met for nearly two years, and the deadly fear I entertained of her in childhood and flapperdom had waned. My nerves were stronger, I felt more independent, I looked on my aunt dispassionately, fought hard to smother my sense of personal antipathy and distaste, and to put myself in the place of a stranger, meeting her for the first time. If my uncle was well featured, and of short stature, his wife was his opposite in appearance; tall and bony, with high square shoulders, a pair of bluish green eyes, a large domineering nose, and a sunken, bitter mouth. A plain woman, who made the utmost of her appearance, had admirable taste in dress, and carried herself with dignity. I am glad to state that I did not quail when we met in the library, and she accorded me a smudgy kiss.

"Delighted to see you, Eva," she said. "Hubert," turning to an elderly gentleman with an eyeglass, "this is my niece, or rather my husband's niece, Eva Lingard."

Sir Beaufort Finsbury bowed, carefully rearranged his eyeglass, and, on second thoughts, offered me his hand.

"Hallo, Eva!" exclaimed Clara, "Here you are! And so you've been hobnobbing with the pater all this time? You look as if you'd grown a foot, but, my dear girl, how abominably you do your hair!"

"She's got stacks of it, anyhow," put in her sister; "no pads, nothing put on, eh, Eva?" Dora had always befriended me.

Clara was my senior by seven or eight years. When I was a small child in the nursery she had been a well-grown girl in the schoolroom, and a cruel and merciless bully. She was tall, with a stoop, and had pale reddish hair, a thick white skin, and heavy white eyelids, half concealing her pale prominent eyes. As Clara had a sharp, merciless tongue, wore glasses and subscribed to the London Library, she was generally spoken of as "the clever Miss Lingard." Dora, on the other hand, was dull and indolent, but good looking, in a lazy dark style, and much more amiable than her sister. She was fond of bridge, and did a little betting on the sly! Was the hereditary failing to reappear in *her*?

The party from London, a gay one, was chiefly composed of Sir Beaufort's friends and some of the Lingard connections who had "handles" to their names. One day we patronised a point-to-point steeplechase, the next a race meeting; at night, there was bridge and dancing. My aunt had brought me some evening dresses, my hair was arranged in the latest fashion, and I no longer looked like Beke—nor felt like it either! I enjoyed myself vastly, and was privately informed by Dora that her mother was pleased with me, and that I had been quite presentable. I really believe that at this time my aunt almost liked me. I was ready to help her by writing menus and notes, giving a last little touch to the table decorations, and "taking on" the bores. Moreover, I was in considerable demand as a partner for bridge and dancing, and possibly my chaperon had agreeable visions of getting me speedily off her hands.

Early in April the wedding took place, after a week of the most strenuous preparations. The house was packed to the very roof, and I confess that I was not sorry when the whole affair was over, the bride had said farewell, the last handful of rice had been thrown, and the departing motor become a mere speck on the avenue.

Bev, who had come down expressly for the day, renewed his attentions to me. He informed me that he found me enormously improved in appearance. Unfortunately, I was not able to repay the compliment in kind. Bev had none of the good looks of the Lingard family. To me he always bore a ridiculous resemblance to a young gander. A very long thin neck, a very long beaky nose, a small flat head and no chin, supported this impression.

We had settled into the usual routine, and my aunt was beginning to talk of a couple of weeks in London and a June Drawing Room, when, to the consternation of the whole family, Beverley reappeared, having been sent down from Oxford. Apparently his scrapes had reached a climax. There were debts, too! Uncle's face looked grim and glum, and even my aunt, always so indulgent, was obviously displeased with her darling.

Suppressed by his parents and sister, Bev turned for consolation to me. He followed me about like a shadow and was absolutely impervious to snubs. If I went out riding he became my escort; if I escaped for a walk, or into the old schoolroom, he tracked me down and joined me. My angry protests were of no avail, and I could not help feeling that my aunt was really unlucky. Here was an idle ne'er-do-well loafing about at home. Here was also the niece, whose attractions she feared—and the pair were continually together!

For my part I sought refuge with Clara or Mrs. Paget-Taylor, but what was to be done upon wet days? On one of these Bev joined me in the old schoolroom, where I had ensconced myself before a good fire with a new novel in my hand. I gave him a very tepid reception, as he drew up a chair, put his long feet on the chimneypiece, and lit a cigarette.

"I have been hunting for you everywhere," he announced.

"Yes," I replied, "like the little boy in the fable, who wanted somebody to play with; but I'm not going to play," I added sharply, "and if you worry I shall go and sit up in my own room." And I returned to my book.

"By Jove, Eva, you are changed!" he exclaimed, "such a grand, stand-off young lady. Do you remember how in this very room we used to roast chestnuts and make horrible toffee? We were great pals then, why can't we be pals now?"

"Everything is different," I replied without raising my eyes.

"Oh yes; instead of being a long-legged flapper, with red hands and a cold in your head, you have bloomed into a great beauty."

"Don't talk nonsense," I said impatiently.

"By Jove, it's true! Old Finny"—thus did he refer to the baronet, his brother-in-law—"said that if you were brought out in London you would make a tremendous stir."

"Rubbish," I ejaculated, "he was pulling your leg."

"Not mine; he was talking to the governor; and young Chambers told me there was no one to touch you at the Belmont hop, that the men were falling over one another to get a dance, and I don't wonder." Here he brought down his legs with a crash, threw his cigarette into the fire, and, turning to face me, said, "Eva, I adore you!"

"Oh, shut up," I answered rudely.

"That's a nice way to talk to a fellow," he exclaimed in an injured tone.

"It's the right way when a fellow is talking nonsense."

"You would be the making of me, Evie; you know that," he continued, towering over me as he spoke; "you are awfully clever, the governor says—so clear-headed and sensible, with a capital seat on horseback, and uncommon good looks. He is dead nuts on you. Come now, say you will marry me!"

"And what about your mother?" I asked.

For a moment he was dumb.

"Well, if she objects and makes the place too hot to hold any of us, I'll marry a chorus girl. After all, I'm one and twenty and the property is strictly entailed."

"You'll be cutting a rod to beat yourself, my good Bev, and I should be truly sorry for the poor chorus girl, and incidentally for you. I like you all right, Bev, as a cousin. I do not forget that you always took my part and befriended me when I was in disgrace— —"

"Well, now the boot is on the other foot," he interrupted, "I'm in everybody's black books, I'm in disgrace with the pater, so won't you befriend me? Turn about is fair play."

"I'm afraid, Bev, that the only thing I can offer you is advice. Why don't you try for a commission in the army?"

"Too old."

"Well then, travel; go and see the world."

"If you will come along with me I'll go like a shot."

Ignoring this suggestion with a wave of my hand, I continued my admonition—

"You really must give up betting and cards— —" History, as we all know, repeats itself; even as I spoke the door opened, and my aunt entered.

"Oh— —" and she paused expressively. That "Oh" was dramatic; it conveyed volumes of disapproval.

"Eva, I have been looking for you everywhere. I want you to collect the books for Mudie's, make out a fresh list, and, as the maid is ill, will you wash two of the griffons?"

She spoke in her normal voice, but her jaw was set and her suspicious blue-green eyes roved backwards and forwards from Beverley to me.

"All right," I said, rising with alacrity, only too thankful to close the interview; and as I followed Aunt Mina down the long flagged passages, I knew from the expression of her back, as surely as if she had told me in words, that her fears respecting Bev and myself were once more awakened.

My life at this period was by no means a bed of roses. Uncle was laid up with a sharp attack of gout, possibly brought on by the shock of Beverley's debts. Beverley persecuted me. He was quite too dreadfully cunning, a domestic Sherlock Holmes, and seemed, in spite of his mother's most anxious precautions, to mark down my exact whereabouts with unfailing accuracy. I snubbed him mercilessly, even at meal-times, and, strange to say, my brusque little speeches aroused Aunt Mina's ire; yet if I had been agreeable she would have been furious and have declared that I was "drawing him on." There was no pleasing her, but, poor woman, the situation was harassing; she could not send Beverley from home, as he was not to be trusted—her only alternative was to make some desperate effort to get rid of *me*! Alas! this was a hopeless undertaking. Consequently, so far as I was concerned, she became the very incarnation of despotism and aggression.

Although I lived in a luxurious abode, shared a maid with my cousin Clara (my share I may mention was merely nominal), had a delightful horse to ride, a superb piano to play on, quantities of books and most dainty food, I was far from being happy or contented. The truth was that the continual strain of holding Beverley at bay on the one hand, and vainly attempting to soothe his mother's fears on the other, was altogether too much for my nervous system. The tension was terrible, a tension that was never relaxed. Just at this particular crisis our good genius, Mrs. Paget-Taylor, came to the assistance of the family. She constantly entertained visitors in her comfortable Dower House; sometimes these were relations, sometimes old friends, and occasionally there were casual acquaintances whom she had picked up abroad or when doing a "cure" at home.

One afternoon she appeared, just before tea-time, accompanied by two guests, a lady and gentleman; the former, who followed her closely across the slippery parquet floor of the vast drawing-room, was entirely uncommon and picturesquely different from our everyday callers. The visitor who approached in the wake of Mrs. Paget-Taylor held herself erect, her head slightly thrown back; her face was strikingly handsome, she had wavy brown hair, straight black brows, extraordinarily expressive eyes, and a brilliant complexion. These details can give but a faint idea of her personality. She wore a costume of some rich dark blue material with little touches of gold, and a hat that was equally *chic* and becoming. The vision was so vivid and impressive that I could do nothing but gaze, and gaze, and gaze.

The strangers were presented as "Captain and Mrs. Hayes-Billington," and Mrs. Paget-Taylor murmured to my aunt that he was "a far away connection, at present on leave from India." Captain Hayes-Billington was a stout well-set-up man of thirty, with regular features and a heavy dark moustache, but his face had a puffy appearance; indeed, he was altogether puffy, and to me his arms and legs recalled inflated air cushions, so tightly did his grey suit encase them. He was not in the least overawed or dumbfounded, as were some, by the magnificence of Torrington, but chatted away to Aunt Mina about "my regiment," "my appointment," and "my mines," and carried round the tea-cups with the address of long practice. Mrs. Hayes-Billington also took part in the general conversation. She had a sweet, rather low voice, and exhibited when she spoke glimpses of beautiful teeth. Her manners were easy and assured, and her smile was radiant. Such smiles thawed Aunt Mina's usual manner of ice and iron. She was always amenable when she realised that people were not afraid of her. This stranger was fearless, and listened to her account of the super-griffon's asthma with an admirably assumed air of absorption and sympathy. It was wonderful how rapidly she stole into my aunt's good graces. They discussed Monte Carlo, and the rapacity of milliners, and compared their experiences of French hotels. The visitor also exchanged a few sentences with Bev, who, instead of fleeing from callers as usual, was sitting, tea-cup in hand, staring at Mrs. Hayes-Billington with wide open pea-green eyes.

She inquired the name of his regiment, which query, strange to say, delicately flattered his greedy vanity.

"Not in the army?" she repeated incredulously, "I certainly thought you were in the Guards."

"Oh, no," he rejoined, "I am going into the Diplomatic Service"; which was the first that anyone had heard of it!

It transpired that the couple were spending a whole week at the Dower House ere returning to India in a month's time, and presently I screwed up my courage and ventured to ask her how she liked the East.

"Oh it's all right, as long as one is young," she answered in a deep, rather vibrant voice, looking at me steadily with her marvellous dark eyes. "We have always been in the Punjaub, but this time we are bound for the Deccan. Herbert has been given a very good appointment there. It will be an entirely new country."

Before the little party took leave, my aunt, much to my astonishment, invited them to dinner, for as a rule she never extended hospitality to the Dower House guests.

No sooner had they left us than a chorus of remarks arose, all in praise of Mrs. Hayes-Billington. Bev was particularly loud and eloquent. His mother and sister agreed that she was handsome, smart, and not in the least the usual type of officer's wife that drifted home from India, washed out, flabby and dowdy.

Mrs. Hayes-Billington's appearance of an evening was positively dazzling; in fact, I may say that the effect of her beauty on a country cousin like myself was almost overwhelming. She wore a rose-coloured gown, very *décolletée*, a diamond bandeau in her dark wavy hair, and was undoubtedly the queen of the company. What was Aunt Mina in dark green velvet? What was I, in my new white *crêpe de Chine*? Merely the background of an exquisite picture.

We were a party of twelve; four from the Dower House, five of ourselves, the rector and his wife (she was a bishop's daughter) and young Tom Champneys, a neighbour. Uncle took in Mrs. Hayes-Billington, who sat between him and Bev. I came next to Bev, with Captain Paget-Taylor on my left hand. At the head of the table Aunt Mina was supported by Captain Hayes-Billington and the rector. Mrs. Hayes-Billington talked away with great animation to my uncle. She discoursed of pig-sticking, jackal hunting, and racing, and asked many questions about our local pack; but somehow I received an impression that she and my uncle did not hit it off. It struck me that my usually voluble relation was somewhat reserved in his manner, though always the polite and attentive host. Occasionally she addressed herself to Bev, and found him eagerly responsive.

From the other end of the table I could hear Captain Hayes-Billington relating experiences and stories to Aunt Mina and the rector in a loud, jovial voice. I caught one or two stories—chestnuts, no doubt—with regard to a certain class called "Baboos." One of them had announced that "the army was a glorious profession in time of peace, but in time of war highly dangerous." Another, who had given his seat to a lady, on her saying she was sorry to deprive him of it, replied, "No depravity, madam!" The raconteur laughed so uproariously at his own anecdotes that his hearers were compelled to join—even my aunt accorded a fixed smile.

Young Champneys, who sat opposite, suddenly addressed Captain Paget-Taylor across the table, and said:

"Last time I was in town I saw Falkland at the club. He was just starting for India. He seemed a bit bothered by a dog he had with him. He told me it had been given to him by a girl."

"Oh, rats!" exclaimed Bev, "Falkland isn't a ladies' man, we all know that. He bought the brute at Whiteley's."

"Funny sort of aide-de-camp he'll make," said Captain Paget-Taylor; "I can't see him escorting women, writing invitations, and doing the carpet knight! Falkland is a keen soldier, his character is as strong as a breakwater, but his manner is short and he has no parlour tricks! I believe the general is a connection of Lady Louisa's, and as Falkland had a pretty stiff time in the Soudan, and as a lad got knocked about in the Boer War, his mother clamoured for this easy billet, but of course *he* knows nothing about that!"

Once in the drawing-room, Mrs. Hayes-Billington and my aunt paired off together and enthroned themselves on a sofa, whilst I was dispatched to the piano and commanded to play and sing. Mrs. Paget-Taylor and the rector's wife discussed the temper of the parish nurse, and Clara wrote letters.

Between my unappreciated songs I noticed that Aunt Mina and her guest were engaged in what appeared to be an absorbing conversation. Mrs. Hayes-Billington undertook most of the talking, and was evidently explaining something to my relative, to which she listened with unusual attention, punctuating the information from time to time with slow, impressive nods.

The next day Mrs. Paget-Taylor came up to Torrington, and had a long private conference with my aunt in her boudoir. Subsequently the Hayes-Billingtons were invited to lunch and the lady was taken for a drive in the family landau—a most unusual favour—and, so far as I could divine, for no ostensible reason. It soon became evident that *I* was the cause of all this hospitality and condescension. To make a long story short, the Hayes-Billingtons were hard up; a year at home had proved unexpectedly costly, and they would gladly undertake the charge of a nice girl, if it were made worth while. Their terms were £150 a year inclusive, to be paid quarterly. All this my cousin Clara imparted to me with considerable zest, for although she and I had never openly quarrelled we were far from being really congenial, and apparently she now saw a happy opportunity for displacing me. In her opinion one Miss Lingard in the landau, or the new car, was amply sufficient, and, with a heavily charged brush, she painted my future prospects in glowing colours, finishing off the picture with the announcement:

"You will have a splendid time out there, Eva, you are so lively and superficial, and such a good dancer—just the right sort of girl to go to India."

This may have been a left-handed compliment, but when, as Lord Chesterfield said, a compliment is doubtful, it is best to accept it. My cousin candidly admitted that my uncle was inflexibly opposed to Mrs. Paget-Taylor's scheme. He thought Captain Hayes-Billington a loud bragging sort of bounder; as for his wife, she was a handsome woman, there could be no two opinions about that, but somehow or other she was not his style. She wore too much scent, made too much use of her eyes, and he couldn't exactly place her; but then he was always particularly fastidious. "To come down to the bedrock of the whole question," said Clara, in conclusion, "what do you think yourself, Eva?"

I was not prepared to give her an answer on the spot, and felt rather inclined to fall in with my uncle's opinion. Captain Hayes-Billington, though good-natured, was loud and slangy, and in spite of her spell there was something odd about his wife. She glowed with beauty like some hard irresponsive gem, and for all her flow of impulsive talk I instinctively felt that she was really as cold as a well-cut diamond. I paced slowly up and down the room with my hands locked behind my back, then I went and stood for some time looking out of the window, endeavouring to concentrate my mind on the "fors" and "againsts." Suddenly below in the Italian garden I beheld Beverley, who, having caught sight of me, halted and signalled violently with his handkerchief. No doubt my aunt was watching him from her boudoir—which was just below—and believed that I was encouraging this frantic demonstration.

Oh, I felt my present position to be absolutely intolerable. Yes, even if I went out of the frying-pan into the fire, I resolved to accompany the Hayes-Billingtons to India!

CHAPTER IX
OUT OF THE FRYING-PAN

What a change in my life a few hours had brought. I was going to India! My dream of dreams was about to be fulfilled. In the meanwhile there were arrangements and obstacles to be talked over. Uncle, Beverley and Lizzie Puckle were strongly opposed to my trip, but for once Aunt Mina and I were agreed, and to every objection we presented an invincible force of obstinate resistance. She gave me enthusiastic support, was my firm and eager ally, generously engaged to pay for my outfit and passage, and assured me that I should have a delightful time and that this accidental invitation was "a great chance!" She even went so far as to hint that I would not be long with the Hayes-Billingtons, but soon comfortably installed in an establishment of my own.

"Really, my dear Eva," she said in an outburst of happy relief, "a girl with your air and appearance, not to speak of connections, ought to marry remarkably well."

Apparently I was about to be specially exported to India in order to be launched on the marriage market! That was my aunt's idea. My own was otherwise. I would be within hail of my beloved Ronnie, and far away from the anxieties and embarrassments which encompassed me at Torrington. With a view to a good talk and to learn my immediate requirements I went to tea at the Dower House, where I found only Mrs. Paget-Taylor and Mrs. Hayes-Billington. As I sat beside the latter on the sofa I was nearly overpowered by the perfume of some heavy Eastern scent, and at close quarters noticed that the lady's face was a little made up and careworn. On her part, she was examining me with an unmistakably critical expression in her lovely eyes.

"I hear you ride well and are fond of dancing, Miss Lingard, so we will keep a pony for you," she said. "We start next month, and as we arrive out there in the monsoon you and I will go to the hills together, whilst Bertie, poor boy, must return to those detestable mines."

I had not the faintest idea of what a "monsoon" might be, but did not venture to display my ignorance by making inquiries.

"We are going out by a cheap liner if you don't mind," she continued, "first class to Bombay only forty pounds. We are obliged to be economical. Your expenses on to Silliram will come to about a hundred rupees. Unfortunately, we arrive in the rains, but, you see, Bertie's leave has expired and it cannot be avoided."

She then proceeded to give a long list of my requirements, which Mrs. Paget-Taylor precisely entered in a little notebook. It seemed that I should require a saddle and bridle, a thick and thin habit, warm clothes, cool clothes, smart clothes, cushions, a folding chair, a good supply of scented soap, sheets, towels, a tea-basket, heaps of silk underwear, silk stockings, and also golf and tennis requisites.

Armed with this list I returned to my aunt. I felt a certain diffidence about handing over such a long array of wants, but she seemed to look upon the matter as a mere bagatelle and even added several items. She also informed me that I had (as I knew) an income of £150 a year of my own. This would go to the Hayes-Billingtons, to pay for board and lodging, and as their funds were low she had agreed to lodge the first six months in advance, also she and my uncle had decided to make me an allowance of an additional hundred a year for clothes and my personal expenses. This was generous treatment, and I thanked her warmly. Now that I was actually departing, placing seas and continents between us, Aunt Mina had become semi-attached to me, and it may seem mean of me to add that I believe she scattered this liberality and largesse as sacrifice and thank-offering, and, as it were, the price of Bev.

My aunt accompanied me to London to select my outfit, which was ordered on the most lavish scale; in fact, I would be justified in calling it a trousseau! When the preparations were well *en train* she left me to spend two or three days with Lizzie in the flat, and to be taken by her to undergo my various fittings.

I found Lizzie comfortably installed, looking years younger than she had done at Beke, and quite smart. She gave me to understand that Mr. Chesterfield, the rector, had urged her to marry him, first by letter, indeed letters; and, as these proved unsuccessful, he had actually come to London and figuratively prostrated himself at her feet, announcing that "he was lost without her, and had never realised her priceless value until she was gone! She was sorely missed everywhere and really must recall her decision and return to Beke as Mrs. Chesterfield."

"I told him," said Lizzie, "that I knew how he had leaned upon me and that under other circumstances I would gladly have become his wife, but now it was impossible. Mrs. Puckle was the obstacle. He might think me unchristian if he liked, but I could not breathe in the same parish with that woman."

So much for Lizzie's affairs, and with respect to mine she said: "Eva, I do hope you will never regret this step. I know you have always longed to go to India and I must confess I envy you. I too would like to flap and spread my wings. But you ought to go out under proper auspices. *Who* are these Hayes-Billingtons?"

She had met them at Rumpelmayers, and somehow they had not coalesced. Mrs. Hayes-Billington was lofty in her manner, and inclined to be condescending to Miss Lingard's late governess—who scrutinised that very beautiful chaperon with keenly observant eyes.

"He may be Mrs. Paget-Taylor's cousin, but these Hayes-Billingtons are not in your class—hard up and pretentious. I may be quite wrong, but the man looks as if he drank, and the woman, although undoubtedly handsome, is so made up. My dear Eva, your aunt must be desperately anxious to get rid of you! If the worst happens cable to me and come back to the flat. I am not sure that your little skiff is sufficiently weather-tight to battle among the waves of Indian society."

"I know you are a good judge of character, Lizzie, and before I 'take to the water' I wish you would tell me something about myself. You have carte blanche to say what you like—I shall not be offended."

"Well, it will be no news to you that you have a strong will, and heaps of vitality and staying power; are naturally impulsive and much too talkative, also, in a way, deceptive. Your real feelings are not easily moved, and, except for sick people and animals, your heart is rather hard."

"Oh Lizzie!" I exclaimed.

"Oh Eva!" she echoed. "This is, in a way, true. When you dislike a person it is for always. For instance, nothing would ever make you really care for your aunt and Clara; or at Beke for Mr. Chesterfield and Eliza the cook. On the other hand, your affections are staunch and unchangeable, you idealise your friends far beyond their deserts, and refuse to see a single flaw in their characters. Take, for example, Ronnie. To you he is absolutely perfect, a sort of little god; if it came to a pinch I believe you would make *any* sacrifice for him."

"Yes," I answered stoutly, "any—and glad of the chance!"

"Ronnie is a good sort and fond of you, but he is by no means a stable character. Yours is by far the stronger of the two."

"Lizzie, how can you talk such nonsense?"

"It is the truth, and you may have occasion to realise it yet. With you it is all or nothing, and when you fall in love I confess I shall feel anxious— you will give so much, and may receive so little. Well, there, no one can help you! Fate shuffles the cards and you have yet to meet your destiny. Shall I give you one or two scraps of worldly advice, my dear?"

"Yes, do," I urged eagerly.

"Well, when you go into the big world be careful how you choose your associates; people are judged by their friends."

"Are they? I should not have thought so."

"Try, if you can, not to talk of yourself."

"Yes, I'll do my best, but I have not much else to talk about, have I?"

"There will be plenty of topics once you are out of your little groove. In Vanity Fair I dare say you may receive a share of knocks and bruises among others hustling in the market-place, but whatever these may be do not show them! All I am advising is simply worldly wisdom, and my most urgent important injunction comes last: do not give your confidence to every agreeable woman, or your heart to the first insidious and good-looking man who gazes into your eyes, and tells you that you are pretty and a darling. Wait and look round, for with you to love, is for always."

I felt unexpectedly embarrassed; my face felt hot, as I listened to these intimate personal directions, and I hastened to turn the conversation to Beke and its inhabitants.

In answer to my questions Lizzie informed me that her uncle had taken over the whole of "The Roost," and paid her a rental of twenty pounds a year. The house was now occupied by Mrs. Puckle's married daughter and her three children; with long visitations from Mrs. Puckle's actor son when—as so frequently happened—he found himself "out of a shop."

The new mistress kept pigs, the garden was converted into a poultry run, the mulberry tree and others had been cut down and sold. According to Mr. Chesterfield the establishment was a continual scene of animosity and wrangling, and the professor's beard was as white as snow!

"At one time," added Lizzie, "I would have asked for nothing better than to live my life and end my days in Beke, but, as you know, I have been driven forth by my aunt by marriage!"

CHAPTER X
THE "ASPHODEL"

During my stay in London I saw a good deal of Mrs. Hayes-Billington; her husband had been hastily summoned to his mines and she was alone, awaiting my company in the *Asphodel,* in which we had secured passages. My future chaperon would often drop in at the flat to offer advice respecting my luggage and boxes, or to arrange for meetings at dressmakers. She exhibited a lively interest in my frocks and invariably accompanied me to be fitted. It struck me as strange—or rather I believe Lizzie suggested the idea—that such a handsome and fashionable woman should appear to have so much time on her hands. Apparently she had taken a fancy to me, called me by my Christian name, and was far more demonstrative than my late governess, who had known me since I was a fretful little creature aged four years. Mrs. Hayes-Billington was also her reverse in another respect, as she fed me with a certain amount of flattery. This was indeed a novelty and I must honestly confess that I was not averse to such nectar in small doses, but from huge spoonfuls I instinctively recoiled.

One day I had been enduring the trying on of a lovely white evening frock, and the fitter had left the room in search of some ribbon; as I stood before the long glass contemplating my appearance Mrs. Hayes-Billington suddenly rose, put her arm round my neck, and gazing at my reflection exclaimed:

"Do you know, my dear, that you are *lovely!*"

Before I could protest she continued:

"I think we shall make rather a striking pair, you and I—such a complete contrast. I with my gipsy face, you with your masses of golden brown hair and sunny blue-grey eyes—sometimes they are angel-praying eyes, and sometimes I see a little devil dancing in each of them! Then, and above all, my dear, you look such an aristocrat."

It was an enormous relief to me when the return of the forewoman and skirt hand put an end to these embarrassing and exaggerated compliments.

Ten days later we sailed from Tilbury Docks. I was seen off by my uncle and aunt, Lizzie, Beverley, young Champneys and two schoolfellows who happened to be in London; my cabin, which I shared with Mrs. Hayes-Billington, was packed with books, flowers, and large boxes of my favourite sweets. I must here confess, hard-hearted creature as I was, that I left my native land with composure. I should add, however, that since I had come to woman's estate I was not much given to weeping, but, on the other hand, Mrs. Hayes-Billington, in a voice choked with emotion, large tears trembling in her splendid eyes, assured my aunt and uncle that she would be a *mother* to me.

Our steamer, the *Asphodel*, corresponded with the passage money in every particular. She looked, and was, cheap, and I think I may add, nasty. The smell of oil from the engine-room almost overpowered the salt sea air, and the saloon reeked of new mahogany and stale sherry. The cabins were small and stuffy. There were but two bathrooms for the first-class passengers, who luckily were few and far between: chiefly individuals like the Hayes-Billingtons who had squandered most of their money when on furlough; one or two railway officials, several planters, and half a dozen missionaries; nothing approaching the smart crowd that one heard or read of as passengers to the East. For one thing, we were outward bound at the wrong time of year; and for another, we had booked by an unfashionable line. There were no dances, no games; the piano was a derelict; but the weather and the novelty consoled me for all deficiencies.

As we coasted down by Spain and put in at Gibraltar and Malta, and endured the usual coaling agony at Port Said, it seemed to me that I was seeing the world at last! Mrs. Hayes-Billington and I shared the same cabin. Here I also shared some of the secrets of her toilet; to do her justice she had no false shame, and allowed me to know that certain portions of her hair and complexion were artificial; nevertheless, much of her beauty was *bona fide*. Living at such close quarters I realised that she was considerably older than I had supposed, and, in spite of some wonderful grease that she applied at night, there were wrinkles round her eyes and lines upon her forehead.

I always rose first, in order to clear out of the cabin and give my companion lots of elbow room for dressing. The operation was a lengthy one, and she rarely appeared on deck before twelve o'clock, but, on the other hand, she seldom descended to her berth till after midnight.

Among our fellow passengers she had discovered an old acquaintance in a good-looking officer of the frontier force. His name was Colonel Armadale; he sat next her at meal times, his chair was with ours on deck.

They promenaded for hours at a time, and occasionally disappeared into a particular lair of their own somewhere about the bows of the ship. Mrs. Hayes-Billington carefully explained to me that Colonel Armadale's sister was her very oldest friend, which fact naturally drew them a good deal together, and this was not their sole tie. They had been in the same station in the Punjaub, and had many acquaintances and topics in common. Her friend was always polite and attentive to me, carried my rug, moved my chair, and occasionally included me in the conversation. Once or twice I caught his eyes gazing at me with a curious, interrogative expression. What did it mean?

As he had, to a great extent, appropriated the society of my chaperon, I was more or less thrown upon my own resources. At first the other womenkind seemed to hold aloof from me, but before long I found myself received into the bosom of the missionary circle. There was a kindly white-bearded gentleman and his wife who were going to Assam, and one tall, distinguished woman travelling alone, *en route* to join her husband in Upper Burmah. Her name was Mrs. Ashe, and she and I became comrades, paced the deck together, exchanged books and new stitches in lace work. Her spirits were depressed, as she had just left two small children at home, but presently she cheered up and gave me a great deal of useful information respecting the country to which I was bound. Undoubtedly Mrs. Ashe belonged to my own class, though I may honestly say it was not for this reason that I made friends with her. She informed me that her father had been the general commanding a division in Northern India. There she had met a zealous young Oxford parson, cast in her lot with him, and departed to work in the mission field, to the stupefaction and horror of her family. "It has turned out all right," she added. "Julian and I are very happy. Our only trouble is in having to be separated from the kiddies."

For my own part I imparted abundant information about myself, and told her that I had no parents, no real home, and was going to India in order to be within reach of my brother, also because the family doctor advised that I should spend the winters in a warm climate.

"And Mrs. Hayes-Billington is taking charge of you on the voyage?"

"By no means," I replied, "she is in charge of me altogether. I am to live with them."

For quite an appreciable time Mrs. Ashe was speechless. At last she said:

"But how on earth did your people come across her?"

"Captain Hayes-Billington is distantly connected with some friends. The Hayes-Billingtons were looking for a paying guest, I was anxious to go to India, my aunt liked Mrs. Hayes-Billington—and so here I am."

Mrs. Ashe said no more on this subject, but I gathered that she did not approve of my chaperon, also that the feeling was mutual. The two ladies "looked down their noses" on the rare occasions when they met face to face.

Mrs. Ashe and I had many talks as we sat together on deck on lovely moonlight nights. Steaming down the Red Sea the water was like glass, but no sooner had we left Aden than I learnt the meaning of the word "monsoon." Directly we abandoned the shelter of the coast we were struck by the full force of what to me seemed a hurricane. It burst upon us suddenly at luncheon time; at the first lurch of the *Asphodel* all the knives and plates and glasses slid off the table, and oh! how we rolled and wallowed! We rolled all the way over to Bombay, the rain descended in torrents, and the knocking about, the clinging, and the crawling were horribly uncomfortable. Our *Asphodel* was what is called "a wet boat," her decks were continually swept by seas, and she groaned and shuddered like some stricken animal.

I must confess that I was by no means sorry when the voyage came to an end and we stepped upon the Ballard Pier, in the animated and highly coloured city of Bombay. Here we did not delay more than a few hours, which we spent at the Taj Mahal Hotel, and then drove to Victoria Station to pursue our journey.

Bombay gave me my first sight of the ancient and picturesque East. I was fascinated by the quaint native craft at the quays, the crowds of people in gay and varied costumes, the painted bullock carts, the jingling trams packed so tightly, the fine imposing public buildings and the beautiful bay—"Bon Bahia" indeed!

The ascent of the great Bore Ghât was to me a most thrilling and impressive experience. How we went up, up, up, and how we went down, down, down! What dizzy views of the plains as we crept along precipices and turned the most paralysing angles! Finally, after steady travelling by rail and tonga, we found ourselves at our journey's end—the hill station of Silliram.

It was pouring the traditional "cats and dogs" when we arrived, and here Captain Hayes-Billington awaited us at the tonga office, his broad, good-looking face wet with rain and wreathed in smiles.

It appeared that he had secured a small bungalow, collected a few servants, and done, he declared, "his best to give us a flying start." The bungalow, which was named "The Dovecot," was old and dilapidated, surrounded by a deep veranda and a small garden or compound which separated us from a high road, at present swimming in mud. Accommodation in "The Dovecot" consisted of four rooms, viz. drawing-room, dining-room and two bedrooms, to each of which was attached a ruinous bathroom; for tub, a half barrel of primitive age. The smaller of the bedrooms was naturally apportioned to me, and here, with the aid of an English-speaking ayah, I began to unpack my small baggage and endeavoured to make myself at home. Coming across from Aden I had learnt the true meaning of the word "monsoon." Arriving in Silliram, I received a practical illustration of the word "rains!"

It was not merely rain, but a cataract that battered on the roof, roared down the gutters and made large ponds in our little compound. Silliram was situated on a spur of the ghâts about 4,000 feet above the plains, but for the moment one could see nothing of the place. The atmosphere appeared to consist entirely of a wet white mist; the roads were ankle deep in red mud, the valleys filled with masses of what looked like cotton-wool clouds. Europeans on ponies and disguised in mackintoshes occasionally splashed by our gate, and the natives went about with long bare legs, the remainder of their persons entirely shrouded in brown blankets.

It was now that I began to see the best side of Captain Hayes-Billington. Always loud and boisterous, he was nevertheless wonderfully good-tempered, cheerful and considerate, and eagerly disposed to make the best of everything. He was also surprisingly energetic, and helped his wife and myself to furbish up our shabby little bungalow. I gathered that we might soon expect a number of visitors, but that it was our business, being the last comers, to sally forth and call upon the station.

We made an expedition to the native bazaar during a few hours' "break," waded about from shop to shop, and picked up some necessities and odds and ends of decorations wherewith to furnish our abode. We bought bamboo chairs, phoolcarries, and pallampores; muslin for curtains; crockery, mats, a few cheap rugs, and a couple of reliable lamps. We also— oh, great adventure!—hired a piano. I stood by awestruck whilst Mrs. Hayes-Billington bargained and gesticulated—talking all the while in the most fluent Hindustani, and ruthlessly cheapening every article. Meanwhile, her husband looked on, now and then making suggestions, indicating deficiencies, and exhibiting the deepest interest in every transaction.

With the fruits of this excursion the Hayes-Billingtons at once set to work to "do up" the rickety old bungalow, to which undertaking I gladly lent a hand. Somehow it reminded me of dressing a stage for private theatricals, such as we had at school. The dreary, damp little drawing-room, its walls streaked with green, was now hung with stamped cotton; the mouldy matting was replaced, and gay rugs laid here and there. Bamboo furniture, a couple of second-hand chairs, a black and gold table, and a paper screen effected a grand transformation.

I contributed photographs in silver frames, my books and silk cushions, to help in the embellishment, and with flowers and a couple of lamp shades we all agreed that the little room was "quite top hole."

We also made a few alterations in the dining-room, cast out the rotten matting and some broken chairs, and now considered ourselves in a position to receive company. I had taken part in all these arrangements *con amore*, for I realised that I had thrown in my lot with the Hayes-Billingtons, and was bound to consider myself as one of the family. In a way, I liked them both; he, strange to say, the better of the two. He was always so cheery, optimistic and busy. He told me he had heard of a smart pony that he was going to buy for me by and by, and said I must ask my brother to run up soon and pay us a visit. For her part she did her best to make me comfortable and to break the shock of squalid appointments, the, to me, unusual cooking— and undesirable insects! I could see that she was anxious we should mix in society and that I should have what she called "a really festive time."

"You must know, my dear girl," she explained, "I am as much a stranger in this part of the world as yourself. I have always been up north, where the natives, the climate, and the manners and customs are altogether different. I shall certainly miss our nice cold weather, but as Bertie has got this good appointment in the Deccan that will be some compensation. He is obliged to go down in a few days, so you and I will have to take care of one another," and she put her arm round my neck and kissed me.

In spite of her endearments and affection I always realised that there was a certain amount of reserve about my chaperon. She never talked of the past, except in a general way, but greatly preferred to throw herself into the future—especially my future—which was kind of her!

I did not grumble audibly or make disparaging comments, but so far, with regard to India, I was painfully disillusioned and overwhelmed with disappointment. As I sat in the driest spot I could find in a leaking veranda I asked myself, where was the sun? Was this wet, cloudy country the gorgeous East? We had been five whole days at Silliram and as yet it had never ceased to rain. Captain Hayes-Billington had paddled out as far as the club and library, put down our names for both, brought back some news, and cheered us with promises of finer weather.

"This is just an extraordinarily bad break they say," he announced with a broad smile; "but the glass is going up and we shall have the sun out and everything all right to-morrow or next day."

The servants ministering to "The Dovecot" were a strange and motley crew. The butler was a Portuguese half-caste from Goa, who had previously been in the service of Captain Hayes-Billington; the Mohammedan cook, a bearded individual in a red turban. My English-speaking Madrassee ayah was sympathetic and even motherly; she turned out the frogs that hopped about my room, destroyed several promising nests of white ants, and slew a venomous-looking black scorpion. The old woman informed me that she had been twice to England with ladies and children.

"England," she said, "plenty good food, good beer but plenty much stairs; journey there very bad, specially the Biscay river, too much jumping that Biscay river!"

I gathered that she was considerably impressed by the style and quantity of my outfit; but, on the other hand, she openly despised the bungalow.

"This too much bad bungalow," she declared, "too old, too cheap, too far from bazaar and the club gur, and all the big mem sahibs."

But of this drawback I had not yet had an opportunity of judging.

By the end of a week Captain Hayes-Billington had taken his departure. His wife seemed unaffectedly sorry; I think they were really attached to one another—almost like a newly-married couple.

They had one rather irritating habit: that of conversing in Hindustani. They spoke it fluently, although they assured me that they had got very rusty at home and were now talking it for practice. Occasionally I had an instinctive and disagreeable feeling that sometimes, in my very presence, they were discussing *me*!

CHAPTER XI
A HILL STATION

Captain Hayes-Billington's prediction was fulfilled; a welcome "break" brought us perfect weather, and at last we were enabled to dispense with umbrellas and goloshes, and sally forth to see the place. Silliram was situated on a high plateau, and, as we emerged from a by-path and stood near a celebrated "point," a world of absolute peace and beauty lay beneath us. The precipices which overhung the low country were heavily wooded and clothed with masses of trees, flowering creepers, orchids and a luxuriant variety of gigantic exotic ferns. The plains which stretched so far below resembled a faintly coloured map, or some delicate piece of embroidery, gradually fading away into a misty blue distance. The atmosphere after the rains was so extraordinarily crystal-clear that we could see for miles, and even trace the outlines of distant towns, forests and rivers. Overhead a few lazy clouds threw their shadows on the wonderful scene, possibly jealous of such beauty and endeavouring to obscure it.

It was no doubt owing to its lofty situation that Silliram dried up rapidly; the roads were no longer merely red mud, the cascades of running water ceased to brawl, and the all-reviving sun had apparently brought the whole population into the open air—also their wardrobes. In almost every compound one noticed long strings of male and female garments fluttering in the breeze.

After our walk to the view Mrs. Hayes-Billington and I bravely ventured into the club. Among the crowd each face we saw was that of a stranger. Apparently we were the only outsiders, everyone else seemed to be acquainted.

I took courage from my chaperon, who was evidently well used to Indian clubs and club ways, and securing seats and a table she issued an order for tea and bread and butter.

"Not buffalo butter," she amended imperiously.

I noticed a number of girls, various soldierly-looking young men, some few matrons and oldish officers with grey hairs, but no really elderly people. There was bridge, badminton in a covered court, tennis, a reading-room and a supply of refreshments. I could not but see that we were observed with interest; who would not look at Mrs. Hayes-Billington? She was unusually animated and in good spirits, and we sat over our tea cups for some time absorbed in our surroundings, enjoying this pleasant change from our damp little "Dovecot."

As we walked back Mrs. Hayes-Billington remarked:

"To-morrow I will order a conveyance of some sort, we will put on our smartest frocks and pay a round of calls from twelve to two. Bertie got a list from the club baboo. We will begin with the general's wife, the commissioner's wife, the padre's wife, and so on. I think I had better write your name on my cards, and then everyone will know that we are living together and that you are under my wing."

"Yes," I assented, "of course, that will be best."

"I hope they will all be out; this calling is a mere matter of form. As soon as visits have been exchanged, we shall be invited to the general's at homes, the club dances, picnics and tennis parties, and you will have no end of a good time."

The following morning, arrayed in our best afternoon frocks, we started out in an ancient victoria to make our round of calls—in short, "to wait upon the station." The general's wife and daughter were at home. They proved to be charming people, and the girl, who was my age, and I took to one another on the spot. Our other calls were more or less satisfactory; we dropped our names into the many "Not at home" boxes, and having dispersed twenty cards returned to "The Dovecot" and tiffin, in a condition of complete exhaustion.

The result of our effort was an immediate shower of pasteboards or visitors, and we were soon in the midst of a whirl of hill gaiety. We went to tennis parties, picnics, and dances. My companion was impressively sedate and correct in her manner—this was not the Mrs. Hayes-Billington with whom I had travelled in the *Asphodel*! She was also an admirable bridge and tennis player, had an unfailing supply of agreeable small talk, and was one of the most popular married women in the station.

My chaperon was an excellent manager, and thoroughly understood Anglo-Indian housekeeping and the art of cutting down the cook's accounts. We lived carefully and economically, but nevertheless entertained in a quiet way; we gave little tiffins and dinners before a club dance, to young men and girls—though our dining-room was a crush with six. On these occasions the table was beautifully decorated by Mrs. Hayes-Billington, and some of the sweets and the savouries were made by her on a handy charcoal stove in the back veranda. She had a deft way of doing things; everything turned out by her delicate fingers seemed so dainty and complete, whether it was a toque, a pincushion, or some toothsome dish. Although Mrs. Hayes-Billington invariably spoke of herself as "a genteel pauper," I had a shrewd impression that once upon a time she had been accustomed to wealth and luxury. Her wardrobe was plain and inexpensive, but she possessed beautiful lace, the remains of various gorgeous gowns, a gold-mounted dressing-bag which had evidently seen much service, a string of pearls and remarkably fine diamonds. Also she was a notable dressmaker, and refurbished and altered some of the satins and brocades, with the aid of a clever *dirzee*; he sat in the veranda from morning till night, sewing, pinning, copying, making marvellous use of his toes for holding breadths of stuff, and was armed with the most formidable pair of scissors I had ever beheld.

The outcome of these exertions were picturesque teagowns and evening toilettes, gracefully worn by Mrs. Hayes-Billington at our weekly bridge party, when young men dropped in after dinner for a rubber and a smoke.

On such occasions I did not take a hand; the stakes were too high and the rubbers were so long—sometimes the clock struck one before I heard the break-up of the party. In a house like ours, with the walls possibly made of old packing-cases, every sound was audible.

My chaperon was a first-rate bridge player; she smoked unlimited cigarettes, used slangy expressions and was more at ease and in "mental undress" than Aunt Mina would have approved. However, she was undoubtedly happy; as I watched her eager radiant face I could not help thinking of some poor pot-bound thirsty flower that had at last received freedom and moisture!

The young men worshipped my companion; no doubt they were flattered by her notice and her sympathetic manner; she was always so beautiful, so vital and so gay. Once or twice I found myself wondering at what she saw in *them*. They were very young and, even in my callow opinion, rather dull and uninteresting. I came upon the answer to this question (if answer it was) in rather an unexpected form. One morning, after one of these weekly parties, I happened to open the old bureau in order to hunt for a piece of sealing-wax, and there, stuffed under bridge markers, cards and scraps of paper covered with figures, I discovered coins and notes to the amount of three hundred rupees!

I must confess that the find was a shock. I had never seen what is called "real gambling." Was this the first nod from our family skeleton, or was it merely the housekeeping funds accidentally muddled up with cards and paper? Mrs. Hayes-Billington was so foolishly careless of money and jewellery, and rarely kept them under lock and key. The only possessions she ever locked up were her letters.

The general's daughter and I became companions and fast friends. We went sketching together, though our poor attempts were libels on the wonderful scenery we attempted to transfer to paper. Besides Dolly Dane there were numbers of nice girls in the station. For instance, Belinda and Sylvia Brabazon, known as "Billy" and "Silly"—for India is no respecter of names!—a plain little couple, matchless tennis players and cotillion leaders, tirelessly good-natured and energetic. Their mother, an amazingly vigorous matron, looked like their elder sister. Colonel Brabazon's activities were confined to collecting butterflies, and telling "good" stories in the club smoking-room. No picnics or dances were considered complete without his belongings.

The commissioner's wife, Mrs. Clayson, a kindly but lethargic lady, was weighed down by the cares of a large small family, and took no part save that of spectator in any social gaieties. Then there were Major and Mrs. Wray of the Grey Hussars, a particularly smart couple, who enjoyed the reputation of giving the best dinners in Silliram, to which none but what I may call the *"crème de la crème"* were invited.

I regret to add that Mrs. Wray figuratively closed her doors on the commissariat, uncovenanted and subordinate railway and telegraph service. She, however, did not close her doors on us, but was Mrs. Hayes-Billington's chief friend, at which I was not surprised, as there were certain points in common between them. They had dealt at the same London shops, employed the same Court milliner, used the same soap, and were equally devoted to bridge.

In all my life I had never enjoyed myself so thoroughly as during these weeks at an Indian hill station. The weather was perfect; the clear exhilarating mountain air raised my spirits to the highest pitch, and when I woke in the morning it was always with the feeling that something delightful was going to happen during the day, and this sensation was usually justified. I had hired a pony from the bazaar—fortunately my new saddle fitted him perfectly—and joined riding parties and picnics all over the plateau. The hard red roads and overgrown lanes wound among wonderful ferns and woods. Here were my old friends the oak and the willow; the delicate tamarind and stately peepul I now saw for the first time. Our expeditions were generally to points commanding clear-cut views of the far-away plains, or the purple gloom of valleys beneath our feet. At some of these "points" we had picnics, *chotah hazree*, tiffin, or afternoon tea, as the case might be.

Besides such rural excursions there were tennis tournaments, small club dances, and active preparations for the great event of the season—theatricals, which were got up by the general and his wife. The piece selected, *The Scrap of Paper*, was undoubtedly ambitious, but where is the amateur who does not soar? The rôles of the Marquise and Suzanne were undertaken by Mrs. Wray and Mrs. Hayes-Billington, and the piece required constant rehearsal. As I had been selected to take the small part of a servant who comes in and dusts a chair, I was always present, and, behind the scenes, was immensely interested and entertained.

Mrs. Hayes-Billington's performance filled me with a glow of personal pride. My chaperon was what might be called "a born actress." It also transpired that she had played in this piece on former occasions.

Dolly Dane was cast for Mathilde, and as our parts were insignificant we had the pleasure of looking on and watching the others perform. Mrs. Hayes-Billington was admirable, Mrs. Wray was also good. In spite of their close friendship I thought I could discern a certain amount of rivalry between these ladies. The general himself, and one or two of our most prominent young men, were in the cast. The date of the great gala night was fixed to take place within a fortnight, and after this, alas! the season would begin to wane.

In almost every letter I sent to Ronnie I begged him to come up and see Silliram and me, holding out such inducements as *The Scrap of Paper* and the Bachelors' Club dance.

"I am longing to see you," I said, "and also for you to see me, and to judge how splendidly I am getting on in India. Already I know a little Hindustani, I can fold and put on a pugaree, and chaffer with the hawkers as to the manner born."

But my invitation fell flat. Ronnie wrote that he could not possibly get leave; the rifle meeting was coming on, also the polo tournament, and a general inspection. He was simply worked to death. Later he might be able to get away. Meanwhile he was delighted to hear that I was having such a ripping time.

Mrs. Hayes-Billington and I had a good many men callers; one day among these, Mr. Balthasar, a friend of Captain Hayes-Billington, presented himself. He was a foreigner—that is to say, not English. His dark skin was in surprising contrast to a pair of very light grey eyes, which he rolled about incessantly. He had thick black lashes, a bullet head, fat clean-shaven face, good features, beautiful hands and a stout, supple figure. Also he was remarkably well groomed and carried himself with an air of confident assurance.

I noticed a slight hint of patronage in his manner towards Mrs. Hayes-Billington, which, with a gracious dignity, she speedily suppressed. He talked with a sort of soft drawl, and informed us he had come from the mines, and had just run up to Silliram to confer with a well-known engineer, and was returning the following day. Our visitor paid me conspicuous attention, his restless eyes constantly rolled in my direction, and he accepted an invitation to dine with flattering alacrity. When he had departed in a motor Mrs. Hayes-Billington said:

"That is one of the directors of the Katchoocan Gold Mines, where Bertie works; he is what is called 'a big pot,' notable for getting valuable concessions from the Nizam's Government. His call was an honour. I believe he is a Greek—anyway, a Levantine of some sort—and enormously rich. I must send to the bazaar and the shops and prepare a really smart dinner—oysters and pomfret, and get some wine from the club, and a tin of caviare. If I entertain him well it may be of use to Bertie. I believe he plays bridge, so I shall ask another man, Captain Learoyd, I think, and be sure you put on a becoming frock."

The little dinner proved a success; it was cooked to admiration. The great man expanded and made himself agreeable, and hinted that he would do great things for "B.B.," as he called Captain Hayes-Billington. Subsequently at bridge I was his partner, and I positively could not endure the way he stared—precisely as if I were an uncertain investment about which he was making up his mind. At the same time he played bridge with skill; was cool, subtly cunning, and had a clear memory of every card. We won two rubbers, to his obvious satisfaction. He and Captain Learoyd played for money, and I think he pocketed about ten rupees, a mere nothing to a millionaire, but he was as pleased as if it had been thousands.

"I look upon our success as a good omen, Miss Lingard. You and I are first-rate partners. How would you like to take me on for life?" he asked boisterously.

"Not at all," I replied brusquely, as I turned my back upon him and moved away. I disliked Mr. Balthasar particularly—his boasting, his grand air, the way in which he looked round our cheap little room—and appeared to see through our makeshifts—also the style in which he had stuck his glass in his eye and peered into the entrées at dinner. He was insupportable, and after I had tidied away the bridge cards I withdrew into my own apartment and put myself to bed. It was a long time before I heard his motor moving off, and immediately afterwards Mrs. Hayes-Billington came into my room and said:

"He has been waiting on for *ages*! Why did you go away and never come back?"

"Because he is too appallingly awful!" I rejoined with energy. "I never saw such manners. I never met such a detestable, odious creature. I felt inclined to throw things at him, and I sincerely hope I may never see him again!"

"He hopes very much that he may see *you* again. He has taken an extraordinary fancy to 'my friend Miss Lingard,' and says if I will bring you down to stay at the mines he will put us up—"

"He will never put *me* up," I interrupted, "and nothing would induce me to put up with him!"

For a moment Mrs. Hayes-Billington stood gravely contemplating me with her wonderful dark eyes.

"Ah well," she said at last, "I grant you that he is a bounder, but then on the other hand he is enormously rich."

"My dear chaperon!" I exclaimed, "surely you are not thinking of trying to make a match for me with a fat foreigner who must be fifty years of age! I would rather be dead than married to such a horror!"

She nodded her head expressively and went slowly out of the room.

As a rule our young men callers were officers upon leave, a nice, cheery set, my partners at dances and tennis. We were always at home on Sunday afternoons, and Mrs. Hayes-Billington and I were most regular attendants at the little hill church in the mornings. One particular afternoon two of our habitués brought a stranger, a certain Captain Vesey. Somehow he was not of the usual type of our visitors, who were simple, unaffected, and genial. This was a fair man, with a long, faded face and a querulous expression. After the first introduction he appeared to freeze into a solid block of ice, and was reserved almost to silence. I noticed him looking hard at Mrs. Hayes-Billington, and, although he reclined in a well-cushioned cane chair and was offered the very best orange pekoe tea and hot cakes, he scarcely contributed a word to the conversation and was obviously dissatisfied with his company and his surroundings. Possibly my name had escaped him, for when someone addressed me as "Miss Lingard" he became faintly interested.

"I know a namesake of yours in the 'Lighthearts.' Any relation?"

"Yes," I answered shortly, "he is my brother."

"Your *brother*," he repeated incredulously.

"Is it so very astonishing?"

"Um—er——" he stammered, "I had no idea that Ronnie Lingard had a sister out here."

"I only arrived six weeks ago—I came with Mrs. Hayes-Billington."

"Oh, did you?"

"I wanted Ronnie to come here for even a week, but he is so busy and so hard-worked he says it is impossible."

"Oh yes—impossible—quite, quite impossible," he muttered, as if talking to himself, and then he got up rather suddenly and took an abrupt departure.

There was certainly something strange about Captain Vesey. He had forgotten his gloves and he had not touched his tea. The two young men who had brought him exchanged glances and grins and one of them exclaimed: "Sunstroke!"

"I hope you don't mind him, Mrs. Hayes-Billington," he added apologetically, "but Vesey is the most eccentric old bird."

"So it seems," she rejoined with a laugh, "and I have not the slightest wish to put salt on his tail!"

The great day of our theatricals was approaching. The evening before it took place we had a full-dress rehearsal—a *répétition générale*, French fashion—at the theatre, to which at least half of the people came, bidden or unbidden, but everyone was more or less interested in the performance. If they were not acting their friends or relations were taking part, or they had lent properties, garments, furniture, or given assistance in dressing and making up.

The little theatre was almost full. I made this discovery by peeping through that indispensable hole in the curtain. Mrs. Dane, the general's wife, was already seated in the middle of the front row, and with her was a lady, a rather austere-looking, middle-aged woman whom I had never seen before, also a grey-haired gentleman, presumably her husband. I may add that the *crème de la crème* of the station were present at this rehearsal, but every one of them would be there the next evening, honourably paying their ten rupees a ticket. Rather a high price, but then it was for a local charity.

I must admit that I was highly excited, being about to make my first appearance on the stage. I dressed myself as a smart parlourmaid; my face had been beautifully painted by Major Wray—who was quite an artist in this line—and I was ready!

After some delay the curtain rose on Mathilde and her companion. Dolly acquitted herself well (although she had been nearly crying with stage fright). I had helped to attire the Marquise; she looked magnificent and wore her diamonds. Having played my own little part and accomplished my dusting I went round to the front to enjoy the performance.

The good-natured Brabazons made room for me between them in the second row, just behind Mrs. Dane and the general, who turned about to compliment me. At this moment the Marquise appeared upon the stage, and received a round of applause. I noticed the strange lady in front examining her programme and whispering to her husband; then she turned her attention to the actors, and looked at the Marquise (the cynosure of all eyes) with a sort of fixed glare. The play was going splendidly, the prompter's voice was rarely heard. The chief honours fell to my chaperon, whose acting was simply magnificent.

During the interval between the second and third acts, I noticed Mrs. Dane and the strange lady engaged in earnest conversation, and caught the name "Mrs. de Lacy." I also observed that Mrs. Dane seemed very much perturbed and upset.

The Scrap of Paper ended in a triumph. There were repeated calls before the curtain, which were accepted by the Marquise and Suzanne, who appeared, curtsied hand in hand, and received a boisterous ovation. This delightful evening concluded with a little supper-party at the Wrays', and it was long after one o'clock in the morning before I found myself in bed.

As the result of such dissipation I was not a very early riser—neither was Mrs. Hayes-Billington. Verbal messages are uncertain in India, and even to someone in the same house you send a pencilled note or "chit." I had received a chit to say "Have an awful headache, do not expect to see me till quite late. D. B."

I spent the remainder of the morning in writing letters, doing a little mending, and finishing an engrossing novel. At tiffin, of which I partook in solitude, the *chokra* was my sole attendant, and when I inquired for Fernandez, our factotum, he replied, "Missie done send Fernandez with one telegram. Fernandez stopping all the time in bazaar."

As our letters had arrived, I concluded that my chaperon had received some important news, and never gave the matter another thought.

Strange to say that morning there were none of the usual visitors; a certain number of our intimates and neighbours generally looked in, in passing, to ask questions, make engagements, exchange bits of news, and to borrow or to lend. To-day not a soul appeared! The veranda was a desert, save for the *dirzee* and myself. This did not strike me as odd, because most people of our acquaintance were fagged after the previous night's excitement, and were no doubt "lying low" in anticipation of the evening's entertainment.

Towards four o'clock I put on my tennis shoes, took my racket and sauntered off to the club, where I had engaged to make up a set with Dolly Dane. I found already awaiting me Dolly, Captain Learoyd and the padre. I noticed that they were talking eagerly together, but ceased abruptly as I approached within earshot, and there seemed none of the usual eagerness about starting a game.

"What is the matter?" I asked. "You all look so very grave. Is anyone dead—or has there been an accident?"

"Well—er—no accident," said the padre, and he glanced significantly at Dolly, who, taking my arm, led me aside.

"My dear Eva," she began. "I am sorry to say I've the most *awful* thing to tell you," and she paused.

"Oh do be quick!" I urged. "It's my brother—is he ill?"

"No, no," she replied, with a jerk of impatience. "It's about Mrs. Hayes-Billington, your chaperon. It seems that she is the heroine of a terrible divorce case. She was a Mrs. de Lacy; her husband had a civil appointment up in the Punjab. She was always lovely, but outrageously fast. Four years ago she ran away with an officer up in Cashmere. Mrs. Hancock, who is staying with us, knew all about it and nearly had a fit last evening when she saw the notorious Mrs. de Lacy taking the principal part in Mother's theatricals."

"Oh, Dolly," I gasped, "it cannot be true!"

"But it is," she reiterated, "and the case was so scandalous and shameless, that the Hancocks are astonished that she had the audacity ever to return to India. They say she is already beginning in her old style, turning the heads of young men, and having horrid little card parties. It is a fearful shock for the whole station. Mother has written to her. There will be no theatricals, the notice has been posted up on the board this morning. Of course she must have got hold of you under false pretences. Mother says you are to come to us at once. W. will send down for your things."

"It's all very dreadful," I said. "I feel completely stunned. Still, I don't think I ought to leave Mrs. Hayes-Billington like that."

"But you must, my dear," urged Dolly imperatively. "It is too dreadful for a girl like you to be associated with such a person. What an impostor she is! Poor Mrs. Wray is in a state of collapse—fainting fits; the doctor has been to see her. The committee have taken Mrs. Hayes-Billington's name off the list in the library and the club, and the sooner she takes herself out of Silliram the better! Come into the club with me," continued Dolly; "I want to fetch my scarf, and I will walk back with you to 'The Dovecot,' and, if you like, help you to put your things together?"

I made no reply. I felt as if someone had banged me upon the head, and I followed Dolly into the club, feeling extraordinarily dazed and nervous. Fortunately it was not yet tea-time, and the place was nearly empty.

As we passed a great black-board, on which notices were fastened, my companion pointed with her tennis racket and I read, inscribed in very large letters:

"Owing to unforeseen circumstances, the performance of *The Scrap of Paper* will not now take place. L. J. Bowen, Sec. Dramatic Society."

CHAPTER XII
THE NOTORIOUS MRS. DE LACY

With considerable difficulty and various feeble excuses I released myself from Dolly's assiduities, promising to send her a chit as soon as I had collected my thoughts, and to let her know what I intended to do with respect to this social avalanche.

As I walked back alone to the bungalow I told myself that it was a strange coincidence that I had been within the last six months involved in the uprooting of two homes, "The Roost," and now "The Dovecot." Was there something malignant and destructive in my personality? That such a scandal should be placed to the credit of Mrs. Hayes-Billington seemed a crazy, incredible idea. She was domestic and prudent, apparently devoted to Bertie, careful of offending Mrs. Grundy, and totally unlike my lurid mental picture of a *divorcée*. Then I suddenly recalled Colonel Armadale on the *Asphodel*, and as I was endeavouring to piece past and present experiences into one whole, I became aware that a tonga and a pair of smoking ponies were standing in front of "The Dovecot," and beheld Ronnie hurrying towards me with a white excited face, on which I could not help noticing a large splash of mud! Judging by his appearance he had travelled far and fast.

"Oh, Ronnie," I exclaimed, "how glad I am to see you!" and I flung my arms round his neck and hugged him. "Why did you not let me know you were coming?"

"Walk down the road a bit—walls have ears! Such an awful business, Eva, and to think of Aunt Mina letting you in for it—to think of your being chaperoned by Mrs. de Lacy! Good Lord!"

"Yes, I know," I replied, "Dolly Dane has just told me. The whole station is reeling from the shock. For my own part I feel as if I were dreaming."

"Wake up then," he said sharply, "you must get out of this at once. I'd a letter from Vesey two days ago and I have been travelling hard ever since. It appears that when he was calling here he recognised Mrs. Hayes-Billington as Mrs. de Lacy, a notorious *divorcée*. Four years ago her case was the scandal of the whole Punjab, and here she is, in another region, and under another name, doing the respectable matron and chaperoning *my sister*. It's a pretty awful debut for you, Evie!"

"Somehow I cannot believe it," I broke in. "I've had such a happy time, and Mrs. Hayes-Billington has always been so kind to me, so careful of appearances, and— —"

"Just a wolf in sheep's clothing," interrupted my brother, "a regular bad lot! De Lacy was a political agent, and she, as Mrs. de Lacy, was celebrated for her extraordinary good looks and her extravagant love affairs. You must get your things packed and be ready to start with me to-morrow morning at nine o'clock. I have ordered the same tonga. Just put a few things together— your heavy baggage and the ayah can follow."

"But to where? Where are you taking me?"

"Why, to Secunderabad, of course. As soon as I got Vesey's letter and had pulled myself together, I dashed over to the colonel's wife and showed it to her. She said at once that you must come to her. Yes, she really is a thundering good sort. Later on a captain's quarters, near to the C.O.'s, will be vacant, and there you and I can set up house. It will be made a special case, and she has undertaken to talk over the old man."

"Oh, how delightful, Ronnie!" I exclaimed. "What a piece of good fortune!"

"Yes, rather," he assented emphatically. "It looks as if your presentiment were likely to come off."

"What am I to say to Mrs. Hayes-Billington?" I asked after a pause.

"Is she up, and visible?"

"I think so, by this time; I have not seen her all day, she has had a most dreadful headache."

"Well, I must have a jaw with her. Yes, I must. I won't sneak you out of her house without an explanation, and I intend to give her a jolly good bit of my mind."

"Oh, Ronnie—*must* you?"

"Yes, I must," he rejoined, as we entered the bungalow; "which is the drawing-room?"

As I pointed to it in silence he pushed open the door and entered. Mrs. Hayes-Billington, who was crouching over the fire, turned on him a ghastly face, and I realised in a second that she was aware of his errand. Then like a coward I retreated and went away to break the news of my impending departure to the ayah.

"Missie going—me, too, going to-morrow morning!" she exclaimed.

I must confess that I rather expected a scene, but the ayah accepted the news with staggering unconcern. Mary was evidently accustomed to these hasty departures. She was a Deccanee woman, she informed me, and not sorry to return to her own country. With astonishing celerity she began to collect my various and scattered belongings, to sort and to fold. Natives love the excitement and hurry-scurry of a hasty move. A native cook welcomes, rather than otherwise, an unexpected addition to a dinner; a butler is never more in his element than when improvising a hasty *tamasha*, an abruptly arranged *shikar* party, or an early morning supper!

Presently Ronnie knocked peremptorily at my door and said:

"It's all right. She says of course you must go—she is leaving too. Now mind you eat a good dinner and get to bed early, for it's a beastly long journey. Ta ta!"

I did my utmost to do justice to my solitary meal, though I experienced sensations both varied and strange. I felt as if I were sitting among ruins, or as if I had been expelled from school, or was standing on the edge of a steep precipice gazing down into the unknown.

After dinner I received yet another little note from Mrs. Hayes-Billington. "Do come and see me in my room. D. B."

In fear and trepidation I accepted the invitation, but did not, as I anticipated, find my chaperon in sackcloth and ashes and tears, but as calm as usual, only deathly pale. She looked a beautiful, tragic figure, as she stood in the middle of the room, wrapped in an old pink tea gown. Like myself, I could see that she was making preparations for an imminent departure. Before she uttered a word she walked over and closed the door—most of our doors stuck, or rattled—then she turned about and faced me.

"Eva, I am most frightfully sorry that this has happened, more for your sake than mine—although to me it means social ruin. You have been a dear girl, so simple and so loyal; I am really fond of you, and as I would not like you to think worse of me than is necessary I have sent for you to tell you my true story."

As she concluded, she indicated a chair, into which I sank in silence, but she still continued to pace about the room.

"You must know," she began, "that I was the daughter of a West Country parson. When I was eighteen years of age Robert de Lacy, who was fishing in the neighbourhood, saw me in church and fell in love with my face on the spot. He soon contrived to make my father's acquaintance and mine. He was fifteen years older than I was, and had a fine appointment in Northern India. As his furlough was nearly ended we were married after a month's acquaintance. I was not in love with him but in love with the idea of going to India—always the land of my dreams—also thankful to be released from a detestable stepmother and a hateful country groove. India enchanted me; in her I was neither disappointed nor disillusioned—but then as the wife of a wealthy civilian I saw the country from its best aspect. I had numbers of servants, horses, and crowds of appreciative friends. We entertained a good deal. At nineteen I was queen of the station! My husband, who was exceedingly proud of me, loaded me with jewels and lovely clothes. At first I was happy—my home and children were all in all to me."

"Children!" I ejaculated.

"Oh, yes, I have two boys; the elder is seventeen. They were sent to England when they were about three years old. My husband had certain fixed ideas. One of them was that no child should remain in India after that age. Another, that a woman's place was with her husband. He did not care about home life; his work and big game shooting absorbed all his interests, but it was *my* duty to remain at my post as mistress of his house. In the hot weather he sent me to the hills, or to Cashmere, and himself went away on shooting trips into Nepaul or Tibet.

"Except as a sort of ornamental figurehead, I believe Robert soon grew tired of me. I had not been well educated; I could sing, and act, and dance, but none of these accomplishments appealed to *him*. He liked a woman who was deeply read, who could talk politics, statistics, Indian famines, and so on, and when we were alone, without guests, we would spend whole days scarcely exchanging a word; and thus I lived, in a sense, solitary—my soul starving. My good looks, which were famous, were something of a drawback; they made me too conspicuous; women were afraid of me. On the other hand, men were my slaves. I had numbers of admirers, and to fill my idle hours I embarked on harmless flirtations, merely *pour passer les temps*—and so the years passed. Then up in Cashmere amid the most romantic and exquisite scenery, I met my other self—my twin soul. He was in a cavalry regiment stationed at Umballa. Well, I need not dwell on this. You have never seen Cashmere or Gulmerg, 'the meadows of roses,' or the Dal Lake, by a full moon; or breathed an atmosphere trembling with an appeal, or looked into the blue eyes of Rupert Vavasour. After struggling for a whole year I listened to him, and the end of it was that we went away together to Japan." She caught her breath, and paused for a moment— standing with her back to me.

I felt myself blushing violently, and was conscious of a sort of undeserved, shamefaced embarrassment.

"Our elopement was not a nine days' wonder," she resumed, "but a whole season's talk! Of course I was divorced. We went to Italy to await the decree nisi, hoping to marry and be happy ever afterwards. Rupert had given up the army and we intended to live abroad until our story was forgotten. But at Florence he got fever, and, to my indescribable anguish, died within a week. His people hurried out from home, ignored me altogether, and wound up his affairs. Captain Vavasour was immensely wealthy, but had made no will, and I, neither wife nor widow, was thrown upon the world, almost destitute. My own people would not receive me, excepting one old aunt, who, like myself, was very poor, and I lived with her until she died. How often and often I wished that I was dead too! I used to walk about the streets of London, with nowhere to go, with no one to speak to, and entirely without friends. I realised then all the loneliness, misery, and despair of a lost dog! I had no interest in free museums, picture galleries, or libraries; my tastes did not tend toward Botticelli prints or blue Hawthorn china; inanimate objects bored me to death, but I hungered and starved for the society to which I had been accustomed, when one lived and experienced thrills! For years I breathed an atmosphere of change, excitement, and luxury; this poverty-stricken, dull isolation was insupportable. The friends I had known and entertained in my palmy days passed me by with blank faces, and people of shady character, who would have welcomed me with open arms, I avoided like the black plague. It was a case of Mohammed's coffin! Then last summer I made the acquaintance of Bertie. It all came about through the loan of an umbrella. I had recovered my looks, and he fell in love with me and asked me to marry him. Of course I told him my story, but it made no difference. Bertie is a truly unselfish man and has been more than good to me. Then I longed with a sort of aching to see the East again, and finding that his work was in the south, where I did not know a soul, and as it was four years since the divorce, I ventured to return to India, hoping that I could make a fresh start. I was getting on, as you know, and beginning to feel so happy and safe, enjoying the old familiar life and surroundings, when Mrs. Hancock descended from that former existence and shattered my house of cards. She beheld me acting the principal character in a play she had once seen me appear in in Peshawar—evidently received in society, and instantly signed my social death warrant. Although she sat in the front row, strange to say I had not noticed her, and I was unaware of my sentence until I received a note from Mrs. Dane early this morning. I wired at once to Bertie. Poor old fellow! I know he will be dreadfully cut up; he will take me away as soon as possible. Meanwhile, I shall remain 'purdah' until I go down to the mines, and will never, never again endeavour to show my face in Indian society."

All the time she talked she had been walking to and fro; suddenly she halted before me and said:

"*I* always said it was a risk bringing you with us, but Bertie thought otherwise, and then your aunt was so frantically urgent, the money was such a temptation, and you were a nice girl, not at all modern, and I hoped and prayed that I would never be found out. I must explain about Colonel Armadale. No doubt, you, like everyone else, thought I flirted with him on board that dreadful old tub. He is a dear old friend and godfather to my elder boy. He meets Bob and his brother whenever he likes, but I, although I am their mother, never. He told me a great deal about them, and that Hugh, the younger, is brilliantly clever; his father is immensely proud of him. The child's only drawback is that he resembles *me*! Although I have not seen my boys I have seen my husband. Not very long before I came out he and a lady sat directly behind me in the stalls of a theatre. Another time we met face to face in the street, looked at one another—and passed on.

"Well now, Evie, you will not think too badly of me, will you—perhaps, some day, you may forgive me?"

"I forgive you now," I said, rising; "indirectly you have done me a very good turn, for in future I am to live with Ronnie. I am really sorry that this has happened to you, and I must tell you that since I came to Silliram I have enjoyed every day of the time we have spent here together."

"And never for a moment suspected that I had a past?"

"Yes, I did think there was something mysterious about you—you were so reserved about your affairs. I thought you had somehow or other come down in the world, and naturally did not care to talk about it. You always said you were poor—but you had some costly possessions. Your diamonds and your pearls——"

"Those pearls are sham!" she interrupted. "I sold my string for seven hundred pounds, and lived on it for years. Well, Evie, as you are making an early start to-morrow morning, I must not detain you any longer. Will you write to me sometimes?—'Care of Captain Hayes-Billington, the Katchoocan Mines,' will always find me, and I shall get so few letters."

"Yes," I replied, "I will certainly write."

"Well then, good-bye, my dear girl. I wish you all happiness, joy and good fortune."

As she kissed me I felt her tears upon my face, and when I had wrenched open the door and blundered out of the room I was crying too.

CHAPTER XIII
A FRESH START

From the nearest railway station to Silliram, our journey south was both monotonous and dusty. The country we passed through was disappointingly flat and uninteresting; a reddish brown plain, broken here and there by serrated hills of red sandstone, which at times gave the illusive impression of castles, battlements and fortresses.

During our long *tête-à-tête*, Ronnie and I had found plenty to say to one another on many subjects, besides lengthy discussions on Aunt Mina's delinquencies and Mrs. Hayes-Billington's past. With respect to these topics Ronnie was forcibly eloquent.

"Of course Aunt Mina wanted to get rid of you at any price, although she wrote me a gushing letter, saying she had made the most delightful arrangements for your happiness; but as far as she was really concerned, you might have gone to the devil!—and you *did* go to the devil in one way when you set up house with Mrs. Hayes-Billington! The more I think of it, the more furious I feel. To have been chaperoned and brought out by such a woman is enough to blast the name of any girl; and if one of the Secunderabad cats were to get hold of this story you would be simply down and out! The sound thing to do is to pretend you have only just arrived from England, and drop those weeks in 'The Dovecot' out of your life."

"That's all very fine, Ronnie," I protested, "but it's not so easy to drop bits of one's life like that. Numbers of people knew me at Silliram. Supposing some of them were to come down here?"

"Not much fear of that," he answered emphatically. "The Silliram crowd seldom travel south—their beat is Bombay."

"After all, Mrs. Hayes-Billington is not such a coal-black sheep," I urged. "In many ways she is a good soul, generous and unselfish, and never says a nasty thing about anyone. I believe lots of women have been divorced and are allowed to creep back into society by degrees."

"My good girl, don't talk about what you don't understand! Mrs. Hayes-Billington's case broke the record. Of course her reputation as a beauty made her rather conspicuous, her track was strewn with victims. There is a legend that more than one silly fool committed suicide on account of her. The man she went off with was enormously rich—it was an absolutely mercenary affair. However, he didn't marry her, and left her to prey about the world. Apparently she picked up with Hayes-Billington, who by all accounts is a thundering ass!"

"The man Mrs. Hayes-Billington ran away with could not marry her because he died," I explained impressively.

"Oh, did he? Well, I don't see that that makes much difference," was Ronnie's amazing reply. "Although you made such a bad start I expect you and I will have a real good time housekeeping together, won't we, old girl?"

"I hope so," I replied. "I have learnt a little about prices and things, and a few words of Hindustani."

"Oh, you don't want Hindustani at Secunderabad. Most of the natives speak and write English. My butler was with a married couple before he came to me; he will help you to run the show, and will tell you all about the Hali sicca rupee, which is worth ninety-six dubs—a dub is like a scrap off an old copper kettle. We shall fix up No. 30 quarter in grand style, and have our little dinners and bridge parties. Mrs. Soames will take you out, and I have a ripping pony that you can ride. You'd think to look at her—I mean Mrs. Soames, not the pony—that she was a stiff-necked old maid, as narrow-minded as they make 'em, but she really is awfully kind and soft, and does so enjoy being a colonel's wife in India, and entertaining the regiment and fussing over soldiers' wives. 'James' is bound to take to you. Between ourselves, it's my opinion that James would like to flirt a bit in his hours of ease. You will like Major and Mrs. Mills, our only other married couple, beside the quartermaster, though Mrs. Mills is wrapped up in her nursery and housekeeping."

Before we reached Wadi Junction, I had received an outline of what my future friends, amusements and duties were likely to be, as described in an offhand sketchy manner by my brother.

As we changed on to the Nizam's State Railway, Ronnie met a racing acquaintance, and, with many apologies, they both retired into a smoking carriage—there to discuss important forthcoming events; meanwhile I made a sort of toilet, arranged my hair and hat, and dusted my frock, in order to assure a presentable appearance on arrival.

At Secunderabad station we were met by Mrs. Soames herself; a slight, smartly-dressed, elderly woman, with a long thin face and an immense unnatural looking fringe. She gave me a cordial welcome, and soon we were trotting up towards Trimulgherry behind a pair of fast bay cobs. After the usual journey talk, I said: "It is so very, very kind of you to take me in—a sort of waif and stray."

"Why of course," she replied, "I am only too glad to come to your rescue. Your brother is one of my favourites, he *is* such a dear fellow. Although so popular he is so thoughtful and unspoiled, and when he brought me Captain Vesey's letter I saw at once that there was nothing for it but that he must go and fetch you here. By and by we shall settle you into a nice quarter, close to ours, and I will be your chaperon. No, no, you really must not thank me so much. I am fond of girls, and I shall be delighted to have your company. Just one little word of caution," extending as she spoke an exquisitely gloved hand, "do not mention Mrs. Hayes-Billington here. If it leaked out that you had been brought to India and associated with such a disreputable character, the result might be most distressing. Although the largest station in India, Secunderabad is extraordinarily proper and correct. I have been here for three years and we have not had *one* scandal! There is the club," she broke off, "our great rendezvous for tennis, dances, bridge— and, I think I may call it, the heart of the station."

I leant forward, and gazed at an imposing two-storey building on my left, which stood in a spacious and well planted compound. Then, bowing to people on horseback, Mrs. Soames continued:

"You ride of course?"

"Yes, I love it," I answered promptly, "Mrs. Hayes-Billington and I hired ponies by the week, and rode everywhere."

"My dear girl, *please* don't mention that woman's name," she protested in a plaintive voice.

"Well, may I say something, just for once? I do not think she was really so dreadfully to blame—her children were taken away—she was so much alone—I cannot help feeling sorry for her."

"What are you saying? *Sorry* for her!"

"Yes, she told me her story the night before I left; it was not so bad—but rather sad——"

"She threw dust in your eyes of course!" interrupted my companion, bristling up and speaking with great asperity. "Those abandoned creatures make themselves out to be martyrs of circumstances; and indeed, my dear, I should not be discussing such a woman with a girl like you. Now here we are, and there is James awaiting us."

As she spoke, we were whirled in between two gate piers and came to a standstill before a solidly built bungalow, with a round, bowed sort of veranda. With hospitable agility, Colonel Soames sprang down the steps to greet me and handed me out of the victoria. He was a wiry little man, with keen granite grey eyes, a small sandy moustache, and a remarkably square jaw. Judging by his figure and youthful appearance, he might have been a mere captain instead of the officer commanding a notable regiment.

I was conducted into a perfectly appointed quarter, a C.O.'s bungalow — light, airy, and furnished to suit the climate. My room was not large, but looked most attractive, with its white bed, pink rugs, and pretty flowered chintz.

"Now make yourself quite at home," said Mrs. Soames, "we have a few people dining, but, if you feel too tired after your journey, as soon as we go into the drawing-room, you can just slip away."

Fortunately my clever ayah Mary had squeezed quite a goodly amount of raiment into a small trunk, and I was able to appear in a smart black evening gown, for which my hopeful aunt had paid no less a sum than twenty guineas. It seemed to me that there was a crowd in the drawing-room as I entered, but we only mustered twelve, including Ronnie and myself. I heard Mrs. Soames inform her guests that I was "just out from home!" Her tone and glance implied that I had arrived no later than yesterday, and I was plied with all sorts of questions by the two men between whom I sat at the dinner table with respect to the latest books, plays and news. As I gave rather vague and unsatisfactory answers, I'm afraid they looked upon me as a stupid sort of girl, or perhaps ascribed my lame replies to my strangeness in this new environment, or the fatigue of a journey from Bombay. So apparently my six weeks at Silliram were to be as though they were not, and I was beginning my career in Secunderabad with a smothered scandal and a secret!

The dinner party, as a dinner, was a great success. The cooking, waiting, appointments, and flowers could not have been bettered at Torrington; these native servants were certainly more deft and light-footed than Baker and his subordinates.

I slept soundly in the delightful "Europe" bed, between lavender scented sheets. This airy solid bungalow (*pucka* built) was a delicious change from the damp and mouldy "Dovecot." The hours of the house were early and of military punctuality, and seven o'clock found me sitting in the veranda, having *chota-hazri* with my hostess, who was, as usual, full of animation and conversation.

As she talked I watched the *bheesti* and a *mali* working in the garden; the former with his great *mussick* filling waterpots and the latter sitting on his heels, wrapped in a *cumblie*, digging very deliberately among tomato plants. My hostess explained to me that our lines were what is called "in the entrenchment," although the officers' quarters were outside the fosse and the barracks. These were built back to back, thus ensuring absolute privacy, and each had its own large compound. She pointed out the double-storey mess-house, which faced us across a maidan, and was dimly seen through clumps of flaming "gold mohur" and other trees. Not far to the left of the mess-house lay the jail, which was castellated, and known by the name of "Windsor Castle." Then, taking me by the arm, she led me to a corner of the veranda and introduced me to yet another scene. Behind our quarters lay the Trimulgherry bazaar, overlooked by its celebrated "Gun Rock." This was merely a large piece of granite, shaped precisely like a cannon, and apparently laid and ready to blow the place to pieces. Presumably it had been in this position for hundreds of years.

On his way from parade Ronnie dashed in to visit me. This was the first time I had seen him in his uniform. He looked very smart and soldierly and was riding a perfect darling of a pony, a bright bay with black points.

"I just dropped in to find out if you were alive after yesterday," he said. "You look all right. I believe Mrs. Soames is taking you to call on the ladies of the regiment this morning. Only Mrs. Mills, the major's wife, and the quartermaster's old woman; afterwards, she is sure to bring you down to the club and show you who's who. I am playing polo up at Bolarum, but keep your pecker up—I'll see you again before dinner," and he wheeled about his pony, and was gone.

CHAPTER XIV
THE CLUB

The station club, "the very heart of the community," as described by Mrs. Soames, lay about two miles from our lines. As we drove down there behind our spanking Australian cabs, my chaperon, who was a great talker, enlarged upon the subject.

"Our club," she remarked, "is capitally situated just half way between the cantonments and Hyderabad city, close to the parade ground, shops and cemetery, with roads diverging in every direction; a modern but not very dignified building, as you see. Its businesslike outline and platform verandas have led scoffers to compare it to a railway station, and hint that it is the work of a railway engineer, who desired to raise a monument to the glory of his line! In this idea there may be a touch of professional jealousy; anyway, 'handsome is that handsome does.' The club is supplied with the latest improvements in the matter of ventilation and comfort. No London club has better billiard tables, more luxurious armchairs, or a superior cook. We women are not suffered to set foot in it, except on special occasions, such as receptions and balls; mankind are a greedy, selfish pack, who keep the best of everything for themselves! Well, here we are!" as we turned abruptly into a large enclosure. "It's rather early," she continued, "I see the bullock bandy with the band has only just arrived, so we may as well sit in the carriage for a little longer and I will point you out the chief objects of interest."

"Yes, please do," I said, "everything, as you may suppose, is new to me. What is the small building where I see so many ladies on the veranda?"

"That, my dear, is the 'morghi-khana,' or hen house; a humble offshoot of the larger establishment, where the ladies of the station forgather to read papers, exchange news and play bridge, for, as I have already told you, we are sternly debarred from the parent premises—so amusing!"

"And what," I inquired, "is the round raised platform with the tea table and chairs? It looks like a large white cake."

"It is called a 'chabutra,' and was originally intended for a bandstand—you see one in every station. People make use of them for tea and talk; they are raised a foot or two off the ground, and keep you nicely out of the way of snakes. Thank goodness we don't have many in Secunderabad—the dry climate doesn't suit them."

As Mrs. Soames imparted information, I had been using my eyes and absorbing my new surroundings. In comparison with the club at Silliram, this was as a city to a village! Dozens of men and women passed to and fro, some making for the club, some for the *morghi-khana*. Many of the men were in polo kit or flannels; the women as a rule were remarkably smart, their frocks and hats were undoubtedly imported, and had no connection with the *dirzee* or bazaar. There were numbers of motor cars as well as carriages in the compound, and the road beyond was thronged with vehicles continually passing up and down.

"Did you notice the three ladies who have just settled themselves at the tea-table?" said Mrs. Soames. "They are always early birds, and are no doubt waiting for bridge or friends. Shall I tell you about them, as you will meet them every day?"

"Yes, do, if you please," I replied, as I glanced over at the trio. Mrs. Soames gave a little preliminary cough, and began:

"The elderly woman, in the creased tussore costume and toque three sizes too large, is Mrs. Lakin. She is not nearly so old as she looks, but the struggle on small means, separation from her children, unhealthy stations, and the burden and heat of the East, have aged her. She comes of a good old Indian family, and was born in the country. At last she has emerged from her early difficulties; her daughters are married, and her husband commands a regiment. Mrs. Lakin is one of the old type of mem-sahibs, now almost extinct, who speak the language fluently, and know the bazaar prices to a dub. Her servants have grown grey in her service, her animals are fat and well liking; she is the soul of hospitality, and the most unselfish and sincere of women—her one weakness is auction bridge," and Mrs. Soames concluded this little sketch with a complacent smirk.

"So much for Mrs. Lakin," I said, "and now for the smart lady with a white aigrette in her hat."

"That is Mrs. Belmont, a typical modern mem-sahib. Her husband is in the Tea-Green Hussars. She had a huge fortune—made, it is said, in glue— and affects to loathe India, which she scorns as a paradise of the middle-classes—her own *milieu* as it happens! Unlike Mrs. Lakin she does not know her retinue by sight. To her, one black man is precisely the same as another. Her housekeeping is in the hands of a magnificent butler, who is amassing a fortune; her personal attendant, a Europe maid—*such* a mistake out here— is amassing admirers, and enjoying the time of her life. Mrs. Belmont is a good many years older than her husband, but wonderfully well preserved, and, considering her class, really quite presentable."

Here I recognised the inflexible attitude of a county lady towards the heiress of thousands made in glue.

"The third on the chabutra is Mrs. Potter," continued my companion. "If you listen you can hear her voice, and her loud rollicking laugh. She is also known as the 'Daily She Mail,' and 'Slater's,' as she is an inveterate, I may say, official newsmonger. Be sure that you are *very* careful what you say to her."

"Yes, but I don't see how *I* can give her much news."

"My dear, you personify news! She will pick your brain in ten minutes; she will know all about your family, your fortune, your tastes, and possibly the price of your hat! It is marvellous how she gets hold of the first tidings of such events as the movements of troops, engagements, quarrels or scandals; and the worst of it is, that in many cases her information is correct. Some say she has a friend at the Post Office; others, that she owes much to her ayah's circle at the bazaar, or that Joe Potter, her husband, has his ear to the ground in the city—where he is a vague 'something.' They live in a fine bungalow in Secunderabad, but have no claim to any social standing. All the same, Mrs. Potter goes everywhere; her card is filled the moment she appears at a dance, she is never 'left out' of any entertainment, and people propitiate her with craven attentions. It is much safer to be her friend than her enemy, for she uses her pen as well as her tongue, and supplies sharp unsigned articles to the press. Well, now I have given you an outline of one or two personalities. Here comes Mrs. Wolfe, that handsome dark woman in the yellow car. She is the wife of an official at Chudderghat, and that is a stranger with her. Let us get out now, and hurry over to the chabutra, or we won't get good seats."

We ascended the steps of the white cake without any undignified haste, and Mrs. Soames formally presented me to Mesdames Lakin, Belmont and Potter, as "My friend Miss Lingard." We all bowed and smiled at one another, and fresh tea was ordered from a bearded butler.

As my chaperon was exchanging civilities with the ladies already established, Mrs. Wolfe and her companion joined us. Mrs. Wolfe was a tall elegant woman, with magnificent black eyes and an intensely animated expression.

"This," she announced, with a comprehensive wave of her hand, "is my cousin Miss Payne. Sally Payne, who, after her arduous labours in globe-trotting, has come to enjoy a domestic holiday with me."

Mrs. Belmont raised her glasses and considered the new-comer with an air of grave appraisement. A little woman with reddish hair, sharp features and a pale clever face; she wore a well-cut white linen, a Panama hat, and carried in a white gloved hand a gold-handled sunshade.

Miss Payne bowed all round with self-possessed grace, seated herself, and began to take off her gloves.

"Just arrived?" said Mrs. Potter brusquely.

"Yes, only yesterday morning."

Then she glanced at me and said, "We came up from Wadi in the same train. You were the girl in that delightful blue silk dust cloak; it made me *so* envious. When you tire of it, please let me have the first offer?"

"Yes, certainly," I answered, in the same key, "but I do not propose to part with it yet."

Mrs. Potter's swift glance gave me to understand she would deal with me presently, but that just now she was particularly interested in Miss Payne, and she once more addressed her:

"Did I not see you at the Cinderella?" she inquired in her judicial voice.

"Guilty!" admitted the stranger. "My cousin dragged me there, but I enjoyed it immensely. What 'go' there was about it!"

"Yes, it was a good dance," agreed Mrs. Potter, "though one of the band had a fit, and the ice-cream ran short; but on the whole, everything was thoroughly well done."

"And what heaps of dancing men and pretty women!"

"Yes, we were just about to discuss the beauties of the evening—'present company always included!'" and Mrs. Potter glanced at Mrs. Belmont with her beautiful complexion, and then at Mrs. Wolfe with her animated, vivid face.

"Oh, pray don't mind *me*," protested Miss Payne, coolly accepting the implied compliment. "At forty I am past the beauty stage. Last night a worried-looking man rushed up to me and asked where he could find my daughter? Imagine such a question for a respectable English spinster!"

"I expect he took you for Mrs. Hastings," suggested Mrs. Soames, "her hair is the same shade."

"Well, I'll make it my business to look out for Mrs. Hastings, and see myself as others see me. I must confess, if I had been endowed with a daughter, I'd have chosen that delightful vision in rose-coloured chiffon."

"Oh, Miss Warren!" said Mrs. Potter with a sniff. "As it happens, she has no mother. Yes, she looked well enough, but her dress—an old one dyed—was too remarkable, especially as she danced with the same partner most of the evening!"

"Where was her chaperon?" inquired Miss Payne, as she helped herself to two lumps of sugar.

"Probably she had none," was the startling reply.

"What!" cried Miss Payne, brandishing the empty sugar tongs. "I know that chaperons are extinct at home—the bicycle killed them—but I'd no idea that India was so emancipated."

"I'm afraid we are," replied Mrs. Potter. "I heard some violent kissing last evening behind the screen where my partner and I were sitting out, and I happened to see the couple later—a girl and a married man!"

"Oh, really!" protested Miss Payne with mock horror, "I shall be obliged to retire. I am *much* too young for this kind of conversation!"

Then she looked across at me and burst out laughing.

"What do *you* say?"

This question drew upon me the immediate notice of Mrs. Potter. Hitherto I had been sitting a little in the background, now she turned round and favoured me with special attention.

"And you arrived yesterday, did you not?"

"Yes," I acknowledged with meek humility.

She stared at me so hard that I felt quite out of countenance, and could not find anything else to say.

"You are Captain Lingard's sister, I believe? How nice it is for him to have you out here!"

"And very nice for me—to be with him," I murmured.

"Your first visit, of course?" she was proceeding, when my chaperon interposed, and, moving a little nearer, asked Mrs. Potter a question about an imminent bridge tournament, and I was for the moment released. I confess I rather envied the independence of Miss Payne, who, having finished tea, had courageously betaken herself to the library.

Mrs. Lakin, hitherto engaged in cutting up cake and waiting on the company, now took a seat beside me and proceeded to break the ice. I noticed that her complexion was a pale biscuit colour, and her blue eyes looked faded, but she had a sweet expression—perhaps once upon a time she had been pretty.

"So I hear you are a new-comer. I wonder what you will think of India."

"So far, I like it immensely," I answered.

"There have been wonderful changes since I set foot in the country. That was thirty years ago. Then this club was a small affair, and stood farther down where the shop is now. Everything is made so comfortable in these days. People rush backwards and forwards to England for a few weeks' holiday. Formerly it was a wonderful thing if you got home once in five or six years. All the same, I liked those times best."

"Did you!" I exclaimed. "But why?"

"Well, it's not altogether because everything was quarter the price, though of course that does make a difference, especially when you have a large family. Things were quieter and easier. Generals did not come hustling round when they were least expected, and you and your friends were left in a station for three or four years instead of being whipped off as now at a moment's notice. The servants were a superior class, and one grew attached to them, and almost every girl that came to India was bound to find a husband."

"And that is all changed, I understand."

"Oh yes, it's as difficult to get off a girl here as it is elsewhere. In these days when the exchange is so low, sending home money is ruination—people bring out their families, and the country is overrun with paying guests, and this, in India, so famous once for hospitality! My two girls are married—not grand matches, but to really good fellows—and I must confess I miss them. My husband and I are alone—just Darby and Joan. I am sorry to say that his time will soon be up, he will be retired, and we go home for good next spring."

"Then you love India?" I said.

She nodded expressively, and added:

"You see I was born out here, as were my father and mother before me. We come of families who have made their home in India for many generations—educated of course in England, they all return like homing pigeons to the Army, to the Civil Service, and to many other posts. India draws them—they *all* hear the East a-calling."

"And so you will be really sorry to retire?"

"Yes," she admitted, "and if we can't stand it we will return and settle down in the hills. I can see us in England, probably established in some London suburb, in a little house, with smoky chimneys, the boiler always out of order, two servants—saying they've too much to do—ourselves with nothing to do, no interests, and none of our accustomed comforts. My! I don't like to think of it! I have heard such tales from friends who have gone back to England, and find the change awful, especially the climate."

"Oh," I exclaimed astonished, "you do surprise me."

"Yes," she answered. "Give me the ordinary honest hot weather out here. You know where you are; when the heat or rains are due, and when they cease. It is so much better than your capricious sun one day and snow the next, and your desperate English winters. Most English die in winter, and no wonder! You are staying with Mrs. Soames," she continued. "Your brother is in Colonel Soames's regiment; they are going home in the spring like ourselves."

This announcement gave me a shock. I understood that there might be a move from Secunderabad, but I never realised that it would be to England, or that I might find myself back at Torrington, before the year was out. As I pondered the subject Mrs. Lakin suddenly rose, in answer to a frantic signal from another matron.

"Bridge," she said, turning to me with a triumphant smile, "they have got up a rubber at last!"

Then she descended somewhat heavily, and hurried away to the *morghi-khana*.

"A good soul, but oh, what clothes!" said Mrs. Potter, looking after the retreating figure. "It is whispered that they are chosen by an envious old maid sister-in-law. I can see a world of spite in that short-waisted gown and the pantomime toque; and yet the poor lady is pleased, and tells us that *now* she gets everything from home."

"Never mind the clothes," put in Mrs. Wolfe, "when the woman inside them is a jewel. She is a sort of godmother to half the station."

Seeing that I had been abandoned by Mrs. Lakin, Mrs. Potter again turned to talk to me.

"As you have only just arrived, you have seen nothing of India so far except railway stations?"

I coloured with guilt, and nodded a deceitful assent.

Mrs. Potter's quick black eyes looked me up and down, and then she remarked:

"I dare say you will have a very good time. This is a most interesting place, if you care for that sort of thing; and you can see something of all conditions of men, Asiatic and European. There is, as you know, the great city of Hyderabad, which we may not enter without a pass. Then comes Chudderghat, where the Politicals and the Resident live; he has the finest Residency in India. There are also colleges and the convent of the Holy Rosary. Next we have Secunderabad itself, all shops, and bazaars, and fine old bungalows. That brings us here. Up your way the Army is sprinkled about—artillery and engineers, cavalry and line; this is the largest garrison in India—and now you have the place in a nutshell!"

"Who are these people?" I inquired, as I observed close to the *chabutra* several handsome dark young men getting out of a large motor.

"Oh, they are some of the Nizam's entourage, mostly noblemen and officers of the Golconda Lancers. They have been playing polo with the Lighthearts' team. Your brother is their captain. Of course, you must feel rather strange at first, not knowing a soul in the place!"

"Yes," I answered. I could not say why, but I found it difficult to talk to Mrs. Potter; her sharp eyes seemed to stab me like knives.

"But you will soon know everybody," she continued, with a little air of patronage. "Out here we are all supposed to be in the same set. The set in Secunderabad is embodied by the club—to be a member is our social hall-mark. All the rest are, so to speak, in outer darkness—where I believe there's a good deal of gnashing of teeth!"

As she was speaking I happened to glance towards the entrance through which people were still coming and going, and there I beheld someone who was not a stranger. It was Captain Falkland, attended by Kipper.

CHAPTER XV
A RENEWED FRIENDSHIP

Captain Falkland presented a striking appearance in his A.D.C. uniform, mounted on a fine black horse. He looked thoroughly at home in the saddle.

"Behold that faithless man!" cried Mrs. Wolfe excitedly; "how *am* I to get hold of him?"

"I suppose the general has been inspecting something, as he is on duty," said Mrs. Potter, "and there is the dog that is always at his heels."

"Lord Runnymede's only son is dead," observed a lady, who was now one of the company on "the cake." "He was always a poor consumptive creature, and Captain Falkland is the next heir. What a chance for some girl!"

"Oh, he's not a marrying man," declared Mrs. Wolfe with brisk decision; "he bars girls, and naturally he would never think of one of our 'spins' out here."

In answer to an agitated signal with a newspaper, Captain Falkland approached. He was now on foot.

"Oh, I've been trying to catch your eye for ages," screamed Mrs. Wolfe. "You never answered my chit, and you know you half promised to take me on the lake to-morrow. Do; come and have tiffin first."

He shook his head, and, before he had time to speak, she hastily added:

"Oh then, I'll meet you at the boathouse! I don't intend to let you off. An hour's rowing on the Hussain Saugur will be *so* good for you!"

Just at this moment Captain Falkland's eye caught mine, and he exclaimed:

"Miss Lingard! Well, I am astonished. When did you come out?"

I was prevented from answering by Kipper, who had also recognised me, and sprang into my lap in a state of hysterical delight, ruining my nice clean white linen with the red dust off his paws.

"So you and Miss Lingard have already met?" said Mrs. Soames, and I noticed that Mrs. Wolfe honoured me with a piercing stare.

"Oh yes, we knew one another at home," he replied, and then this bold man stepped up and took a chair on "the cake"—the one just vacated by Mrs. Lakin.

"When did you arrive?" he repeated.

"Only the other day," rejoined Mrs. Soames, evidently afraid that I would give myself away, and I sat by in helpless acquiescence. "Miss Lingard is staying with me."

"Kip is awfully pleased to see you," he said, addressing me particularly.

"Yes, isn't it nice of him?—and it is more than six months since we parted. He was once my property," I added, looking over at my chaperon.

After this evidently unexpected announcement there was a significant pause, and some of the ladies exchanged glances.

"How did you leave them at Torrington?" inquired my neighbour.

"Oh, very well, thank you. They all came to see me off from London."

"What steamer did you come out in?" demanded Mrs. Potter, but I pretended not to hear, and said:

"Dora is married, as I dare say you know, and Bev has decided to go into the Diplomatic Service."

"Sorry for the Service," muttered Captain Falkland.

"I wonder if you came out in the *Modena*?" persisted Mrs. Potter, who I could see was boiling over with questions, but Mrs. Soames, an efficient general, now rose and said:

"I promised to look for a book for Jimmy, and I had nearly forgotten it— something to do with military law—arrived in the last batch. Come along, Miss Lingard, and I will show you the library."

Captain Falkland rose to attend upon us, but was instantly arrested by Mrs. Wolfe, who figuratively flung herself upon him. She was one of those women who triumphantly capture the attention of men—be they never so wary—and thrust the rest of her sex ruthlessly aside. We left her holding her prey by the sheer force of her volubility, and talking with surpassing gesticulation and animation; but presently with surprising adroitness he managed to escape and joined us.

"So you and Miss Lingard were acquainted in England?" said my chaperon.

"Oh, rather—we are connections. My people and Miss Lingard's have lived within a few miles of one another for centuries. The Falklands and the Lingards are old and trusted friends."

"How amusing! I had no idea of this," said Mrs. Soames; nor had the poor deceived lady any idea that the speaker and I had only spoken to one another on two occasions!

"You must come and dine with us," she continued hospitably, "just a quiet little family dinner."

As they were arranging the day and hour, I stood aloof talking to Kip, and was astonished to behold yet another familiar face and form. Could I believe my eyes? There was Mr. Balthasar descending from an imposing grey motor.

He crossed the compound quickly and accosted Ronnie, who had just ridden in from polo; they talked eagerly together as the latter dismounted and his pony was led away. I noticed that Ronnie took Mr. Balthasar familiarly by the arm and spoke to him earnestly for some minutes, whilst from time to time Balthasar nodded his close-shaven bullet head in emphatic agreement. Undoubtedly Balthasar had heard of my arrival, had possibly seen me and informed Ronnie of our former meeting, and Ronnie had pledged him to silence. Now, including Captain Vesey, there were four people who held the secret of my past.

As Mrs. Soames and I moved towards our victoria, escorted by Captain Falkland, Ronnie took a few steps towards us, but his companion stood stock-still, and looked at me as blankly as if he had never seen me before. Then one of his thick black lashes quivered slightly. Yes, it was an unmistakable wink!

As our carriage wheeled about to thread its way among a crowd of other vehicles I beheld Mrs. Wolfe "descend upon the fold." She seized the helpless A.D.C. and carried him off in triumph to the *morghi-khana*.

The next afternoon Mrs. Soames and I drove up to the polo ground to witness a match, in which Ronnie greatly distinguished himself. He was captain of the regimental team, rode splendidly, and was remarkably well mounted. I could see that he was an important factor in the local polo world. I noticed Mrs. Lakin in a dreadful old phaeton, drawn by a bony chestnut horse. As she caught sight of us she waved her hand with effusion.

"Isn't she a funny old thing?" said Mrs. Soames. "She lives down at Begumpett, where her husband commands a regiment, and she dresses like a caretaker, but is such a good, generous woman, so kind to the natives, Eurasians, and poor whites. She spends on others—saves on herself. To my certain knowledge she has had that toque ever since I came to the station. If anyone is ill, it's Mrs. Lakin to the front; if anyone is in trouble, they turn to Mrs. Lakin. Her husband is a smart, well-set-up man, and looks years younger than his dowdy wife. Their bungalow is on the style of forty years ago, quite a curiosity. They have queer old furniture and Argand lamps, but give capital dinners in the good solid style; everything in the most lavish profusion. Masses of servants, dozens of courses, wonderful curries, and such tender mutton! She is the secretary of our Mutton Club. It is really an historical object lesson to dine with the Lakins, and to learn how things were done—say at the time of the battle of Plassey."

"I wish she would invite me to dinner," I replied. "She is a nice, confidential, motherly old thing, adores India, and cannot endure the idea of leaving the country."

"No, I dare say not," said Mrs. Soames; "all her children were born and most of her relations are buried out here. Her sons and daughters are scattered about this Presidency. I don't suppose she has anyone belonging to her at home, and would be rather at a loose end in Bayswater or West Kensington."

"She might write her memoirs," I suggested, and here Ronnie and several of his friends surrounded our carriage and claimed our attention.

The night that Captain Falkland dined with the Soameses the only other guests were Major and Mrs. Mills, the chaplain and his wife, and ourselves—a somewhat sober party. I must confess that I took unusual pains with my appearance. My ayah and luggage had arrived. Captain Falkland had never seen me in full war paint, that is to say in evening dress, for at what he called the "beanfeast" I had worn a demi-toilette. I think Mrs. Soames was a little impressed by the fact of our former acquaintance; at any rate, she sent us in to dinner together, and we talked away gaily.

We discoursed about Torrington and Beke, the "Beetle," and also the "Plough and Harrow."

"That was a ghostly old place," he remarked. "I spent two nights there and heard the most extraordinary noises, as if someone was ploughing up and down the passages."

"Oh, how amusing!" exclaimed Mrs. Soames.

"Surely you don't believe in ghosts?" I said.

"No, I'm not sure that I do," he replied, "although we own one ourselves—appearance guaranteed only to members of the family—but I have a sort of sneaking belief in those horrible things called 'Elementals.'"

"An Elemental—what is that?" I asked.

"Oh, a sort of half ghost, half reptile, a hideous animal—or even a too frightful vegetable! Germans call them 'House devils.' They are the most modern and fashionable article, and have entirely cut out the old sheeted spectre and clanking chains business."

"And what do they *do*?"

"All manner of hateful tricks; for instance, supposing you've laid down a book or an umbrella for a moment, you turn about, and it's gone! After a protracted search and considerable loss of time and temper, behold it once more before your eyes! Say you have discovered something important in a newspaper and particularly wish to show it to a friend, you may hunt the paper through and through until you're nearly crazy, and there's not a sign of it. That's the work of an Elemental. When you have written, with painful labour, a most particular letter and tip over the ink—Elemental again! Or when you are late and in a terrific hurry, and your only collar stud jumps out of your hand, rolls away and falls into a hole in the floor, you tear your hair, and delight the Elemental! Some go so far as to say that bruises and pinches for which we cannot account come from the same quarter."

"Horrible!" I said. "I'd a thousand times sooner have to deal with a banshee."

"Well, yes," he replied, "they only sit outside the window and howl and wail; but they will never wail for *you*, as you are not Irish."

"No," I said, "I rather wish I were."

"Do you, my dear girl?" said Mrs. Soames. "How very amusing!"

"They are an attractive nation, a most happy-go-lucky lot," resumed my partner. "I sometimes go over there to hunt with a friend. The very last time I crossed I told the porter to label my luggage for Bristol. Luckily, I caught him just in time as he was pasting on 'London.' I asked him what the dickens he meant? 'Shure, yer honour,' he replied quite calmly, 'I'm bound to put *something* on—and these is the only ones I have!' He seemed to think he was doing his duty, and looked so genial and so pleased with me that I believe I gave him sixpence."

"It's wonderful how *you* get Captain Falkland to talk," said Mrs. Mills when we forgathered in the drawing-room; "with me he is generally as dumb as a fish."

"He is an example of a man who makes a little conversation go a long way," said Mrs. Soames. "Rather a drawback for an aide-de-camp. However, what he does say is generally to the point, and he has the most beautiful manners. He must have learnt them from his mother Lady Louisa—she belongs to the old school, and is as proud as Lucifer! I don't envy the unfortunate girl who will be her daughter-in-law. I do not think that in her eyes anyone short of a princess will be a fitting match for her dear Brian; however, he is a nice fellow, and one of those rare, unselfish individuals who enjoy listening to other people."

"Then I should imagine he has a thoroughly happy time with Mrs. Wolfe," said the major's wife. "She must nearly talk his head off, and with her great black eyes, enormous mouth and flashing teeth, she sometimes looks as if she were going to *eat* him!"

It was painfully evident that this lady was no favourite with Mrs. Mills.

"Oh, she just talks as easily as she breathes," declared Mrs. Soames good-naturedly. "It's her second nature. She is a brilliantly clever woman, and *so* amusing."

"Well, I much prefer her cousin Miss Payne," declared Mrs. Mills; "she is really unique; so original, independent, and interested in the whole world. Mrs. Wolfe is merely interested in herself and her admirer for the time being; she cannot exist without some attaché. Whether he likes it or not she has a way of annexing a man that there is no resisting. Her tactics are excessively bold and open. If she takes a fancy to any particular individual his struggles are useless; he is condemned to dance, to ride, to boat, and to play tennis with her, until she is tired of his society."

"But it's all so absolutely harmless," protested Mrs. Soames. "Mabel Wolfe is an excellent wife; her three children are at home, and I suppose she thinks, being young and gay, that she is entitled to some distraction!"

"I don't know what you call 'entitled,'" rejoined Mrs. Mills, "but I know for a fact that she was at the bottom of the breaking off of the Wallington-Allan engagement, and there was 'distraction' if you like! I grant you that she has a wonderfully animated manner. Her descriptions are vivid, her 'take offs' are inimitable. She entertains the men, and they like her, but, for my part, for a woman with three little children——" She paused abruptly as the lords of creation were now sauntering in, and the subject of Mrs. Wolfe and her shortcomings was postponed to another occasion.

After some desultory conversation, Mrs. Soames uttered the words "A little music," and I was conducted to the piano—a rich-toned Schiedmayer—and Colonel Soames begged me to sing something he had heard me trying over that morning.

After one song I was urged to many. My efforts were unexpectedly appreciated. Captain Falkland was evidently fond of music; he stood by the piano turning over the leaves, and begging for his special favourites, and I was retained at the instrument until it was ten o'clock, the hour for the departure of our guests—all early birds.

"Are you riding in the mornings, Mrs. Soames?" inquired Captain Falkland, as he was about to take leave.

"Yes, to be sure I am," she replied briskly.

"Well then, if I may, I will call in on Thursday and take my chance. We might have a gallop round Moul Ali racecourse."

On Thursday, which was the garrison holiday, a large riding party assembled outside our quarters. Colonel and Mrs. Soames, Major and Mrs. Mills, Ronnie and his greatest friend in the regiment, Mr. Arkwright, Captain Gloag, the adjutant, Captain Falkland, Colonel Grey (a colonel of the artillery in Trimulgherry—not very far from our lines), his two daughters and myself.

The Misses Grey, Emily and Mabel, were not remarkably pretty, but were very popular in the station. Their mother being dead, their father enacted the part of an effective chaperon. He was a wonderfully dapper, active little widower, and looked young to be the father of these well-grown young women, was a capital tennis player and an indefatigable dancer. It was certainly rather hard upon the girls that he laid such heavy toll upon them for partnership on tennis court or in ballroom. At every dance it was an unwritten law that each had to reserve three dances for her parent. As they danced beautifully their young men friends considered this claim an outrageous exercise of parental authority. Certainly the little colonel danced amazingly well. If by any chance one of the girls "cut" her father's waltz, domestic matters would be more or less disagreeable for some time. In all other respects he was a pattern to chaperons.

Moul Ali, an otherwise forsaken racecourse, was often the scene of morning and evening gallops, and the forlorn, dilapidated stand made a suitable resort for *chotah hazri*, afternoon teas, or even moonlight suppers. The course and stand were the sole attraction to people from the cantonments, as this portion of the Deccan is surprisingly ugly, and has to depend for its beauty on sunset and moonlight effects. The land is barren, covered with low-growing shrub and enormous red sandstone boulders of every size and shape. So numerous are these that there is a native legend to the effect that when the Creator had completed His work, He discharged all the rubbish in this part of the world. For miles and miles it is a sea of stones, with not even a palm or a mango tope to break the monotony.

On this particular Thursday morning the sun was scarcely over the horizon when we moved off *en masse*. I rode with Colonel Soames. Our way lay along a rough cart track, full of ruts and rocks, bordered with bleached jungle grass and thorny, leafless bushes. At last we arrived at our destination and there let ourselves and our horses "out." How I enjoyed that delightful gallop with the fresh morning air beating in my face! Captain Falkland's great waler and my stud-bred raced along together side by side, and we were soon far ahead of the rest of the party.

"Your animal has a turn of speed; that was a good stretcher," he remarked, as we subsided to a walk. "You love riding, I can see."

"Yes," I replied; "and here it is all so nice and free. One is, as it were, off the road," and I waved my hand at the enormous stretch of open country.

"That's so,"he assented. "There are no farmers to head you off new wheat, but it's pretty bad going. You have not yet come across any of our big nullahs." Then turning round, so as almost to look me straight in the face, "I say, do tell me, now we are by ourselves, how you happened to come out to India."

"I wanted to come," I replied. "I have always longed to see the East."

"That you particularly wanted anything would be no reason for your getting it, if I know Mrs. Lingard. Rather the other way I should say; so tell me the truth, the whole truth, and nothing but the truth."

"Well then,the real reason— —" Here I came to a full stop.

"Yes, go on please—the *real* reason."

"Was Beverley," I brought out with an effort. "He was so horribly fond of me."

"Good Lord!" exclaimed my companion. "What a way to put it!"

"And although I couldn't endure him, and snubbed him fiercely on every occasion, still my aunt was afraid— —" And again I hesitated.

"That you might be tempted? Yes, I see."

"There were no grounds for her fears I do assure you, but when Aunt Mina saw a chance of shipping me to India, naturally she seized upon it—and of course I was only too glad to come."

"Did she ship you to your brother?" inquired my companion.

"Well—no—not exactly," I stammered.

"Oh, then, there *is* something behind!"

"There is," I admitted.

"Nothing much, I'll bet my boots. You haven't it in you to keep a deadly secret."

"I'm not so sure," I replied. "For all you know to the contrary, I may deserve the kettle. I heard you talking to Mrs. Potter about truth."

"Yes, I hope I didn't put my foot in it? Truth, between you and me and the doorstep, is not her *most* prominent virtue. Now, you have it written all over your face; you couldn't tell a lie if you tried."

"Please don't hurl these compliments at me," I protested, "especially as I don't deserve them. I may not tell a lie—but I might *act* one!"

"What do you mean?" he demanded, reining up suddenly; and Kip, who had caught us up at last, sat down to pant.

"I do not see why I should explain. You seem to expect me to tell you everything about myself and my affairs as a matter of course. On your side, you divulge nothing."

"I am not as good at talking as you are and I have but little to say for myself. Possibly, like the parrot, I think the more. Perhaps, some day, I may tell you something that I would never say to another soul. Although you and I have met so seldom, we know one another extraordinarily well, and if there is any truth in the fashionable doctrine of Theosophy, we were united by a close tie in some former existence. Do you know I had that feeling when we passed one another on Slacklands Marsh? Well now, won't you tell me the great secret?"

"Yes," I agreed, "but not at present. Do you see," I continued, pointing over at the stand rendezvous, "everyone is there already!—they are waving what looks like a tablecloth."

"By Jove, so they are!" he exclaimed, as we put our horses into a canter. "All right, then," and he looked at me expressively, "your thrilling story must be continued in our next!"

CHAPTER XVI
AN UNWELCOME VISITOR

When we dismounted at the stand we found that *chotah hazri* had already started, and was, so to speak, half-way round the course. As I received my teacup from her hands, I gathered that my chaperon was displeased with me—my tardy arrival was not "amusing." Perhaps she thought that I had made myself too conspicuous in riding off and having a long *tête-à-tête* with Captain Falkland, although we *were* old friends; therefore, on the way home I carefully avoided his company and gave him no opportunity of resuming our conversation, keeping close to Major Mills and Ronnie.

Within a week of my arrival at Secunderabad I seemed to have slipped into my place in the station as Mrs. Soames's guest and Captain Lingard's sister, and as they were both popular everything was made pleasant for me. My singing was extravagantly praised. I loved music, but satisfaction in my own performances had hitherto been cheapened and damped, especially by Aunt Mina, who had no ear, and assured me that my execution on the piano was all right, but my singing was far too dramatic and theatrical, also that I *screamed* like a curlew!

We had tennis, riding parties, dinners, dances, sports on the Futeh Maidan, and boating excursions on the lake. Besides this, there was plenty of work for the garrison—manœuvres, night attacks, field days and route marching. As the weather was now cool, the general, a particularly active soldier, kept his staff incessantly occupied, and I saw but little of Captain Falkland. On the other hand, I saw far too much of Mr. Balthasar. He appeared to be continually about the club, and had been actually introduced to me by Ronnie!

I felt secretly comforted when Mrs. Soames agreed with me that he was "a most odious person."

"Of course, my dear," she said, "he is in the club, and that says all. He has lots of money and subscribes to everything, has a fine house down in Chudderghat, gives men's dinner parties, and is said to have extraordinary influence in the city—not of London, but of Hyderabad. All the same, in my opinion, he is just an adventurer, but he is received at the Residency, and Secunderabad people have him at their houses. He shall never enter mine! He gives me the idea of being some horrible human bloodsucker, and I believe—though I dare not say it in public—that he is a money-lender."

Mrs. Soames was very intimate with Lady Dynevor, the wife of the Resident. We frequently went down to Chudderghat to tiffin and to tennis parties, and I was taken to see something of the great Mohammedan city: for instance, the Char Minar, the Nizam's palace (the finest in India), standing on a high terrace; the façade, a double row of Corinthian columns, the interior with its marble stairs, statues and treasures—truly the Palace Beautiful!

At the Residency I made the acquaintance of a delightful Mohammedan lady. Her name was Zora; she came to tiffin when there were no men, arriving in a closed car and heavily veiled. She was no darker than an Italian, and very handsome. Her figure was slight and willowy, and she was undoubtedly the most graceful creature I had ever seen. Her father, a Nawab of great wealth, was one of the ministers to the Nizam; she was his only daughter—and a widow. Zora was an accomplished musician, and played the piano magnificently. As she spoke English fluently we soon became friends. Zora informed me that she had often been in England, where she dressed and went about precisely like other people, and was often taken for an Italian!

"I used to go to your theatres, dinners and garden parties, and enjoyed myself immensely. In London I often rode on the top of a motor-bus, but as soon as I come back to India I become *gosha*."

Mrs. Soames and I visited her at her father's palace, an imposing abode, with many servants in livery, wide staircases and long corridors, the floors of which were covered with white linen. Zora's own apartments were furnished English fashion, though there were divans piled with cushions, and wonderful Persian rugs; here, too, was a splendid Steinway piano, a writing-table, Chesterfield couches, and bookcases crammed with French and English books.

At tea-time we were joined by her father (the minister), a handsome elderly man with suave, courteous manners and an expressive voice. He spoke English perfectly, talked with ease, and told us many interesting things about the city. The Nawab had two sons who had been educated at Harrow and were now in the Nizam's forces, but I could see that Zora the beautiful was the pride of his life.

I had now been a whole month with Mrs. Soames, and made many acquaintances—for instance, all the officers of the "Lighthearts"—and began to feel myself almost one of the regiment. I had also been made known to most of the people at the club and a number of girls—among these my particular friends were Emily and Mabel Grey, and we met almost daily.

As Quarter No. 30 was vacant I insisted upon moving into it. I hated to feel as if I were imposing, though I believe Mrs. Soames really liked me; I did my best to help her in every way I could, by writing notes, reading aloud—as her sight was indifferent—going messages down to the bazaar when she was busy, and shopping at Cursetjee's or Spencer's and various places in Oxford Street, Secunderabad. I liked Colonel Soames, too, but somehow he resembled the countryman and the claret—one never got much "forrarder." I rode with him, danced with him, and sang to him, but he was often preoccupied and inaccessible, and had no real interest in the world beyond the regiment. The regiment was his fetish; its fitness, smartness and fame were all he cared for, and I could see that he ruled his officers and men with an iron hand, encased in a somewhat thin velvet glove.

Hospitable Mrs. Soames was reluctant to part with me, although I was to be such a near neighbour. Quarter 30, or the end bungalow, faced towards Trimulgherry Rock. Our abode was a good size; three large lofty rooms, and two slips at either side. The compound was considerable; the late occupant had kindly started a vegetable garden, our avenue was lined with cork trees in flower, and the whole front veranda was enshrouded in luxuriant creeper. With fresh matting and pretty bamboo furniture, chintzes, cushions, and solid indispensables, Ronnie and I made the end bungalow very nice indeed. He took great pains in hanging pictures, putting up heads, and fixing draperies. Kind Mrs. Soames lent me some plate just for the time, as she had more than she wanted, and I could return it to her when the regiment went home. This was a move which I could not bear to contemplate, but I kept my thoughts to myself.

Ronnie and I instituted a most happy ménage. We shopped together in Oxford Street, and there picked up glass and china, lamps and stores. Our stables held a smart dog-cart and horse, my stud-bred grey and Ronnie's three polo ponies, which he also hacked. Our household consisted of a cook and *tannyketch* (an individual who carries the market basket, plucks fowl, and is, in short, the kitchen slavey). There was Michael the big butler, a dressing *chokra*, my ayah—now happily situated in one of our go-downs, with a whole brood of relations—and the usual *mali* and *bheesti*, etc.

I had invested in a ponderous account book with a lock and key, and was the household purse-bearer. We boldly adventured on little luncheons and dinners; numbers of people called, and, if we had been so disposed, we could have dined out nearly every night. On Sundays we always had supper at the colonel's. I sat with Mrs. Soames in the garrison church, accompanied her to dances, and though I now was a "Miss Sahib" with an establishment of my own, was still more or less under her friendly wing.

Besides Mabel and Emily Grey and Mrs. Mills, I had two friends who were a considerable contrast, Zora and Mrs. Lakin. Ronnie and I had dined at the Lakins'—a most overwhelming repast—and now and then Mrs. Lakin herself came to see me and gave me hints about housekeeping and kept me well posted in the proper price of ghee and charcoal. I could see that she took a motherly interest in me, now that her own girls were far afield, and I was grateful for the same.

Mrs. Wolfe had honoured me with a visit, so had Mrs. Potter. I instinctively felt that she did not accept me for what I may call "my face value." To use a common but disagreeable expression, I think she figuratively "smelt a rat"! Our interview was a long series of sharp questions and nervous answers, and I was nearly exhausted and at my wits' end, when, to my great relief, Ronnie and his friend Mr. Arkwright made their appearance and she took her departure.

Among my other visitors was Zora, who came by special appointment when I was alone, and we mutually enjoyed music, tea and conversation. Captain Falkland also called, and one who was not equally welcome—Mr. Balthasar. I think when I beheld his great big grey motor turning into the compound, I would have said "Durwaza bund," only that Ronnie, who seemed surprisingly excited, cried:

"By Jove!—here's old Balthasar!—just the very man I wanted to see."

He was just the man I did *not* want to see, but naturally I was bound to be civil in my own house, and although he oozed affability and admiration at every pore, I was not softened. No! Could I ever forgive his insolent wink? However, Ronnie and he appeared to be on excellent terms, and he accompanied my brother into his little office or writing-room, there to confer together on some important subject, which they declared would not interest me. Later, as Ronnie was obliged to go to barracks, I was left to entertain Mr. Balthasar alone.

After discussing a recent gymkhana, Ronnie's prowess in the Loyd-Lindsay and tent-pegging, he worked the conversation round to Silliram.

"Do you ever hear from your friends there?" he inquired.

"I do not know that I have any friends there at present," I answered evasively. "All the people I knew have gone down to the plains."

"I was over at the Katchookan Mines last week for a couple of days and put up with the Hayes-Billingtons," he continued.

"Oh, did you? How is she?" I asked.

"She looked awfully seedy—no beauty *now*, so thin and faded. It's a horrible hole for a woman; nothing to do, hardly a soul to speak to. Billington is in the mines all day, and of course for a lady accustomed to a very—er—er—flash sort of life, as she was, when Mrs. de Lacy, it must be a sort of hell on earth—minus the company. She was asking for you; she seems awfully fond of you. I say," and he hitched his chair a few inches closer and lowered his voice, "it's a pity that your people at home were so slack about making inquiries, eh?" Here he rolled his pale grey eyes at me. "It's an awful handicap for a girl to start out in this country as the companion of a woman of loose character."

I clenched my hands tightly, but held my tongue.

"Luckily for you," he continued, "the matter has been kept dark down here. There are only one or two people in the know, and I am one of them, and, my dear young lady, you can always rely on *me*." As he made this unctuous announcement he patted me on the arm with odious familiarity. "Your brother and I are tremendous pals; he is an awfully clever chap, and I would do more than that for him—and for *you*—but you must not be so stand-off, you know—let us be friends, *great* friends. Ronnie must bring you down to tiffin and I will show you my little bungalow, and you will let me take you for some drives in my new car. Perhaps you would like to go out to the mines one day and see Mrs. Hayes-Billington?"

These astounding invitations almost took my breath away, and as I was endeavouring to invent some polite excuse he resumed. "Not a soul need know about the little expedition; it's only a run of a hundred miles, and if we went next week—there is a full moon."

"Thank you very much," I said at last, "but I could not possibly accompany you to see Mrs. Hayes-Billington, although I am really sorry for her loneliness."

"Then why not come, my dear young lady? Your visit would do her so much good. It would be a charity, for, upon my soul, she looks as if her heart were breaking. No one except your brother will ever hear of our trip. It will be quite under the rose! Come, come! Why not do good by stealth?"

"I am afraid I do not care to do anything by stealth," I answered stiffly.

"And what about false pretences?" he demanded, now changing his tone, and once more patting me on the arm.

"What do you mean?" I asked sharply.

"Well, here is a beautiful young lady"—he rolled his eyes expressively—"she is the belle of Secunderabad—as even the women allow. She shines like a star; the station is full of her praises, she is so sweet and unspoiled; so simple and so *innocent*! Her singing and her dancing are the admiration of everyone who has the happiness to be in her company. She is supposed to have just arrived from England—yet all the time the poor foolish people are being deceived. Previous to her arrival here, the beautiful innocent young lady has been living in a hill station with a notoriously bad woman. Of course I shall keep all this as secret as the grave—but, my darling girl, what are you going to do for *me*?"

For a moment I was too stunned to speak or to stir. At last I got up, walked over to the door leading into the veranda, and beckoning to our butler, said:

"Please order this gentleman's car!"

Then I turned my back on Mr. Balthasar and retired to my own apartment, feeling, as Mrs. Paget-Taylor had once expressed it, "completely unhinged."

CHAPTER XVII
A COMPROMISE

Our modest ménage at No. 30 was a very happy one, at any rate for the first three months. We were like a pair of children playing at housekeeping, and often when we sat down to dinner at our daintily arranged table we would nod and laugh at one another, for somehow it all seemed unreal and too good to be true. Here was indeed "a place in the sun."

I looked carefully after Ronnie's comforts, ordered his favourite dishes, and was always up early, ready to give him *chotah hazri* in our shady veranda before he rode off to parade. I did my utmost to entertain his friends, especially Roger Arkwright, who soon became my friend as well. He was a tall fair young man, with square shoulders and a pleasant square face. He came in and out as often as he pleased and we called him "The tertium quid." I wondered if, occasionally, his visits were not nicely timed so as to meet Mabel and Emily Grey—especially Mabel—who were often with me, practising new songs or just running over merely to idle and talk. However that may be, Roger Arkwright gave me valuable help with our garden. We had a splendid show of roses in pots, and a respectable amount of lettuce and tomatoes. He also took a personal and greedy interest in my flock of ducks, who every morning, after their early breakfast, departed *en masse* for some distant pond, returning quacking and hungry at sundown. So punctual were they that one could almost set a watch by these worthy and business-like birds.

Mrs. Mills, my next-door neighbour, would often step over the wall dividing our compounds and bring her work and talk to me. She had two small children with her and a boy at home, about whom she was always anxious, as he was a delicate little fellow and had no grannies. The Millses were not well off; she often discussed ways and means, the cook's accounts and bazaar bills, and I agreed with her that in the East rupees seemed to vanish like mists in the sun!

"You see," she said, "this is a smart regiment and the mess bills are heavy. The colonel will have everything done in the most expensive style, and when I see the monthly amount my heart goes into my boots—and yet

I don't want to be mean; as George says, 'the reputation of the regiment and its traditions must come before everything else.' For you it is all right, of course, as you and Ronnie have lots of money."

"I don't know about that," I answered. "Speaking for myself, I have just a hundred and fifty pounds a year, besides an allowance from my uncle."

"Oh, but your brother is well known to be wealthy. Why, last year he gave three thousand rupees for a polo pony! He offers prizes for the men's sports, he entertains at the club, and is always most generous and open-handed."

To all of which statements I could but assent. Ronnie and I did not interfere with each other's arrangements, or rather I never interfered with his. We rode together, drove down to the club in the afternoon, and at balls danced the first waltz. When at home we were rarely alone; there was sure to be somebody dropping in for breakfast, lunch or dinner. In India these casual guests make practically no difference in the menu, just a little more water to the soup, another cutlet and another savoury. My cook was really a treasure; we were on excellent terms; I never cut him down, or weighed his purchases, or fined him, as Mrs. Mills did her man, and he took a real pride in his work. I, too, cooked, and had installed a small stove in the back veranda, where Mabel Grey and I experimented with recipes and made delicious meringues, rock cakes, and original savouries. The little dinners at No. 30 enjoyed quite a regimental reputation. Sometimes Ronnie dined at mess—always on Guest Night—sometimes there was a bachelor dinner at the club. On these occasions I dined with the Millses or the Soameses, or enjoyed in preference a quiet meal (such as a poached egg) at home, made up accounts and worked off arrears of correspondence. Somehow, now that I led such a busy life, with continual goings out and comings in, I was exceedingly thankful to have a short breathing space. Ronnie, too, had rarely a spare minute; what with parades, orderly room, guards, rifle-shooting, arranging polo matches, and playing cricket, he was always busy. Sometimes I had known him to sit up in his little den writing till midnight.

All our lives we had been the best of friends and comrades. Sad to relate, our first difference of opinion was about Mr. Balthasar. One evening Ronnie came home from the club looking alarmingly put out. At first I thought he might have had a bad evening at bridge, or that one of the polo ponies had broken down, but I knew I should hear all about it after dinner, when we smoked in the veranda—I too enjoyed a cigarette, an accomplishment I had learnt from Mrs. Hayes-Billington. I took to it by her advice on one of our gloomy, depressing wet days. She declared that smoking soothed the nerves. So far as I knew I had not any nerves to soothe, but I snatched at a new experience!

As soon as we were comfortably installed in two deep chairs Ronnie began:

"I say, I've an awfully big crow to pluck with you, old girl."

"All right," I answered gaily. "I have got a bag to put the feathers in—now show me the crow?"

"I met Balthasar in the club this evening. He has been away for a week or two; he was frightfully black with me for some reason, and then, when I asked him why he had the hump, it all came out! It seems that that day when he called upon you to pay his respects in full state, and was talking to you and advising you with regard to a certain affair—of course I mean Mrs. Hayes-Billington—you actually rose and summoned your servant and turned him out of the house! Now I want an explanation?"

"And you shall have it," I answered with some heat, and then as rapidly and as forcibly as I could find words I poured out my wrath and the whole tale. I spoke of Balthasar's insinuations, his vague threats, his loathsome familiarity, and his audacious suggestion that I should accompany him to the mines to see Mrs. Hayes-Billington. I declared that when he threatened me and insinuated that I was in his power and living under false pretences, I naturally got up and commanded Michael to send for his car. At last I ceased, breathless. For a moment Ronnie did not speak, but I felt instinctively that he was impressed by my information.

"I see," he said, "the fellow lost his head—I know he admires you enormously."

At this announcement I stamped my foot—old style.

"But, Sis, you must remember that he is a foreigner and make allowances; they are all so hasty and emotional. Balthasar assured me he had come to see you with the kindest intentions, and that you threw him out of the house as if he were a mad dog! He says he shall never forget the way you drew yourself up and looked at him."

"I am delighted to hear that," I answered heartlessly. "I hope I have planted an evergreen in his memory, and that I may never see him again."

"Oh well, for that matter," and Ronnie gave a rather nervous cough, "it would not do for you and him to be really at daggers drawn, for he has been awfully useful to me; in fact, I may say I am under some obligation to him. And so are you, old girl, if he continues to keep his mouth shut."

"Oh, my dear Ronnie," I protested, "*why* should we have anything to do with such a horror? I'd a thousand times rather be under an obligation to Baker, the butler at Torrington."

"Yes, but that's a different affair. He is one of our own race; and, if it comes to obligations, I have borrowed a sov. from Baker before now! These Levantines are different; so emotional and sensitive, and childishly thin-skinned. With them you are either black or white. I prefer to be on good terms with Balthasar. He works many strings in the financial world—half the people here run after him——"

"And the other half run away from him," I supplemented.

"Well, anyhow, he gets stacks of invitations; he is our local Rothschild, and quite an *ami de la maison* at the Residency."

"I can hardly believe that," I said rudely; "and anyway, he is not, you will admit, what we would call a *white* man."

"I can tell you this, Sis, that his face was grey with rage when he was talking to me this evening. Look here," and Ronnie rose and stood before me with his hands in his pockets, "you will have to patch up a truce with old Balthasar, and I will bear the olive-branch. We can ask him up to lunch or dinner to soothe his wounded feelings, and you must put your fastidiousness in your pocket and assume a virtue if you have it not! I say, I don't often ask you to do something—but I do beg of you to oblige me in this one thing, as a great favour."

His expression was so grave and anxious that I could not but yield.

"All right, Ronnie, you know I never can refuse you anything. I will do my best to smother my feelings and, much as I loathe him, be civil to Balthasar in order to please you."

Then Ronnie kissed me warmly, and said:

"That's a good old girl! I dare say he rubbed you the wrong way. He's not a bad sort, I assure you, and rather a friend of mine. Now, I'll tell you of a friend of yours who always rubs *me* the wrong way—it's that fellow Falkland! I can't stand his slow, deliberate manner. Of course the women here have spoiled him and run after him because he'll have a title some day; and he's such a strait-laced beggar, thinks gambling is wrong, at least for anything more than eight annas a hundred at bridge. He doesn't bet, and he scowls if you tell him a sultry story; and this comes well from a fellow who is in the fastest cavalry regiment in India!"

"I don't agree with you about Captain Falkland," was my bold reply. "I'm sure he's not a bit of a prig, and I think he's right about betting, when many of the young fellows here have no money to spare. However, you keep your friend and I'll keep mine."

"All right," agreed Ronnie, "only don't let's invite them here together, for I happen to know that they hate one another like poison. And now I'm going to send off a chit to Balthasar. I'll tell him you're very sorry, but that he quite misunderstood you; you were going out to tiffin at the general's with Mrs. Soames, and were already late."

"What a frightful story!" I exclaimed.

"Oh, it'll be all right," said Ronnie as he passed into the drawing-room. "I expect he'll take it with a grain of salt."

CHAPTER XVIII
THE RESIDENCY BALL

It was the middle of November, months had flown like weeks, and days like hours. The annual great ball at the Residency was imminent. For a ball no more auspicious place could possibly be selected than the splendid Durbar Hall, with its fine teak floor and crystal chandeliers—said to have been "borrowed" from the French at Pondicherry. Everyone on Government House list had received invitations, and guests were flocking not only from the city of Hyderabad and the cantonments, but from Raichore and even far distant Poona. I had a lovely new ball-dress held in reserve for this supreme occasion. It was the white and silver gown which I had worn when Mrs. Hayes-Billington told me that I was "lovely." Of course she was a flatterer, but, whatever I might be, I don't think there could be any question with respect to my frock.

Just as my toilet was completed and I was taking "a last fond look" the ayah introduced an enormous bouquet on a tray. It was not my style of bouquet in the least—tight in structure and overpowering as to perfume; moreover, I had grave suspicions as to the donor.

I inspected it, sniffed at it, and then handed it back to the ayah and told her that she might keep it for herself.

"What for I doing such stupid nonsense?" she asked in her most querulous key. "I putting in missie's bath tub for to-night; to-morrow the mali will arrange in best vases in drawing-room."

"I do not wish to see the flowers again," I replied impatiently, "take them away—*throw* them away!"

Whilst I was still commanding, and she entreating, my official chaperon called for me in the brougham. Ronnie and the colonel had driven down together in the dog-cart. It was rather a long journey to Chudderghat, and when we arrived at the Residency we found the great steps encompassed with such a crowd of carriages and motors that we were obliged to wait for a quarter of an hour before it came to our turn.

The scene in the ballroom was dazzling. Such brilliant functions are rarely witnessed in England; putting aside the vast well-proportioned hall, its blazing chandeliers and banks of tropical flowers and palms, the company was unique—crowds of pretty women and girls in fresh smart gowns, officers in all sorts of uniform, from the ordinary volunteer in black and silver to a gorgeous Golconda Lancer. There were present many nobles from the city, wearing magnificent satin and brocade coats encrusted with gold embroidery, their turbans glittering with aigrettes of diamonds, their throats encircled with enormous pearls, their belts a mass of precious stones. These—members of the Court of the Nizam—were merely ornamental and dignified spectators.

Most of the other guests were swinging round and round to the strains of a delightful waltz, swaying and revolving in time to the beguiling violins. What a riot of colour and movement, of costumes and figures!

With difficulty we made our way to the end of the room to speak to Lady Ryder, and there we halted for a moment and looked about us. A waltz was over and people were walking about or talking in groups. I noticed Mrs. Lakin in a much-creased black velvet, old-fashioned Swami ornaments and two-button kid gloves.

"She hasn't had a new dress since she married her daughters," explained Mrs. Soames, who was herself excessively smart in a mauve confection direct from Jay's. "She rarely goes out," she continued, "but feels it a duty to be present on this occasion. I expect she will sneak off home before supper."

Mrs. Wolfe flared by in a wonderful orange garment; she was looking unusually brilliant, her black eyes blazing with excitement. Partners were beginning to discover me, and in a short time my programme was crowded, even "extra extras" were bespoke. The band was playing another delicious waltz, and I was soon swimming round with Ronnie, an absolutely perfect partner—we always danced the first waltz together. My next was with Roger Arkwright; after him with Captain Gloag the adjutant, a stiff formal individual who invariably wore a harassed and careworn expression. Captain Gloag was succeeded by Captain Falkland, who had coolly put himself down for two waltzes and the supper dance. Although we had met pretty often at polo, tennis parties, gymkhanas and the boat club, yet, since that day at Moul Ali, we had never had any really serious conversation. Recently he had been away with the general on a tour of inspection, and had only returned to Secunderabad on the night of the ball.

Just towards the end of our second waltz we were resting after a long round, looking on at the gay and whirling crowd and remarking on various people. There was Colonel Grey gyrating with Mabel, and Roger Arkwright leaning against the wall following the couple with an expression that was all but murderous. Suddenly I was accosted by Mr. Balthasar, glossy, prosperous and heavily scented, wearing an enormous diamond as a shirt-stud, and a pair of skin-tight lavender gloves. We had in a way patched up a truce, and he had actually dined with us at No. 30—but not to meet my present partner. Having bowed himself before me, he said:

"As I was so unfortunate as to find your programme full, my very good friend your brother has given me his second dance, which I think is number fourteen?"

For a moment I was speechless with annoyance, and then I said: "I didn't know there were such things as second-hand dances."

"Oh, yes, when charming young ladies are in great demand such things can be arranged. Will you not dance number fourteen with me?"

"What is it?" I asked brusquely, "a square?"

"No, it is a waltz."

Now, I found myself in a most disagreeable dilemma. For Ronnie's sake I must not offend this creature; for the sake of my own self-respect nothing would induce me to waltz with him.

"You may have a square, number thirteen," I said haughtily. Balthasar rolled his eyes alarmingly, and became a shade more sallow, but rallied and said:

"Thank you, Miss Lingard; half a loaf is better than no bread," and without another word he retired.

During this little scene Captain Falkland had stood beside me in rigid silence. I thought he might have helped me out. In some ways an A.D.C. is expected to be ready with expedients. But no, he remained stiff and immovable, as if he had been a figure in armour.

"Just one more turn before the band stops," he said, and I was whirled away.

When the waltz was over we strolled into the great veranda to look for seats, and came to a large chintz-covered lounge on which Sally Payne was enthroned in conspicuous solitude. As usual, she was beautifully dressed and wore a string of fine and unquestionably real pearls. When we approached she patted the seat beside her, and I sat down.

"Hallo, Sally!" said Captain Falkland. "Patience on a monument, and all alone! What does it mean?"

"It means that I have sent my partner to fetch me an ice. Did you know that Captain Falkland and I are cousins?"—addressing me. "He did not recognise me at first because I had changed my name, although I am still 'an unappropriated blessing.' Formerly I was Sally Rivers. A relation died and left me a fortune"—and she touched her pearls significantly—"and the name of Payne. So for once pain brought pleasure! I remember Falkland as a dreadful little boy. I had not seen him for twenty years until the other day; he has grown up better than I expected."

"Sorry I can't return the compliment, Sally," he broke in. "It is most unseemly for you to be privateering round the world all by yourself."

"By no means," she rejoined. "I led a very pinched, narrow sort of life for years, and now I'm having my little fling. Some day perhaps I may settle down. After my forty-fifth birthday has passed I shall marry the first man that asks me. There! You are both witnesses. Miss Lingard, you haven't spoken a word. A penny for your thoughts?"

"I have been thinking that we are all related," I answered. "Captain Falkland pretends that the Falklands and the Lingards are cousins."

"Pretends!" he expostulated, "I do like that! Allow me to refer you to the family pedigree."

"If Captain Falkland and I are cousins and you are his cousin, and Mrs. Wolfe is your cousin—we must belong to the same tribe!"

"Very well, Miss Lingard," said Sally, "in future I shall call you by your Christian name, and when I die you must promise to go into second mourning. Ah, here comes my ice at last! Strawberry, I hope. And now you, my two nice new cousins, may pass on"; and without further discussion we took her at her word.

Captain Falkland had put himself down on my card for the supper dance, and I was just about to go in to supper with Roger Arkwright when he appeared, and stood before me and said:

"May I have the honour of taking you in?"

"I have promised Mr. Arkwright."

"But you are engaged to me for the supper dance. You must have supper before the dance—otherwise how is it a supper dance?"

"That is a funny argument," exclaimed Roger, and he glanced at Falkland and laughed.

I don't exactly know how it came to pass, but my cavalier good-naturedly relinquished me, and I presently found myself walking away in company with Captain Falkland. As we passed down a corridor I saw approaching a rather striking pair, a tall man in uniform and a tall girl in white. As we came nearer I discovered, with a mental start, that the couple were ourselves!

"I had no idea it was a mirror," I exclaimed. "I thought we were meeting two strangers."

"Yes, a study in gold and silver," he replied, referring to the gold on his uniform and the silver on my dress. "Now that we have seen ourselves as others see us, what is your opinion?"

I found this question rather embarrassing, and made no reply, but I could not help recognising the fact that we had made an effective picture.

The supper-room proved to be crowded; it looked as if every chair and every knife and fork were in use. After steering me through blocks of guests and waiters my partner managed to secure two places by squeezing in at the corner of a table occupied by a large and noisy party, including Mrs. Potter; by bad luck Captain Falkland's seat was next to hers. I say "bad luck," as I knew they were as inimical to one another as cat and dog. He was never to be seen in her train. For her part, if she found an opening for giving him a nasty thrust she did not overlook it. It was her openly expressed opinion that "he was a shockingly bad A.D.C., and totally wanting in manners and tact." Fortunately this verdict was not supported by the station.

As we talked together of trivial matters I was aware that all the time Mrs. Potter, though ostensibly carrying on a conversation with her neighbour, was listening to every word we said and only waiting for an opportunity to burst into our *tête-à-tête*. Presently she made an intrusive remark, and instantly she and my partner began to spar. I did not take any share in the conflict, but talked to a major in the Tea-Green Lancers, who was on my left—a most amusing neighbour, and the best amateur actor in southern India. As we talked and chaffed I found myself enacting the rôle of Mrs. Potter, and endeavouring to overhear what she and Captain Falkland were talking about. Their voices were low, and among scores of other tongues and the crash of the band near by I was not particularly successful. I gathered that repeatedly he attempted to cut short her flow of speech, but such efforts were paralysed by her tireless volubility. At last her companions began to move; they were giving parting toasts. Turning to my friend with lifted champagne glass I heard Mrs. Potter say:

"Come now, a pledge, Captain Falkland!"

"All right then, I will," he answered in a tone of angry decision, and lifting his glass and looking her full in the face I distinctly heard:

"Here's to the light that lies in woman's eyes!

And lies—and lies—and *lies*!"

"How dare you!" she exclaimed in a furious undertone. "How dare you insult me!"

"I mentioned no names," he replied in his coolest manner; "you asked for a toast, and I gave the first that came into my head."

Mrs. Potter listened to his lame explanation with an expression of concentrated ferocity, then hastily collecting her party she turned her back upon him and left the supper-room in what was a most realistic presentment of high dudgeon!

"I could not help overhearing your toast," I said as soon as I had recovered my partner.

"I suppose not. Now, thank goodness, we shall have elbow room. May I get you some quails in aspic?"

"No, thank you," I replied, "I've had soup, and I never eat at a ball. I believe you have driven Mrs. Potter away, and made her your enemy for life."

"She was always *that*," he answered with amazing nonchalance; "she knows me, and I know her. She cannot spare infants in arms or even the dead. What a tongue! Mrs. Potter does not leave a feather on any woman in the station. In the good old days she would have found herself sitting in the public stocks."

"Who is she so particularly down on this evening—a friend of yours, I imagine?"

"Yes, if you will allow me to call you so."

"So then she was talking of *me*!"

"Yes, you will laugh when you hear her latest. She warns me that you have a mysterious past; that you came out to India and lived with some disreputable people long before you dawned on Secunderabad. I gave her one for her nob, I can tell you!"

For a moment I could not think of any appropriate reply, and at last I brought out Mrs. Soames's well-worn expression, "How amusing!"

"Yes, isn't it? Well, now shall we go and dance, or are you dead tired?"

"I'm never tired of dancing," I answered, as I rose and collected gloves and fan.

"And what about me?" he said. "I was on horseback the whole of yesterday, an early inspection and long railway journey to-day, letters and telegrams to answer on arrival, gobble down dinner, dress, come here and reel off a dozen duty dances. I tell you what! I know a nice cosy nook up in the gallery where we can sit and talk, or rather you shall talk and I will listen."

"You are reckoning without me," I protested. "I don't think I'm as great a chatterbox as I used to be."

By this time we had ascended into a gallery which commanded a splendid view of the hall, and as I sat down Captain Falkland turned to me and said:

"I say, Miss Lingard, I can't stand that fellow Balthasar. I can't imagine what your brother sees in him."

"Neither can I."

"Well, I gathered as much from the way you choked him off just now, and flung a square dance at his head."

"I wouldn't have even given him that but that Ronnie has asked me to be civil to him. I think it's something to do with racing and that they have a mutual interest in a speculation."

"Ah! My own impression of Balthasar is that he is a wrong 'un, a sort of parasite hanging on to the Nawabs in the city, and squeezing out money and concessions for his schemes in gold and coal. He has a bad influence over young fellows. Gets them down to his house in Chudderghat and encourages them to gamble and drink champagne—and I can't stand seeing him talk to a woman. As he was jabbering to you this evening I felt half-inclined to knock him down and wring his neck."

"That would indeed be strong measures!" I answered with a laugh. "Ronnie says that, making all allowances for his foreign blood, he is not such a bad fellow."

"He is a *beast!*" declared my companion with vicious energy. "Don't let's talk about him any more. And now," suddenly sinking into the chair beside me, "behold, this is the hour and the moment for you to tell me that *secret.*"

"Must I really?" I asked with a start.

"Yes, I've hardly been able to sleep for thinking of it," and he laughed. "You know you broke off just in the most interesting place that morning we rode on the racecourse at Moul Ali."

"And that was ages ago," I said. "Fancy restless nights for weeks—how too dreadful!"

"Well, now, please put an end to my misery and impart your awful tale."

"It is rather awful," I said gravely, "and I believe you will be shocked."

"Oh, no fear of that," he answered. "It would be absolutely impossible for *you* to shock *me*."

"Well then, you shall judge," I said. "There is never smoke without fire. Mrs. Potter has some grounds for her story," and sitting up and grasping my fan tightly in both hands, I turned towards him and continued with my usual volubility. I described the visit of the Hayes-Billingtons; her extraordinary beauty and charm, my aunt's fascination and temptation; how Mrs. Hayes-Billington and I had come out together in the *Asphodel*.

"Why, she's just a ditcher," he interrupted.

"If that means a horrid old tub, she was," I assented, "but Captain and Mrs. Hayes-Billington could not afford the P. and O."

I next proceeded to draw an attractive, not to say rosy, picture of the delights of Silliram—tennis tournaments, dancing and picnics. Then I came to a full stop and an appreciable silence ensued.

At last Captain Falkland said abruptly:

"So you were up there for six whole weeks and have never said a word about it?"

"There is a reason for it," I answered, looking at him steadily. "Ronnie and Mrs. Soames know, and so by great bad luck does Mr. Balthasar. He was at Silliram and dined with us one night."

"Well, for Heaven's sake hurry on and tell me this mysterious reason, before I go clean mad."

For a moment I paused, figuratively to pull myself together. At last I said:

"Did you ever hear of a Mrs. de Lacy?"

"Why do you ask?" he said sharply. "What can *you* know about her?"

"Only—that Mrs. Hayes-Billington was formerly Mrs. de Lacy."

On hearing this announcement Captain Falkland turned hastily round so as to confront me face to face; he looked almost pale.

"*What* did you say?" he demanded, speaking in a hard voice, strangely unlike his usual tone.

"Exactly what I have told you," I replied. "Of course I need not assure you we never knew this at Torrington, but you can't very well ask a lady for her reference or character as if she were a housemaid. Mrs. Hayes-Billington was received with open arms at Silliram, she became a great social success, and was taking the principal part in *The Scrap of Paper* when one of the audience recognised her and gave her away."

"So I should hope. Fancy that woman daring to undertake to chaperon a young girl! Well, tell me what happened next?"

"A man who called on us recognised her and wrote down to Ronnie. He arrived the very morning after the explosion and took me off at once. The whole station was shaken to its foundation; there was a tremendous social earthquake, and Mrs. Hayes-Billington was cast out of the club just as if she had been a live cobra. I may confess to you that in my heart I pitied her. Like some drowning creature she had struggled to the bank, but was seized and flung back into deep water."

"*Now* I can understand why Mrs. Soames was so anxious to conceal the date of your arrival in India," he observed, entirely ignoring my protest, "and so far she has been wonderfully successful."

"Mr. Balthasar may give me away," I suggested.

"In that case, I'll shoot him! But he won't. More likely he'll try and blackmail you. If he does, just hand him over to me."

"Did you ever hear of Mrs. de Lacy?" I inquired.

"Hear of her!" he repeated. "Why, I knew her. She ran away with Vavasour of my regiment. We met her up in Cashmere. She certainly was extraordinarily beautiful, and he went clean off his head. As far as looks and manners went, she snuffed out every woman in the place—like the sun among a box of matches. Her husband was a tough old civilian, who left her, by all accounts, to run her own rig—her career was erratic and notorious."

"I don't think she was really so black as she was painted."

"*Don't* you?" he said, considering me with amused, sarcastic eyes.

"She was always very nice to me," I persisted, "and somehow I could not imagine her otherwise."

"Oh, she was 'very nice' to lots of people! I agree with you there. She was so awfully nice to old Holliday the judge, that he gave her——" He paused and said: "Well, well, well, we will let bygones go and say no more about her, but I'd give ten pounds to see your Aunt Mina's face when she hears the history of your chaperon! I must say I blame her for the whole thing. It all came from her indecent haste to get you out of the country.

However, every cloud has a silver lining, and it was a very nice silver cloud that brought you down here to *me*."

As he spoke he took my fan in his hand and was about to say something more. I felt my heart galloping like a fire engine, when I heard soft footsteps and a rustle behind us; Mrs. Wolfe and her partner had invaded our retreat.

"Oh, you dreadful, faithless man!" she exclaimed, dangling her programme before Captain Falkland, who sprang to his feet. "I'm afraid I shall be obliged to report you to the general for conduct unbecoming an officer and a gentleman. Our dance has already begun, so do come along! Captain Stainforth will take charge of Miss Lingard, who is no doubt also hiding from her own legitimate partner!"

As Mrs. Wolfe concluded, she put her white-gloved hand under Captain Falkland's arm and led him unresistingly away.

Her taunt was based on truth! I met my "legitimate partner" as I entered the ballroom. The poor man had been hunting for me everywhere, and as we prepared to launch into the vortex I noticed my late companion and a yellow gown whirling together in the middle of the room. He and I did not exchange another word that evening, though once or twice—especially in my set of lancers with Balthasar—I noticed him watching me fixedly. It was four o'clock in the morning, and a sort of green light of dawn was glimmering along the horizon, when Mrs. Soames and I drove away from the Residency. I was very, very tired; as I sank into my corner of the carriage I felt like a limp rag doll. Mrs. Soames, on the contrary, was unusually brisk and lively. She had enjoyed supper, not once, but twice, whilst I had tasted nothing but an ice and a cup of soup, and that was scarcely sufficient to sustain even a girl in hard training for six hours' incessant dancing.

"My dear," said my companion, "you were an immense success. I don't mean to flatter you—the young men will do that—but I quite agree with Lady Ryder, when she said you looked like the princess in a fairy tale. Wasn't it amusing?"

"Oh, Mrs. Soames," I murmured, in an exhausted voice.

"I saw that you gave a square dance to that dreadful Balthasar, but I must confess that you did not look as if you were enjoying yourself. More like the goddess of war with a drawn sword in your hand, or our dear Lady Disdain—so amusing!"

"I hated dancing with him," I said peevishly, "but Ronnie likes me to be civil to everybody."

"I danced twice with Ronnie; he is a dear, good fellow, and never forgets that an old married woman may still enjoy a waltz. Jim went home about one, but I, as you see, played the conscientious chaperon. Thank goodness to-morrow will be Thursday, and there will be no parade, and everyone can enjoy a Europe morning."

"I feel as if I could stay in bed all day," I murmured.

"No, no, my dear," protested my companion, "you must come to tiffin with me. We will talk over the ball; how everyone looked and behaved, and you shall tell me about your partners, and which of them you liked best?"

As the ayah was undressing me that morning, she asked me in a drowsy voice:

"Where got missie's fan?"

Where indeed! Then I suddenly remembered how Captain Falkland had taken it away. What had he done with it? There are no pockets in uniform. In the surprise caused by Mrs. Wolfe's sudden descent upon us he must have stuffed it into the breast of his coat. I rather hoped that he would keep it!

CHAPTER XIX
"YES—OR NO?"

Two days after the ball, Captain Falkland called at No. 30 and left my fan with a nice little note, and I must admit that I was sincerely sorry to have missed him.

We were now beginning to make a certain amount of preparation for a move; the regiment had been three years in Secunderabad and was due to go to England by the season's reliefs. Many people were sending round their auction lists, their *dirzees* were contriving warm clothes suitable for an English winter, horses and traps had been bespoke, and most of the polo ponies were already sold.

"There is no use," said the colonel (who always gripped time by the forelock), "in leaving everything to the last moment, and we shall probably find ourselves on the high seas some time in February."

I confess that I could not endure this prospect, although I prudently kept my own counsel. Already I had learnt that it is unpardonable to announce that you are not delighted to go back to England, but would much prefer to remain in India. With respect to this guilty secret Mrs. Lakin and I were of one mind. I should mention that after all I had only enjoyed the best of India, and I loved the country; I had never experienced a hot season, and had only seen the bright side of life—beautiful Silliram, imposing Hyderabad, the dignified noblemen of the Nizam's Court, and the warm-hearted Anglo-Indian community.

At this time—which was shortly before Christmas—Ronnie was unusually busy. He rarely had a spare hour to ride with me of a morning, or to drive me down to the tennis courts. The colonel was "so beastly fussy," he said, and there was such a lot to do when a regiment was under orders for home. Ronnie was often late for dinner, as he would gallop down to the club for a game of rackets or billiards—"something to work off orderly room and red tape"—and there he often forgot both time—and me!

One evening I was sitting in the drawing-room, patiently awaiting his return, when I heard someone ride up, and called out: "Oh, Ronnie, I'm afraid your dinner is a cinder!"

As there was no reply I looked over my shoulder and, to my amazement, beheld Captain Falkland standing in the doorway. It was after eight o'clock. What could have brought him? Perhaps he had come to break the news of an accident to my brother—who rode and drove at headlong speed.

"Has anything happened?" I asked, springing to my feet.

"Nothing to anyone that concerns you," he answered; "only to *me*."

"I hope it is not serious?" I said, feeling not a little bewildered by this late visit. "Won't you sit down?"

"I had a cable from home," he began, and I knew from his voice that he was nervous. "My father has had a paralytic seizure, and I'm off to England to-night. The general has been most awfully kind about it," he paused for a moment, and then went on: "I need scarcely say that I could not leave the country without saying good-bye to *you*."

I felt my face glowing, and murmured a civility that was I am afraid unintelligible.

"You remember," he continued, "that morning at Moul Ali when I declared I would say something to you that I could never tell to another soul. Well, now I am here to say it. I have come to ask if you will be my wife."

For a moment I felt almost stunned by this unexpected question, and then filled with a sense of exquisite tremulous joy.

"I have always been in love with you, as you may have guessed, and I've rushed up here in this abrupt unceremonious fashion to put my fate to the touch before I go home. What is my answer to be—Yes or No?"

"They say you will be a lord some day," I remarked irrelevantly. "I—I would never do for a countess."

"I entirely disagree with that; but don't meet troubles half-way. My cousin is hale and hearty and only sixty-five; I may die before him. I'm afraid I'm rushing you, but I should like to know before I leave that you belonged to me; and yet probably I am a presumptuous idiot, and you may not care a straw about me. I know I'm not the only fellow that is in love with you, and I've heard you called the prettiest girl in India."

I could not restrain a wild hysterical laugh as I exclaimed:

"You are nearly as bad as Mrs. Soames—she compared me to a fairy princess."

"I'm sure you are a good fairy, who will make allowances and forgive this precipitate descent on you; and now without any more figures of speech—can you give me your answer?"

I looked up at him and met his anxious dark eyes. The "yes" was trembling on my lips when Michael our big butler flung back the curtain or *purdah* between the drawing-room and dining-room and said:

"The captain sending salaam, dining at club." Glancing interrogatively at my companion he added: "This gentleman dining with missy?"

"No, no," protested my late caller, "I have only a few minutes to spare. Shall we go into the veranda?" was his bold suggestion.

I rose without a word and led the way.

"I am taking silence for consent," he said, and there, in the scented darkness, he drew me into his arms and kissed me.

Sitting hand in hand in the dim light we talked, and how the time flew! A few minutes became half an hour. I was surprisingly silent for me, thrilled with the dawn of first love and the vibrant attraction of my companion's voice.

"I may return before long," he said. "All depends on my father; under any circumstances you will be home in February, and then we will be married. Meanwhile, I will leave you in charge of Kipper."

"Yes, if you like to put it in that way," I answered gaily. "And about our engagement?"

"It is 'done finish,' as they say out here."

"I would rather it was not given out yet. Time enough when you return or I go home."

"I see," he answered; "you think if you were ticketed 'Engaged,' you would lose half your fun!"

"No indeed," I protested indignantly, "but I should hate all the talk; it is not as if you were to be here—that would be different."

"Yes, very different indeed," and he gave an audible sigh.

"People might say that it was not true—and—and——"

"You have a humble opinion of the lovely Miss Lingard," he interrupted with a laugh, "but if you insist I could put up a notice in the club, signed and witnessed; and the general might allow it to be mentioned in orders. I say, Eva, you *are* a little goose."

"I wonder what your people will think? I'm sure Aunt Mina won't give me a good 'chit,' and you know I've no money."

"Don't talk of money," he protested impatiently, "when every second now is worth gold to me. I shall have you, you will have me, and I feel sure we shall be awfully happy together. We must tell one or two friends here about our engagement; for instance, Mrs. Graham and Mrs. Soames."

"Yes, I should like to tell Mrs. Soames—I know she will be so pleased—and, of course, Ronnie."

"I'm not sure that *he* will be so pleased—somehow your brother and I have never hit it off. I know he is immensely popular and a capital sportsman. I believe he thinks me a prig—which I'm not. I'm a bit older and steadier, that's all. By the way, darling, do you know that I am fourteen years your senior?"

"As if it mattered!" I retorted with scorn.

"Not now, no doubt, but later—much later—you must promise not to throw my bald head and grey hairs in my face."

I burst out laughing.

"Captain Falkland—no, I mean Brian—how can you talk such nonsense!"

"I suppose because I'm so happy; if the poor pater were all right I'd not have a wish left! By the way, about Ronnie, you must influence him, my little girl. I hear of high play, racing bets and wild-cat speculations. Try to get hold of the purse strings, and do your level best to cut him loose from that repulsive ruffian Balthasar."

"I'll try, but lately Ronnie is so changed; not the least like himself."

"Then be a good fairy, and turn him into a reformed prince of brothers. I'm giving you one commission—another and more important one is, to take great care of your precious self, my little sweetheart; be happy, write to me by every mail, and think of me every hour."

"You may be sure I shall do that."

"I often wondered if you ever cast me a thought after I came to India. Certainly you never answered my letter."

"I cast you many thoughts," I admitted, "and often wished that we might meet. As for your letter, this is the first I have heard of it."

"It won't be the last! Your aunt shall hear of it, too. It was properly addressed to Miss Eva Lingard, Torrington Park. Well, now, time is up."

"Must you go?" I pleaded impulsively, laying a detaining hand on his arm. "Oh, we have had such a few minutes'——" I could not control my voice.

"Happiness," he supplemented. "I must have another inspection before I am off," and he took my arm and led me back into the full light of our kerosene wall lamps. "I know my mother will love you, Eva, and I want to carry away your picture in my mind, and describe you faithfully. Well, it has to come—our good-bye!"

Brian's eyes and voice expressed something I had never known before— the deep emotion of a reserved man; and his parting kiss told me all that his lips found it impossible to utter.

Then he summoned his syce and horse, and, without another word or glance, cantered out of the compound. I listened to the ring of hoofs till they grew fainter and fainter, then died away completely in the distance. Rejecting the butler's sonorous invitation: "Dinner ready on the table!" I retired into my own room in a strange, anomalous condition; rapturously happy yet desperately miserable. Presently I sat down on the side of my bed and enjoyed a thoroughly exhaustive cry.

CHAPTER XX
CLOUDS

When I whispered my news to Mrs. Soames she instantly ejaculated her usual formula:

"Oh, *how* amusing!"

The colonel's lady was no less delighted than surprised, and as full of excitement and importance as if the match was one of her own contrivance. She was anxious that we should make the engagement known. I saw her cast a longing glance at her writing-table, and knew that she was eager to send nice little notes to Lady Ryder, Mrs. Wolfe and Mrs. Mills, but against such a proclamation I set my face, and implored her to keep the matter, at least for the present, a dead secret.

Of course I took Ronnie into my confidence; at first he looked scornfully incredulous, then stupefied.

"I never dreamt it would come to that!" he said at last. "I can't think how you two made it up. I never saw you much together."

His feelings were contradictory, I could see. He was not pleased—and yet again he was pleased.

"You will take the *pas* of Aunt Mina," he remarked. "Won't she be furious? And, of course, in a way it's a grand match. The Falkland family is as old as the hills, and as proud as Lucifer, but I could never cotton to Falkland, he has such strained ideas of honour. You must never discuss a woman in public, and all that sort of old-fashioned twaddle. I think you are right to keep the engagement dark as he is not here. Envious people might say that the whole thing only existed in your imagination, and, as I have already observed, you and he were never very chummy—although I now remember that he used to ride up to church here on Sunday evenings, and always sit where he could see you."

The news of Captain Falkland's sudden departure for England made quite a stir at the club. Mrs. Soames assured me that everyone was talking about it and saying all manner of nice things about him. In spite of his rather slow manner it appeared that he had a very active brain. The general and

Mrs. Graham were completely lost without him, as he had been invaluable to both, as a smart officer and a tactful A.D.C., never mixing uncongenial people or sending guests into dinner in wrong seniority and thereby causing much heart-burning and enmity.

As I did not appear at the club for two or three days, having a bad cold, I was honoured by a visit of inspection from Mrs. Potter. She came ostensibly to see Mrs. Soames, and dropped in on me on the way in her fine motor-car. She found me sitting in the veranda with Kipper on my lap, and I think the spectacle startled her not a little.

As I ushered her into the drawing-room she said,

"As I was up in this part of the world I thought I would just look in on you. I heard at the club that you were rather seedy."

"Only a cold and a little touch of fever; I shall be well by to-morrow."

"Is that *all* that ails you?" and she looked at me with a malicious glance and added: "Someone told me that it was a serious heart attack!"

I laughed. I think my laugh annoyed her, for she said:

"And so your friend Captain Falkland has gone! That *was* a sudden flight."

"I believe his father is very ill."

"I wonder," she murmured meditatively; "or was it just an excuse to clear out of a compromising fix and a dangerous neighbourhood?"

As I saw that she was bent on being excessively spiteful and disagreeable I remained silent.

"I see you have got his dog," she continued. "Love me love my dog, eh?"

"The dog was originally mine," I said.

"Ah, then I suppose you both love him! So you and Captain Falkland know one another at home?"

"Yes."

"It is doubtful if he will ever come out again. We shall all miss him tremendously. Do tell me, is it true that your brother is not going home with the regiment, but is trying *very* hard to get into the Indian Army?"

"I don't know," I answered, "but I do not think it's the least likely, or he would certainly have told me."

"Ah, my dear," she said, "brothers don't tell their sisters everything, and possibly you have your girlish secrets from him. I think you have some small trifle up your sleeve—a little mystery about your coming to India."

"I came to India in the usual way," I answered, "by sea."

"And were a most delightful importation! Well, now I must be going. As you have a sore throat you really should not talk. Au revoir! I suppose you will turn up at the club in a day or two?" and with a smiling farewell she swept out.

It seemed to me about this period that my happy time was coming to an end. It was not only that Brian Falkland had gone home and that I missed him dreadfully—missed the pleasure of looking forward to meeting him—I even missed the little disappointments when he failed to appear. The sun did not shine so brightly, nor were the skies now so blue; also I was haunted by the unpleasant presentiment that trouble was approaching. Ronnie was changed. He was strangely altered in the last few months. His spirits were fitful—sometimes he was too noisy, talkative, and excited; sometimes so silent and in such a mood of black depression that I feared he was sickening for an illness. To my anxious inquiries the invariable reply was, "Only a touch of fever." His face was paler, there were lines about his mouth, his eyes had lost their glance of irresistible gaiety; he often looked haggard and worried—especially, I noticed, after he received cables and telegrams. At night I could hear him pacing the compound long, long after he had ostensibly retired to bed. Ronnie, who had always been so polite and considerate to our servants, was now impatient, irritable and overbearing. I had known him to throw a boot at the *chokra* and an oath at Michael.

Although I was secretly miserable I followed Lizzie's sage advice, and kept my trouble to myself, nor did I, such was my moral cowardice, venture to appeal to or question my brother, but maintained our intercourse on the ordinary everyday level. Since my early youth at Torrington I had a shrinking horror of scenes and rows, and once when I had thrown out a timid feeler it had been brusquely repulsed.

Money, with which Ronnie was once so lavish, had now undoubtedly become scarce. When I asked for my monthly allowance for wages and bazaar I was put off with an impatient excuse. The mere hint at the payment of bills appeared to exasperate him, and so, for shame's sake, I settled the smaller accounts and servants' wages out of my own pocket. Hitherto I had shared expenses, contributing ten pounds a month towards housekeeping, and this I handed over intact to my brother. Shop bills, bazaar bills, that I thought he had paid, now poured in in shoals, and the club account was appalling. A talk with Roger Arkwright made me even more uneasy. He joined me one day as I rode back from Secunderabad, and after a little commonplace conversation began rather nervously:

"I say, Miss Lingard, you will forgive me if I am taking a most awful liberty—you know that Ronnie and I are old friends and schoolfellows, and all that sort of thing. Just lately I'm afraid he has got his money affairs into a hopeless hash. He won't listen to a word I say, and though I don't like doing it I feel obliged to ask you to try to get him to take a pull. He gambles."

"Only at bridge—for small sums."

"You can lose very heavily at bridge," said Roger gravely, "and also at poker. Ronnie plays high at the club, and also down at Balthasar's."

"Balthasar's!" I echoed in dismay.

"Yes, fellows drive down there, dine, and play chemin de fer. On these occasions I'm afraid Ronnie tells you that he's on guard, or dining at some mess. He is not our old Ronnie; no, he has come under some bad influence this last year. Don't you notice how he has changed and aged, and that he's not half as cheery as he used to be? He has become so terribly restless, and seems always in a condition of feverish excitement. I believe he and that chap Fox, of the Tea-Green Lancers, who has loads of coin, cable home and back horses, and lately I fancy they have both been rather badly hit."

"This is terrible!" I gasped at last. "I knew that Ronnie was short of money lately, and he certainly does not look himself; but I never dreamt of what you have just told me."

"It's partly the fault of Fox," he replied, "who eggs him on and has a bottomless purse. I think there is a sort of rivalry between them. Ronnie has always been so popular, with his polo and rackets, quite a celebrity in his way, and inclined to be a bit extravagant. Then he went home last year and, apparently, got hold of a good sum of money. Well, I'm afraid from all I hear that he has come to the end of that now. The colonel has had hints of his debts and I am told is rather uneasy in his mind, and if something, or someone, does not interfere, Ronnie will find himself in hot water. I believe he has borrowed money from that fellow Balthasar."

I felt so shaken that I could not speak—only stare at my companion with what, no doubt, was a face of horror.

"Always remember you can rely on me, Miss Lingard," continued Roger. "Whatever happens I will stick by him—and here he is now," as Ronnie cantered up behind us with his pony in a lather.

"You look as if you'd come far and fast," said Roger, with a quick change of manner.

"Yes, I've just been down to Chudderghat," he answered, "something to do with the next gymkhana on the Futeh Maidan."

I felt positively certain that this was an untruth. Ronnie had been down to interview Balthasar. As I rode towards home I made no attempt to join in the conversation. My mind was in a tumult. What was I to say to Ronnie? How could I economise and help him? I would send away the *dirzee* and one of the table servants. I had nearly a thousand rupees with Bunsi Lal the banker. I must speak to Ronnie about his affairs without delay, and was screwing up my courage to the sticking-point—as Ronnie was always so irritable whenever I mentioned money. But as it happened I need not have troubled myself, for as soon as Roger Arkwright had cantered off towards his own quarters Ronnie turned and attacked me.

"I know what's coming!" and his face was livid; "you and that fellow Arkwright have been laying your heads together about *me*."

"Do you mind if we did?" I rejoined courageously—but my voice was shaking.

"Yes I do. Now understand, I won't have either of you meddling in my affairs. What's he been saying?"

"That you gamble."

"That I gamble," mimicking my voice. "And if I do?"

"He says you have lost a great deal of money; that you go to Balthasar's to play chemin de fer, and are heavily in debt. Oh, Ronnie dear, don't be so hard and reserved, so unlike yourself with *me*," I pleaded. "I have money at the bank—do let me help you! I shall sell Tommy Atkins and economise in every possible way. Do take me into your confidence—for, after all, there are only the two of us."

"Well, since you put it like that, as the professor used to say, I don't mind telling you that I *do* owe some thousands of rupees. Balthasar has got me out of a pretty big hole, and I shall be able to settle up everything before long and be clear."

"Oh Ronnie—how splendid!" I exclaimed, now inexpressibly relieved.

"Yes—if Collarette wins the Calcutta Cup; and if not I shall pull through somehow. I cannot think how my affairs are known; the morghi khana is a hotbed of gossip—those women have tongues of fire. The colonel was quite shirty with me yesterday about my mess bill, and Mrs. Soames, who always takes her cue from him, was as cool as ice when I met her at the boat club. But don't be uneasy, old girl," he concluded, as he assisted me to dismount. "I shall go slow for a bit and it will all be as right as rain."

But *I* was not so sure. I was sensible of gathering clouds, and that very day I drew my balance from the bank, cleared off the hateful bazaar bills and wrote home for more money. Letters from Brian were such a comfort now; they gave me great happiness and support. He had written from Bombay, Aden and Port Said. These epistles were not long but they were most satisfactory, and written in the clear deliberate hand that accorded with himself.

For a week or two, so far as bills and money troubles were concerned, there was a great calm. I had not sold Tommy Atkins, and I rode, played tennis, and went about as usual. I noticed, however, that Mrs. Soames was by no means so intimate or confidential as formerly. On the contrary, she had adopted an attitude of freezing reticence. I think she was painfully exercised in her mind. On the one hand she saw her protégée the future Countess of Runnymede (a match that when made public would glorify her as a chaperon), and on the other was Ronnie, her former chief favourite, in deep disgrace with her autocratic husband. Although nothing serious had been said or done there was a coolness; we were no longer invited to supper on Sundays, and at an afternoon club dance Mrs. Soames refused to honour Ronnie with her usual waltz!

During these socially grey days I received the following letter from Mrs. Hayes-Billington. It was written in a feeble and almost illegible hand:

"My dear Eva,—I have to thank you for your kind, cheerful little notes, but I am past cheering. I seem to have arrived at the end of all things. My health has been on the wane ever since I came to this awful place, and I am glad to say that I shall not be here long. As it is, hours seem endless. I have no companions, nothing to do but lie and think; I close my eyes and contemplate the days that are no more, and the people to whom *I* am no more. I live some happy scenes over and over again. Then I open my eyes to find myself alone and dying, and the worst of it is that I suppose I have deserved my fate. I offended Mrs. Grundy and she has killed me! Poor old Bertie, he will be sorry. I cannot tell you how kind and unselfish he is, but he is obliged to stick to his work, which claims his time like an insatiable monster, and it is reported that the mine is not paying. How I wish I could see your bright, happy face once more! but I know that such a wish is folly. Good-bye, my dear girl, try and think of me as kindly as you can. Bertie will write to you when all is over.

"D. B."

I must confess that this letter made me shed tears.

After the scene with Balthasar, when he told me of Mrs. Hayes-Billington's loneliness and illness, I had written to her pretty often, and sent her newspapers, books and sweets—remembering how she loved chocolate. I wondered what Brian would say if he were to come in and find me weeping over a letter from Mrs. Hayes-Billington. Perhaps Ronnie was right, and Brian was a *little* bit straitlaced.

Another letter that I had recently received was of much more cheerful character. It came from Lizzie Puckle. She wrote to announce that she was about to marry a Canadian engineer, and was sailing for Montreal in a month's time. I was delighted for Lizzie's sake that she, too, was about to flap her wings and see the world—but sorry for myself. Somehow Canada seemed so far away, and I felt as if she were about to pass out of my life entirely.

At last the sword that I half dreaded fell! The beginning of the trouble was an order from headquarters announcing that the regiment was not to be relieved for twelve months. This was a blow to some, a relief to others, and a surprise to all. There was a hasty cancelling of sales and a general readjustment of plans. I wrote the news home to Brian and said: "As your father is so much better, I shall look forward to seeing you here very soon." I felt that in a crisis, or the storm that was approaching, he would be my mainstay. I had always realised that Brian was a strong man.

Immediately after the order respecting reliefs was known, I was conscious of a still greater change in Ronnie. Collarette had been ignominiously defeated; this was a serious blow, and our financial affairs were far from flourishing. I disposed of two of my best scarcely known or worn frocks to the Greys, dismissed the *mali*, and left off sugar and claret; but to cope with our difficulties was beyond my powers. Instinctively I grasped this truth, and my spirits, once so high and exuberant, now fell to zero.

One Sunday night I noticed that Ronnie, who had been out all day and returned an hour late for dinner, was looking unusually haggard and dejected. He scarcely uttered a word or ate a morsel, but swallowed two very stiff pegs, and when the meal was over rose and said abruptly:

"I have a lot of work to do, Sis; do not mind me but go to bed, and on no account sit up."

Obediently I retired into my room and put on a dressing-gown, and as soon as the ayah had brushed my hair dismissed her. There was not the slightest use in attempting to go to bed, for I knew that I could not sleep. I was oppressed with a premonition of some imminent disaster; so acute was this sensation, that it seemed as if the horror were actually present in the bungalow. I tried to read, but the attempt was a failure; then I got up and crept into the dining-room. Ronnie's office and dressing-room opened out of it and I peeped in. He was sitting with his back to me at a table, his head resting on his hands; I wondered if he were asleep. At any rate, he was totally unaware of my presence, and I crept away as stealthily as a thief in the night.

In an hour's time I returned, resolved to insist upon his going to bed. On this occasion I made no attempt at concealment, but boldly pushed back the purdah till the rings jingled.

Ronnie heard my footfall on the matting, and started. As he turned about, I felt my heart contract, for I saw that his face had a ghastly, glazed appearance, and that he held a revolver in his hand.

CHAPTER XXI
RONNIE'S CONFESSION

"Good God, Eva!" exclaimed Ronnie. "What do you mean by creeping on me like this?"

My answer was to throw myself with all my force upon his wrist and wrench the revolver out of his hand. He rose unsteadily, and stared at me. The expression on his face was something inhuman and terrible—and I could see that he was trembling from head to foot.

"Give it here!" he commanded hoarsely. "You *must*—and clear out—it will be all over in a couple of minutes!"

I made no reply, but held the weapon behind my back in a vice-like grip.

"Eva, do you hear me?—give it back," he reiterated, seizing my arm and shaking it violently.

"Hear *me* first," I panted breathlessly. "Oh, Ronnie, how can you think of doing such an awful thing? Have you the heart to leave me out here all alone to face—whatever you shrink from?"

His expression changed, the rigidity relaxed, and he dropped my arm with a hasty gesture.

"Think, Ronnie, of death—and what it means."

"My dear Eva, I have been thinking of nothing else the last two hours. At seven-and-twenty there's a big bit of life due, but I have no alternative. I'm in a hideous fix, and there is only one way out."

"There must be another," I said; "this one is the coward's path. Oh, Ronnie, I implore you to take me into your confidence. *What* has happened?"

"The family curse has overtaken me—that's all."

"Gambling?"

"Yes. What's bred in the bone there's no getting away from—it is part of oneself."

"Two heads are better than one. It may be the case of the mouse and the lion. Promise me that you will put this idea out of your head. Listen. I will make some hot coffee at the stove, and we will go and sit out in the veranda and you shall tell me *everything*. But before I leave you I must have your promise," and I looked him full in the eyes.

"All right," he agreed. "I give you my word, and you can go and make the coffee. You are a level-headed girl, and perhaps you may be able to see some glimmer of light in the darkness."

I glanced fearfully round the room trying to discover if there were any other weapon, then I went back into my own apartment and hid the revolver; returning, I lit the oil stove and prepared the coffee. As soon as it was ready I brewed two large cups and took one to Ronnie, who was standing by the table in the dining-room.

"I feel better for that," he said, "it clears my head. The other thing would have cleared my head too."

"Oh, don't!" I expostulated. "How can you?"

"Come on, then. Shall we sit in the veranda?"

I rather shrank from this suggestion, remembering my happy half-hour with Brian. That had been a love tale; now I was probably about to listen to a history containing the elements of life and death.

"No, let us go into the compound and walk up and down—it is a lovely warm night."

"Day," he corrected. "In another half-hour we shall see the dawn."

We strolled to the gate in silence, and came to a full stop. Kip, who had accompanied us, much astonished at our proceedings, settled down on the tail of my dressing-gown and curled himself up for sleep.

"Well, Sis," said Ronnie, drawing a long breath, "I'll tell you everything now. You and I have always been such tremendous pals, that I suppose you think you know me, but you've only seen my best side. Even as a small boy I had a taste for gambling and betting—if the stake was only a few coppers or stamps. All the same, I did well at school and at Sandhurst, where, as you know, I passed out first, and got the sword. Before I was launched upon my own, Uncle Horace gave me a tremendous talking-to; told me our family history and warned me that the vice of gambling was in the Lingard blood. Cards were my father's curse—betting is mine! Even in my teens I followed racing with the deepest interest, and could have passed a pretty stiff examination in 'Ruff's Guide to the Turf.' The first few years I spent out here I was just as happy as a king. I was awfully keen and liked the

Service; I'd heaps of friends, four hundred a year besides my pay, and I took to polo like a duck to water. At gymkhanas and small race meetings I was extraordinarily lucky, riding my own ponies and winning all before me. Racing people offered me mounts—you see I'm a light weight and can ride—so I got mixed up with the turf and was gradually sucked into the whirlpool. I backed horses at Lucknow and Calcutta, and on the whole did well. This regiment is not a racing one—they go in for cricket and polo—but I found a kindred spirit in Fox of the Tea-Green Lancers. He has tons of money, is mad keen about racing, and we used to go shares in cables and expenses—for we both backed horses at home. Once I pulled off a double event on the Lincolnshire and Grand National, and bought new ponies, gave champagne dinners at the club, and made a great splash. Well, I wasn't long a winner, but had some truly awful facers."

He paused for a moment and then continued:

"It was one of these facers that took me home last year. I'd been nibbling at my capital for some time, and, as I wanted to handle ready coin, I sold out a lot of stock. Naturally I made the most of my leave in England—at Ascot and Goodwood. Lately my luck has been dead out, and yet, like all gamblers, I have been fighting and striving like mad to get my own back, and have gone in up to my neck!"

"Why did you not tell me? I might have helped you," I broke in.

"No, no, Sis, you could not do anything. Balthasar has given me a hand a couple of times; he is a money-lender—under the rose—the financial pose is all rot. He gives ripping dinners with top-hole champagne—afterwards his guests play poker and chemin de fer; it is all kept dark. He has, as I say, helped me out once or twice, but somehow, since you and he had that scrap I have a feeling that he is no longer my jovial and open-handed ally, but as hard as the Gun Rock!"

Here Ronnie came to a dead stop, and appeared to be suddenly engrossed in his own sombre reflections.

"But what is it *now*?" I ventured. "What has brought your affairs to such a terrible crisis?"

"Crisis indeed!" he echoed, turning to face me, and in the soft light of an Indian night I could see that his face was convulsed with emotion. "Eva, you will be horrified when I tell you that—I have laid hands on the regimental funds!"

"Oh, Ronnie!" I gasped.

"You may well say, 'Oh, Ronnie!' That's the awful part of the whole thing—my rage for gambling goaded me to mad recklessness; that and the sudden change in the reliefs have done for me."

"But what have the reliefs to say to *you*?" I stammered.

"You know we were all supposed to be going home in February and everyone was selling off. We sold our polo ponies for a long price, and the sum was set aside for a team at home."

"Yes, yes—I know that."

"The canteen fund was rich, and the colonel was holding over a big surplus towards setting up in our next station."

"How could——" I began.

"Just let me go on—you'll soon understand," interrupted Ronnie. "The polo money was taken over by Mills, our treasurer; he lodged it, in spite of the colonel, in a bank. It's in a way a private fund, and the C.O. could not stop him. Mills is dead keen about coin, being poor and thrifty; he said even for six weeks four per cent. was worth having."

I leant heavily against the gate. How much longer would these details torture me?

"Mills and the colonel had a regular set-to over the business; I heard them arguing in the anteroom. The colonel is shy of local banks and temporary investments—he was once badly hit up north—so he insisted on keeping the canteen funds locked up in the safe in the orderly room—and I stole them."

"You—stole—them!" I repeated in a whisper.

"Yes, but only under the most frightful pressure. You see I knew all about this money. I have been acting adjutant whilst Gloag got a month's leave to see his people in the Neilgherries. I counted over the canteen notes, reported all correct, stuffed them into a drawer in the safe, and never gave them another thought till last week. Then the mail brought me a letter from my London bookie, saying that I must pay up my losses—about £400—or be posted and run in. He gave me a fortnight's grace. I hadn't a penny in the bank—in fact I'm overdrawn. On the other hand, I had a splendid book on the Calcutta races and was confident I'd get home on Collarette. Meanwhile, I was at my wits' end to find the ready money for Hawkins. I knew if I was posted that it meant ruin; then some little black devil whispered: 'What about that canteen money? It won't be wanted for a couple of months; you can settle up with Hawkins, and the Calcutta winnings will refund the loan. It would only be an extra big risk and gamble.' To make a long story short,

I took the coin; I told myself it was only a loan, and everything combined to make the job dead easy."

Here Ronnie paused; his voice sounded husky, as if his throat were dry. For my part, I could not have spoken if my life had depended on it.

"For two or three days I struggled," he went on. "I am not a hardened scoundrel. I fought off the temptation, but I was pinned fast between the devil and the deep sea. If I did not pay my debts of honour, I would be smashed; and if the canteen money was suddenly missed and had not been replaced, I was also smashed. At last I gave in. Late one sultry afternoon, I happened to be alone in the orderly room copying the summary of evidence for a court martial; the head clerk had finished and I had given him leave to depart. All the time my pen was scratching along the paper it seemed to say, 'Take it! take it! Here is your chance.' You know the orderly room is in the old barracks, where, by all accounts, queer things have happened. There was something in the warm atmosphere that relaxed my will. Although I saw nothing, I felt acutely sensible of a dominating other-world presence between me and the window. Eva, I'll swear that some sort of evil spirit was urging me to take my chance and just *one* more risk!

"For a good while I hesitated. At last I got up and closed the door into the clerks' room, and when I took the keys and opened the safe, I declare my heart was thumping like a motor engine. The money was in a small drawer; ten days before I had counted over the notes and reported 'all correct,' and I knew that a sum of seven thousand rupees was intact. I drew out the dingy bundle, greasy and discoloured—but good paper for all that—thrust it into my pocket, and locked the safe. Once the deed was actually accomplished, I felt relieved and even cheerful. Next morning I gave the notes to Bunsi Lal's agent, in exchange for a cheque on London."

"Yes?"

"So that load was off my back; and then I hedged in case Collarette failed me, and wrote by the same mail to Uncle Horace, begging him to lend me five hundred pounds. I told him that it was a case of the most terrible necessity, and implored him not to fail me. I expect his answer in ten days—but by then it'll be too late. Collarette, as you know, ran a cur; she shut up in the last fifty yards. Then followed the bomb about our reliefs being cancelled. Last, and worst of all, Mills came to me on Saturday and said: 'That canteen money is going to be invested after all; I've been telling the colonel we may as well get some interest this next six months, it is to be made over to Loughton and Law on deposit receipt. I suppose they'll give four per cent., so will you let me have it, Ronnie, and I'll fix it up? A bit over seven thousand rupees, isn't it?'

"I declare to you, Sis, that I felt as if the sky had fallen in. That was Saturday, and here is Monday. If I cannot put the money back in the safe—or rather produce it and pretend I've taken it out—by Wednesday morning, I'm done for. I shall be convicted of making away with the regimental funds, be tried by court martial and cashiered. *My* alternative was better than that!"

"Oh, Ronnie, Ronnie, don't say it!" I protested in agony.

"Just fancy my being proved to be a regular 'budmash' and thief—if I were out of it all things would be hushed up. I'd just have been bundled into a hole in the cemetery—and nothing *said*. I know the colonel would move heaven and earth to smother the scandal. He thinks so much of the reputation of the regiment, and if one of his officers were to be tried by court martial, and the case came out in all the papers, it would turn his hair white."

"And so you have only until the day after to-morrow," I faltered at last. "Something must be done—can't I cable and get out money?"

"No," he replied, "there would be no end of formalities; anyway it would be too late. My one chance is *Balthasar*. I sounded him about a loan, but I must confess that he was not responsive—even though I talked of big interest. He is my only hope. I clutch at him as my very last straw. He said he might turn up here to-morrow afternoon, and I believe if you were really most awfully nice to him he would come to the rescue—it's just my one chance."

I clenched my hands tightly on the top bar of the gate; the prospect was too hideous. That I should have to put forth my utmost efforts to cajole and mollify my most detested acquaintance was, indeed, an overwhelming enterprise—and yet, looking over the whole situation, it seemed to me that in Balthasar's assistance lay our only road of escape.

"I will do my best," I murmured at last.

"Oh, if you will do *that*, you will certainly pull me through. I know you dislike him and I hate asking you to influence him, but you see my position is desperate. Perhaps you might bring a little light into the darkness; and there," he said, pointing, "the light is coming. I see the pale dawn beginning to creep along the horizon—I shall accept it as a good omen. And now, my dear sister, I will turn in and get some sleep. I have not closed my eyes for three whole nights. I shall want to have all my wits about me when Balthasar appears, though it is *you* who will deal with him." So saying he kissed my bare arm and strode off towards the bungalow.

But I still remained leaning over the gate, trying to face things and to realise the situation. I seemed to take no count of time; I felt as if I had been turned into a block of stone. If Ronnie could get the loan and pay the canteen money he would be relieved from an awful situation, though, from what I could gather, he would be obliged to leave the "Lighthearts." (It was not a regiment in which a captain could exist upon his pay.) I would stay with him as long as possible, and see him through his trouble. He would probably exchange into the Indian Service and I would return home. That was the best side. On the other—the worst—supposing that Balthasar still remained hard as a stone? Ronnie would be tried by court martial and disgraced. I too would be disgraced and ruined socially. As for Brian Falkland, how could he marry a girl whose brother had been convicted of stealing? There must be an end to that, and I buried my face in my hands and rested my head upon the top bar of the gate. I believe I remained in this position for a long time, but at last I was disturbed by the ducks. They had disposed of their breakfast and were now quacking and waddling all round me, urgent that I should bestir myself and suffer them to pass forth.

CHAPTER XXII
PUNISHMENT

As I leant against the gate, with my head resting upon my arms, I felt bowed to the earth with abject misery and quaking fear. It was as if an impenetrable black cloud had suddenly descended on my life, and blotted out every gleam of hope and happiness. From this sort of hideous nightmare I was aroused not only by the ducks but also by a bugle call; the early-rising world of India would soon be afoot, and I wrenched myself back into the present actual moment and turned towards the bungalow, which faced a by-road. No one had noticed me so far, beyond a few passing market coolies and the *tannyketch*, whose affair it was to provide for the poultry.

As soon as I had entered my room I removed the revolver from its temporary hiding-place, and buried it in a large tub of hydrangeas that stood outside door; then I threw off my dressing-gown and scrambled into bed. I usually rose early, and too soon Mary ayah would appear, bringing me tea and toast. Already I heard her anklets jingling, and feigned sleep. I endeavoured to make the pretence real, as a strenuous day and a dreadful ordeal lay before me, but I found it impossible to rest. My head seemed to throb and burn; I imagined I could feel it thumping on the pillow, and no wonder! My brain was racked in torture, striving to find some clear, straight road out of our difficulties—for Ronnie's difficulties were mine. I lay thinking hard for nearly an hour, and then rose and felt considerably refreshed after my bath and breakfast. Ronnie had sent me a little note to say, "I expect to be on the ranges till four o'clock. *He* will be here about three."

Evidently I would have to meet Balthasar alone. Perhaps after all it would be best. I spent the morning in making out a list of the contents of the bungalow in a long narrow bazaar book supplied by the cook. Pencil in hand, I carefully counted up our glass and china, our pictures, ornaments, furniture—even the very ducks—and in short everything available for "a sale," for, of course, if Ronnie were now penniless, we must speedily shift our quarters.

All this business occupied my mind and kept me from thinking, yet now and then I was seized by a horrible sort of mental nausea. How was I to beg from Balthasar—to implore, to abase myself—and to succeed? As the dreadful hour approached my heart beat fast. Oh, how much I would have preferred to be about to face a surgical operation! However, I made a great effort to prepare for the ordeal and to look my best. I waved and re-dressed my hair, and selected a pretty pale blue summer muslin over silk far too smart for the occasion, but I knew it was becoming. As I looked in the glass I saw that my cheeks were unusually pink, my eyes unusually bright. Outwardly all was well; inwardly I was on the verge of a terrible outburst of tears, and tears were the last thing I must yield to, that was certain! Balthasar was not the sort of man who would be touched by these. I started violently as I heard the hoot of a motor, and rushed to my little medicine chest and fortified myself with a dose of sal volatile—a detestable expedient, but it might give me composure and courage—how badly I needed both!

When I entered the drawing-room our visitor was already in the veranda, and as he strutted in I instantly realised that here was the Balthasar of Silliram—truculent, overbearing and hateful.

"Is your brother here?" he asked, after our first greeting, rolling his eyes all over the room in search, no doubt, of Ronnie.

"No, he has been on the ranges all day," I replied, "but I expect him home shortly."

"He asked me to come and see him on most particular business." Balthasar spoke with an injured air as he sat down and carefully hitched up the knees of his trousers. "Well, this is a nice affair," he continued, "your brother has no doubt told you that he has been playing the very devil?"

"I am afraid he has been imprudent," I murmured.

"You call it imprudent?" raising his voice. "Well, I call it by another name, and the fine young gentleman wants me to lend a hand with a big cheque in it to pull him out of a hole."

"I am sure you are kinder than you make yourself out to be, Mr. Balthasar. Can you not help him?" I ventured timidly.

"No; why should I?" knitting his black brows. "He would go ahead and back horses. What a young fool! Only for me he would have been in big trouble before this. I have lent money—certainly it has been repaid—but then there was the risk. No, no; I can do no more."

"Then in that case, why did you come?" I asked with a touch of temper. "I believe Ronnie was trusting to you for assistance."

He looked momentarily taken aback and then replied in his slow drawl:

"I came just to see how he was going to work his head out of the noose, and also because it gave me a chance of meeting *you*, which is always such a pleasure."

"You say that you have lent Ronnie money before and been repaid. Can you not do so again? I believe you are a very rich man, Mr. Balthasar, and a sum that would be salvation to Ronnie is a mere trifle to you."

"Where is my security?" he demanded sharply.

"I can give security. I have money in England. See," I said, rising and going to the table; "here is a letter I have written to my bankers, asking them to sell out stock, and remit the amount to me."

"Oh, oh! Then you are of age?"

"Yes, I was twenty-one a week ago."

"Ah, I should not take you for more than eighteen." And he stared at me with a solemn air of deliberate speculation. "Your fair hair and skin belong to the *teens*."

"Won't you lend Ronnie the money now?" I pleaded, anxious to divert the conversation from my personal appearance, "and I will repay you, as you can see, at once. You may, if you please, cable to my bankers, and——"

"How much do you want?" he interrupted abruptly.

"Four hundred pounds."

"And when?"

"To-night—to-morrow it may be too late."

"Oh, oh!" And he gave a horrible sort of chuckle. "Then matters are serious." He sat for a moment contemplating his neat patent leather shoes. At last he said:

"Well, supposing I do advance this will you give me a formal paper, stamped and witnessed?"

"Of course I will," I answered eagerly, "and be most grateful to you for your kindness."

"Grateful!" he repeated, with cynical insolence. "My dear young lady, gratitude is of no value in business—but I'll give the cheque."

"Not a cheque, if you please, but money; notes will be best."

"All right," he agreed, "you shall have the money in notes. I will send it up to-night by ten o'clock, in charge of a special messenger."

"Oh, thank you, thank you—how good of you!" I began.

But again he interrupted me with a wave of his beautifully manicured hand:

"Besides a speedy return of this large sum I must call upon you for something extra in the way of—shall we say—interest? No, not money, but—er—consideration and appreciation. You have always held me off; can I ever forget my dance with you at the Residency ball, or the memory of what happened in this very room?"

Something in the tone of his voice and the peculiar expression of his eyes frightened me. My hands were locked in my lap that he might not see how they were shaking.

"Do please forgive me," I pleaded tremulously. "I was a proud child with a fiery temper, and I'm afraid I cannot always control myself."

"You have openly snubbed me, my beautiful young lady, and to tell me you have a temper and are sorry is of no use. You must be prepared to pay me in my own coin."

I waited in agony to hear my sentence.

"Oh, you need not go so white," suddenly leaning over and stroking my cheek; "I prefer the pretty roses." As I recoiled he added, "And the payment I require is a mere nothing. In the eyes of the whole station you have always scorned me in your cool, haughty English manner. Now, you shall appear in public as my dear friend, make what is called 'a demonstration,' and let all the world see that we are on the very best of terms. My new motor is here. Go and put on your smartest hat and come with me, and show yourself in my company. First of all, we will drive up to the polo at Bolarum. There is a big match to-day—the Hussars and the city team. From there we will run down to the Hussain Saugur and look on at a boat race. Afterwards we will go to the club and have a nice little tea together, and then I will bring you home. How do you like the programme?" His interrogative grin was frankly diabolical.

How could I like the programme? I was aware that to be seen in Balthasar's great grey motor would, so far as the world was concerned, cast me socially into outer darkness. Everyone would believe that we were engaged. This motor drive round Secunderabad and its principal resorts would amount to the precise equivalent of an announcement in the London *Morning Post*. My heart sank. I was painfully alive to the effect of this ostentatious tour, and realised my hateful fate. I was the slave who was about to be dragged at the conqueror's chariot wheels; nevertheless, I resolved to make the sacrifice for Ronnie. After all, it would not be of such deadly consequence, since he and I would soon disappear from the station. As I rose to get ready my companion said:

"If you will draw up your acknowledgment of the money and receipt now, I can take it with me. It is merely a form, and I'll send up a trusty messenger to-night."

Strange to say, some lingering sense of prudence compelled me to reply, "I will have it all quite ready when your messenger comes."

"How suspicious we are!" he exclaimed with a shrug. "Well, run along, my beautiful young lady, and put on your best hat—the one with the white feathers; it looks so nice and honeymoony. Ha! ha! ha!"

I believe our retinue could scarcely believe their eyes, when they beheld me come forth and, though every fibre in my being rebelled against the situation, take my place beside Balthasar sahib in his great grey car. Soon we were gliding towards the R.A. lines and away to the polo ground. I met, alas! many of my acquaintances; there were the Greys and their father, General and Mrs. Graham and Major and Mrs. Mills—riding. Their stares of incredulity were as so many stabs. At the polo other people also gazed—my friends with amazement and it seemed to me a sort of incredulous horror. One or two men strolled over, and accosted me, and talked perfunctorily of the game and the weather. I believe they really came to see if they could believe their senses, or if it was somebody faintly resembling me who was sitting there beside Balthasar. My hateful companion discoursed in a loud, guttural voice; bragged of his new car and its cost, and said that "with a little practice, a lady," here he nodded familiarly at me, "would *soon* learn to drive it."

I was too paralysed to repudiate the suggestion, but my face probably spoke volumes. In Balthasar's car I could sympathise but too acutely with the sensations of a rabbit in a snake house! Presently, when all the world and his wife had enjoyed every opportunity of beholding me, we went away at great speed down to the boathouse, where I was once more placed on show! Finally we drove to the club, and there, in the most conspicuous place that he could select, Balthasar and I had tea. Every eye was upon us, and as he kept muttering: "Talk, talk, talk; try and look as if you were enjoying yourself! If you don't play the game and do *your* share, you can't expect *me* to do mine," I was compelled to chatter any nonsense that my dazed brain could invent, whilst he lolled in a chair, enacting the part of a complacent and well-entertained potentate. People who knew me well nodded, but no one approached, except good kind Mrs. Lakin, who came over to where we were seated, and said:

"I am going up to Trimulgherry, my dear" (which remark was a most barefaced untruth, as her home was in the opposite direction), "and I can give you a lift, so that you won't be taking Mr. Balthasar out of his way, and there is a little matter I want to consult you about."

"It is too good of you, my dear madam," replied my companion in his most unctuous voice, "but Miss Lingard is in my charge. She *loves* motoring, and I am sure you would not wish to cut short her pleasure."

Vanquished Mrs. Lakin, with a sympathetic glance at me, withdrew in helpless silence, and was presently lumbering out of the compound in her dilapidated victoria.

By and by, when the club had scattered to bridge, billiards, or the library, I was relieved from my rack and carried back to the cantonment. As I stepped out of the car I said, in a tone of humble apology:

"I know I've not been good company, but I am sure you must realise that I am most dreadfully unhappy about my brother."

"Yes, yes, of course," he assented; "he is an infernal young ass."

"And you will keep your promise," I added, resting my hand on the car; "we may rely on you? You *will* send it by messenger as soon as possible?"

"Of course, you may rely on me," he answered impatiently; "my clerk will be with you at ten o'clock to-night. I'll see you again before long," and he signed to the chauffeur to proceed.

After this agonising experience I felt mentally prostrated, and sank exhausted into a long chair in the veranda. Ronnie, now at home, came quickly forward, and when I said "It is all right," the relief in the expression of his drawn, worn face was some recompense to me.

After dinner we sat out in the compound, watched the dancing fireflies and listened to the distant band, for it was "guest night" at the mess.

"He said the clerk would be here at ten o'clock." I repeated this more than once—the announcement seemed to give me confidence. "It will be all in notes," I added.

"So much the better," said Ronnie. "In fact nothing else would do. I'll take it up early to-morrow, get hold of the key, stick it into the safe, and hand it over to the old man. Oh, *what* a load off my mind!"

Ten o'clock struck and we listened intently; in the still Indian night there were no sounds but the distant barking of a dog, the stamping of a pony in the stable and the thrumming of tom-toms in the Trimulgherry bazaar. Eleven o'clock—oh that agonised hour of long-drawn suspense! At last a *gurra* sounded twelve distinct strokes.

"Eva," said Ronnie, suddenly breaking our poignant silence, "that black-hearted devil has played *you* false, and ruined *me!*"

"Don't give up yet," I said, "as soon as it's light take my receipt and Tommy and gallop down to Chudderghat and fetch the money yourself."

"Right O!" he agreed eagerly. "Yes, it's our one chance. I shall have to be back before orderly-room, which is at eight o'clock."

Long before eight o'clock Ronnie had returned, and I knew at once that the worst had happened! With a ghastly, rigid face he staggered into the veranda, as Tommy Atkins, dripping with sweat, was led away.

"The whole thing was a fraud—a devilish fraud!" said Ronnie, as he leant against a pillar and mopped his face. "Balthasar was not there. He left the station last night, and no one knows where he has gone or when he will return. He always had his knife into you, Eva, ever since the day you turned him out. Get me a peg; I must try and pull myself together before I go to the orderly-room and face the music. Hallo, here is Gloag!" he exclaimed, and to my astonishment Captain Gloag rode into the compound. He pulled up at the steps, threw the reins to a syce, and clanked into the drawing-room, where we followed him in silence.

"Good morning, Miss Lingard," he said, looking more wooden-faced than ever. "Good morning, Lingard. Ahem—I've come on a rather unpleasant duty. Your presence is required in the orderly-room. The colonel has told me to receive your sword, and to place you under close arrest."

With a face as wooden as the adjutant's, and without a word, Ronnie went inside in search of his sword, and Captain Gloag turned to me and said:

"This is pretty awful for you, Miss Lingard. There has been some sort of mystery about the canteen funds, so the safe in the orderly-room was opened this morning—the drawer and the partition in which Lingard was understood to keep the notes was found empty. The safe has two keys; he had one when acting adjutant. Of course he *may* be able to explain all this, but the colonel is in a terrible state—regimental funds should never be removed."

Here Ronnie appeared with his sword and handed it over in silence.

"Better start at once," said the adjutant. "Will you send for your pony?"

Ronnie gave the order, but otherwise remained dumb, and in less than five minutes I saw him ride away with Captain Gloag, who carried his sword in the sight of all spectators—our servants, and the Millses' servants—every one of whom realised what this portended as well as I did myself.

CHAPTER XXIII
A HAVEN

After the departure of Ronnie I sat as if stunned; possibly I could not have felt more utterly wretched had he been dead. Indeed, it almost seemed to me as if there were an element of death in the bungalow, such was the silence. Not a sound to be heard, except the dripping of a tap and a casual lizard pattering on the matting; all the servants (and other people's servants) were collected in our cookhouse, discussing the catastrophe. As a rule the usual daily routine is carried on, no matter what trouble overtakes a household, and presently I saw the butler preparing breakfast in the dining-room. Then he came to the door, salaamed with both hands, and said:

"Please, missie, to come and take something. Last night missie no dinner having; missie will be sick, and that plenty bad business for everyone."

This was true. If I were to collapse I would be of no use, nor able to face the struggle and strain which lay before me. I accepted the kind advice of Michael, ate a little breakfast and felt better. If Ronnie was about to fall into this awful trouble, I must consider how I could best assist him. I had already written home for money; I would arrange for the sale of everything, and if the worst came to the worst, we should have to go away somewhere together and hide our heads until the first fury of the storm had abated.

It was now ten o'clock, and Ronnie had not yet returned. As I was pacing up and down the veranda, a prey to misery and impatience, I heard a light step in the drawing-room, and there was Mrs. Mills. Without a word she took me in her arms and kissed me, and I could see that she had been crying.

"My poor dear child," she sobbed, "I have heard all. George has just returned from the orderly-room, and we want to know what we can do to help you. We are so desperately sorry for you. So is everyone."

"You must not be too hard on Ronnie," I protested, "but a little sorry for him too."

"Yes, yes," she said; "we all liked him so much, and were so proud of him too. It's that dreadful gambling—he's not the first young man that it has ruined."

"Ruined!" I repeated.

"Yes," she answered, "at least in a way. The canteen money is gone and he can offer no explanation. The colonel is nearly beside himself, and your brother will have to stand a general court martial. Meanwhile he is to be confined to his quarters in close arrest. There will be an officer in charge of him and a sentry on duty, day and night."

I attempted to speak, but my voice completely failed me.

"Under these circumstances, dear, you cannot remain here. These are the colonel's instructions, and George and I wish you to come to us at once."

"You are most awfully kind," I replied, "and of course I will not remain if it is irregular, but before I do anything I should like to have a talk with Ronnie."

"Very well, I expect he will be back directly. Do tell your ayah to pack up your things. George says you are to have his room; he will move into a tent in the compound."

"You are more than good, dear Mrs. Mills, and I will let you know my plans. Here comes Ronnie," I exclaimed, as he and one of his brother officers entered the veranda together. Mrs. Mills hastily disappeared over the wall into her own premises, and as I could not face Ronnie's companion in my present state of mind I withdrew towards my room and beckoned to my brother to follow me.

"Can I speak to my sister for a moment, Carr?" he inquired.

"Oh yes, by all means," replied Mr. Carr, who I must confess looked excessively uncomfortable—yes, and miserable.

Ronnie then led the way into his den and drew the purdah, but no one could overhear us, as the little room was entirely cut off from the veranda. I sat down and waited for him to speak. As he leant against the wall he looked almost death-like. The wear and tear of the last few months had entirely dimmed his good looks; his eyes were sunken, and there were great hollows in his cheeks.

"I went up there," he began in a husky voice, "and found that *everything* was known. The colonel ordered me to explain, but if I had been shot I couldn't have uttered a word! How could I describe the frightful temptation that overpowered me when I fingered that roll of greasy notes and firmly believed that I'd be the winner of more than double the money before they could be missed? If I had been posted at home—just think of it, and uncle's feelings—I should have been obliged to leave my London club, not to speak of the regiment; so, as you know, I took the bull by the horns, grabbed the coin and gave the notes to Bunsi Lal in exchange for a cheque on London; then, by infernal bad luck it appears that one of these notes was passed in the bazaar—a thousand rupee note which was peculiarly marked. Fryer the paymaster spotted it, and smelt a thousand rats, and no doubt he gave the C.O. a hint, hence these—er—tears. I wrote the whole story home to uncle. His answer is due in ten days. Whatever it may be, it comes too late now. Well, in the orderly-room I made no defence; just stood there tongue-tied. At the court martial, of course, I'll have an advocate—but all the same I'm bound to get the boot! The colonel is beside himself—in a stone-cold rage—for it seems that no officer of the 'Lighthearts' has ever before been court-martialled."

I nodded my head, and Ronnie continued:

"Carr or another will be on duty, and so you must turn out, as *you* are not under close arrest; and I hope you will get away from the regimental lines. It will be rather awkward for everyone if you are hereabouts, though I know that the Millses wish to take you in."

"Yes," I replied, "Mrs. Mills has been here."

"You must go to someone outside the regiment, to the Greys, the Babingtons or the Campbells, to await the finding of the court martial, and then you and I will clear out. I say, I wonder how Falkland will take it?"

To this I made no reply—the thought of Brian was agonising.

"If I know him—and yet I don't know him—I believe this business will make no difference. If I were a thief—well I *am* a thief—let's say a murderer, I believe he would stick to you all the same—he is that sort."

"Do you think so?" I murmured tremulously.

"Yes, sure, and now to business. I'll get Arkwright to sell the stable, Cursetjee is to take the auction. I know you've made an inventory, and that thanks to you we have no small bills. If you happen to have any money, you might give it to Michael to run the house, as I shall always have a fellow here on duty. I understand that they will do their best to assemble a court martial soon, but a general court martial with a brigadier as president takes time—at the earliest it will be three weeks."

"How dreadful!" I exclaimed. "What ages to wait in suspense. Do you suppose you will be what is called—cashiered?"

"Bound to," he answered curtly.

After a moment I said:

"I have a hundred rupees I will give to Michael, for which he will account to you. I suppose I shall be allowed to come and see you?"

"Yes," he replied, "and you had better come after dark."

"Well, whatever happens, Ronnie, remember that *I* shall stick to you through thick and thin."

"Then if you do, you will be an awful fool! I shall only drag you down. When this business is over, I'll go to the colonies or South America, and you must return home and marry Falkland."

At this moment the ayah pulled back the curtain. She had a chit in her hand.

"For missie," she said, coming forward. I opened the note; it was from Mrs. Lakin, and ran:

> "Dear Girl,—I have heard of your great trouble, and am so sorry for you both. You must come to me to-day. I shall fetch you about three o'clock, and bring a cart for your luggage. Down here at Begumpett we are out of the world, and you can just be as quiet as you please. There are only my husband and myself. We are, as you know, neither young nor smart, only dull and old-fashioned, but we'll do our best to take care of you and will look upon you as one of our own girls.—Yours in affectionate sympathy,
>
> "Lucinda J. Lakin."

"That's the place for you!" said Ronnie, who had been reading the note over my shoulder, "she's a rare good sort, and you'll be out of the way of prying eyes and the talk. Lord! *how* people will talk! Old Mother Lakin is one of the best. You can get her to bring you up and see me of an evening. And now I must go back to Carr; he is bound to be starving for his breakfast. He or another officer will have this room, so tell your old ayah to hurry up and pack. Well, Eva," and his voice shook, as he put his hand suddenly on my shoulder and looked me straight in the face, "I must say this is beastly hard on *you*." Then he kissed me with burning hot lips, and swung back into the sitting-room.

In order to prepare for Ronnie's guard, Mary ayah and I worked vigorously for hours, and put together and packed my multitude of belongings. This task accomplished, I interviewed Michael and the cook, wrote business letters to Cursetjee and Spencer, and when Mrs. Lakin called she found me ready to accompany her. As we drove out of the compound I turned to look back on the bungalow with its cork tree avenue and veranda veiled in creepers, for three months the abode of happiness, and the theatre of so many experiences: the scenes with Balthasar, with Brian, and with Ronnie.

Kind Mrs. Lakin did not attempt to make conversation as we rolled along side by side behind a shabby coachman and an ancient screw, but from time to time she pressed my hand with silent and comforting sympathy.

On the steps of his house Colonel Lakin received me as if nothing particular had happened and I was a visitor whom he delighted to honour. My room was prepared, and oh, how comfortable! Such large down pillows, such deep roomy chairs and a delightful sofa. Most of the furniture, I subsequently learned, had been bought from Deschamps in Madras, when Colonel and Mrs. Lakin started housekeeping, and since then had travelled hundreds—I may say thousands—of miles over the Madras Presidency. On this inviting couch I lay down to rest, worn out between emotion and the loss of sleep. Dusk had come and I must have enjoyed more than the traditional forty winks, when the ayah announced:

"Mem sahib Soames."

The heavy chick was thrust aside and Mrs. Soames entered without apology. The moment I saw her I sprang up.

"My dear child," she began, "I simply *had* to come and see you." She put her arms round my neck and kissed me. "I am just heart-broken, though, after all, what am I to you?"

We sat down together on the sofa, and she held my hand in hers.

"Ronnie must have been mad, poor boy; but gambling is like a disease, it is in the blood. My grandfather had it, and only for the mercy of my mother's fortune we would certainly have all been in the workhouse. Ronnie is the last young man I'd have dreamt of getting into such trouble. I would have fetched you the moment I heard of——" and she stammered "of—of——" then wisely abandoned the detail. "James, although he likes you immensely, said it would be better if you were not in our lines. You could not help seeing and hearing things that might jar and pain you. So dear Mrs. Lakin is quite the right person to receive you, but Eva—you believe, don't you, that I am always your sincere and loving friend?"

"Yes," I replied, "I am quite sure of that."

"James is frantic," she resumed. "I have never seen him in such a condition; he cannot eat, he cannot rest, he paces up and down the dining-room like some caged animal. There has never been a scandal or a court martial in the regiment—at least, not within the memory of man—and he takes this affair most fearfully to heart. He says it will be in all the papers at home, and that if he had done the deed himself he could not feel the disgrace more acutely. Oh, if I had only known that your brother wanted a loan I'd have lent him the money without hesitation. He was always one of my best boys—and I do try to help them. If he had just given me one little hint—and you, my dear?" turning to me.

"I knew nothing, dreamt of nothing, till the night before last, when I found Ronnie with a revolver in his hand." Here I broke down and sobbed in her arms.

When I had somewhat recovered and was able to speak more coherently, I told my friend the story of Balthasar's revenge and perfidy.

"Oh, you poor, poor darling!" she cried. "How dared he? I heard that you had been seen with him in his car, but did not believe it; and so you sacrificed yourself to Balthasar's vanity and malice, and all for nothing. Well now," drying her own tears, "I shall come and see you again, of course, and we will lay our heads together and make plans. If there is anyone I can write to, any possible thing that I can do, you have only to send me a line by one of Mrs. Lakin's chuprassies. Now I am afraid, dear, it is getting late and I must go."

Mrs. Mills, Zora, the Greys, and various other friends came to see me. Their visits were most kindly meant, but undeniably painful for them and for me. It was not as if I had lost Ronnie by death; I had been separated from him by disgrace, and their condolences were vague and embarrassing.

How I longed to hide myself and be alone, although Mrs. Lakin's company was never unwelcome. Her large heart overflowed with tactful human kindness, and I was treated as something between a spoilt child and a pampered invalid, and oh, the solid comfort of her ménage! What well-oiled wheels in all departments; what soft-footed servants, what cream, eggs, and butter (Mrs. Lakin had her own cows and poultry); but in these days I could not eat, and supported existence on tea and toast.

Every evening about sundown my friend took me for long drives into the country; the boulder-strewn plains looked soft and beautiful in the moonlight, and as we bowled along behind the old chestnut—a surprisingly free goer—she told me tales of former days, on purpose, no doubt, to keep my thoughts from dwelling—as they did—on the one subject. She also related the history of scandals, social convulsions, courts martial and civil trials, beside which Ronnie's iniquities were pale and insignificant. The kind woman exerted herself in this manner in order to cheer me and give my future a less hopeless outlook.

Colonel Lakin was also active on my behalf. He got rid of our ponies and cart, Ronnie's guns and saddlery, all for a good price; and Zora's eldest brother bought my dear Tommy Atkins and promised him a happy home.

On several occasions I had visited Ronnie, and found him more like his normal self and less depressed.

"Now that I have no anxieties and nothing to *hide*, I feel better and I can sleep," he announced. "Arkwright tells me that I have a capital chap as my advocate, and I must say the fellows in the regiment have been extraordinarily forbearing and staunch. Grimes sends down the papers, Waller brought me a box of the best Havana cigars, and I go for a drive every evening when there's no one about. The one thing that I cannot stand is the sentry always in evidence. I believe the court martial will soon assemble now. They are bringing members from Bellary, Poona and Bangalore, and I don't suppose it will last longer than a couple of days. Is it not extraordinary that I've had neither letter nor cheque from Uncle Horace?"

"Not when you remember that all his correspondence is overlooked by Aunt Mina."

"And she always pretended to be so fond of me—and now, as far as she is concerned, I may drop into the pit."

"Well, you and I will drop down together," I declared. "Keep up your heart—they say the troubles we most fear are those that never happen."

Alas, the dreaded event arrived only too soon. I heard of the date from my kind friend Colonel Lakin. The members assembled, and sat in the regimental ante-room. On the first day the business was chiefly technical and formal; the second held Ronnie's fate, and it seemed to me to be as long as an average week. I had declined to go for my usual evening drive, but waited within doors for the return of Colonel Lakin, who would bring us the result of the finding.

It was late when he returned to Begumpett and the wheels of his dog-cart rumbled under the lofty porch. Mrs. Lakin was awaiting him in the veranda, but I was too anxious and shaken to venture beyond my room. In a condition of breathless tension I heard him enter the drawing-room and exchange a few words with his wife. Rooms in the Madras Presidency are merely separated by thick curtains, with a wide space open at the top, and as I overheard her sharp exclamation I was a little prepared when she came to me with a troubled face and said:

"Dear child, I don't know *how* I am to tell you, but they have found your brother guilty of the misappropriation of regimental funds——" She paused, and the tears ran down her cheeks as she added in a broken voice: "They have given him two years' imprisonment."

As soon as I had grasped the real meaning of this speech I seemed to feel as if I were crumbling to pieces, and sank on the ground in a dead faint.

CHAPTER XXIV
THE FLIGHT

As a special favour I was granted permission to have an interview with Ronnie before he was removed, not to "Windsor Castle," as Secunderabad jail was nicknamed—for the regiment had protested—but to Bangalore, a second-class establishment.

"I wish to goodness they were going to *hang* me!" was the first thing Ronnie said, and there was agony in his voice. "I swear I do—only for you and Uncle. Well, Eva, you must go home and try to make the best of things."

"What! and leave you out here?" I cried. "No, indeed, I shall live at Bangalore until your time is up."

"Now that is the very craziest nonsense; you must return to Torrington and marry Falkland."

For the moment I failed to think of an appropriate answer. Why remind poor Ronnie that as the sister of a convict I could never be Brian's wife, or presume to enter his proud and exclusive family?

"I do not wish to marry," I muttered at last, and then hastily turned the subject by asking him if he wanted money.

"No, no," he replied, "a paternal government provides everything, kit and all, and I start to-morrow under escort. It was decent of them to let you see me, and in my own clothes. Good-bye, dear old girl; you've been a real brick to me. Now I implore you to take your own line and not bother any more about your scamp of a brother. Do you remember when we sat on the bridge at Beke and had presentiments, and I swore that I was going to make the name of Lingard famous? I've jolly well done *that!*"

"Don't say such things," I burst out hysterically.

"I'll behave like a lamb," he continued, "and possibly receive some indulgence, but I'm bound to be the only officer and gentleman among a very queer crowd, and I hope the prison diet will put an end to me long before my term is out."

At this moment a man whom I had never seen before entered and signalled that the time was up, and we embraced in silence. The next morning I was informed that my brother had been taken away by night, the authorities sparing him as much publicity as possible. Having ascertained that Ronnie had really departed, I proceeded to lay my own plans before Mrs. Lakin, who protested in long and eloquent speeches packed with objections; but my mind was made up, my decision immovable.

"Dearest, kindest Mrs. Lakin," I said, "Ronnie and I are all in all to one another; where he goes *I* go."

"What—to jail?"

"No; but perhaps I can find some quiet family in Bangalore who will be absolute strangers to me and my affairs. I can see Ronnie from time to time, and send him books and papers—he will like to feel that I am near him."

"But this is sheer madness, my dear child! You don't know a soul in Bangalore."

"So much the better," I replied with significant emphasis.

"If even one of my girls was there—but Susan is at Trichinopoly and Alice at Saugor."

"Do, do help me," I urged, and slid down from my chair and laid my hands on her knees. "I would like to start to-morrow."

My petition was backed up by Zora, who at this propitious moment had called to see me, and warmly approved of my project. That a woman should make the most absolute sacrifice for a man was naturally her own (the Mohammedan) point of view.

"Eva is right," she declared. "Imagine the comfort and joy her visits will be to that poor fellow, cut off from all his friends and associates. I should think Eva could find a home in some quiet family—not perhaps in her own class—and she can steal away quietly from here, and no one need know what has become of her—only we two. I can take her the whole way to Wadi in my car; the ayah will go ahead with luggage and wait there—and so Miss Lingard will disappear."

"Two years in some back-road bungalow in Bangalore will be a sheer sacrifice of Eva's youth; of course she should go home to her people," protested Mrs. Lakin, who had sacrificed so much herself.

"But I have no near relations except Ronnie," I announced; "we are orphans. Do you know Bangalore?"

"To be sure I do, my dear. It was there I was married—in Trinity Church."

"Then probably you can tell me of some people who would receive me?"

"Oh, as for that, I could. I know a nice old widow, who was my mother's English maid and married a half-caste clerk. She is comfortably off, lives in the infantry lines, and has no family."

"It seems to be just the place for me!" I exclaimed.

"No, no," she protested. "I won't have any hand in your crazy scheme."

"Oh, dear Mrs. Lakin, don't say that. If you do, I shall be living in Bangalore, possibly with people you might not approve of—unless you or Zora can suggest something better."

"I do know people down there," she admitted, "but they are in your own class."

"That would never answer," I rejoined. "They would want references and to hear all about me and my business—even supposing they'd receive me as a paying guest."

I could see that Mrs. Lakin was relenting by degrees when she said:

"Even if you *did* go to Mrs. de Castro, it would take a couple of weeks to make arrangements."

"But you can telegraph—'reply paid,'" I suggested.

"I can't imagine why you're in such a hurry to get away; I know the rules, and you won't see your brother for at least three months."

"Oh, I'll see him before that," I replied with conviction, "even if I have to go on my knees to the governor."

"And, my dear Eva, you have not the faintest idea of what you are undertaking. Mrs. de Castro will not charge you more than thirty rupees a month, but everything will be very coarse and rough. Native vegetables, bad bazaar bread, second-class fish, and *goat!*"

"I don't mind in the least," I answered recklessly.

"Well, I suppose a wilful girl must have her way," and after long persistent arguments and an inexhaustible amount of persuasion I prevailed on my kind friend to write to her Bangalore acquaintance on my behalf.

By return of post we received a reply from Mrs. de Castro, saying that she would "be glad of the young woman's company—and money for her board."

When the shock of the verdict had somewhat abated, I wrote several important letters; it was a new experience for me to be relying solely on myself. First I wrote to my bankers, and instructed them to pay to Colonel Soames the sum of four hundred pounds, the amount of the missing canteen money. I felt a great sense of relief as I closed and addressed this missive; at least the regiment would not experience any pecuniary loss—it was their good name which had suffered. My next letter was to my uncle. I sent him a long, detailed and truthful account of the whole tragedy; carefully pointing out every extenuating circumstance, and endeavouring to touch his heart. So far he had not answered Ronnie's appeal, but I was determined that he should take notice of mine. Ronnie's cry was for money—mine for sympathy and forgiveness. I also wrote to Mrs. Paget-Taylor, and implored her to use her influence to soften my uncle and aunt with respect to my brother; and last, but not least, I wrote to Brian. Without any attempt at softening facts, I related the history of Ronnie's temptation and disgrace. I said in the course of the letter:

"Ronnie is already a convict in Bangalore jail. I know that this news will shock you; the whole affair fell upon me as a thunderbolt. It has all come from Ronnie's passion for gambling, which I honestly believe is his only failing, but has brought him, as the world can see, to the most frightful grief. I am sure you will remember how popular he was with crowds of friends. Well, at the present moment he has not a single one in the world except myself, and of course I shall stick to him. He would to me under similar circumstances. Ronnie was always the best and kindest of brothers. This sudden and dreadful trouble will, of course, put an end to our engagement. My dearest Brian, how could you possibly marry the sister of a convict, who is serving his sentence, and whose case has rung through every club and every regiment—not to speak of the whole Press? I cannot express to you what this blight on my future costs me. I know that you will be sorry for me, and perhaps a little sorry for Ronnie. Please do not write, it would only make matters worse, for I can never come into your life, and must do my best to put all thoughts of you out of my mind. I leave here in a few days to await in some quiet place, and among total strangers, the date of Ronnie's release."

Now that my correspondence had been dispatched by the English mail, I began to make arrangements for departure, and here I had an active assistant in Zora. My scheme had her enthusiastic approval. By her instructions all my pretty, smart dresses, jewellery and dainty belongings were duly collected, packed, and sent away to be stored under her father's roof till better days dawned. For the next two years I would have no occasion for smart frocks or ball gowns, and with only a modest outfit in two boxes I was ready for my journey. Under my present circumstances I did not require an ayah, and old Mary and I separated with mutual regrets. As for the Lakins, they could not have been kinder or more sympathetic if I had been their own daughter. The evening before I departed the colonel beckoned me mysteriously into his office, and told me in a low voice that if I wanted money I was to be sure to apply to him.

"I know," he added, "that you have a bit the sale brought you, and I have paid it, as you wished, into the Bank of Madras; but later on, if you find yourself getting a little low, you've only to drop me a line, just the same as if you were one of our girls."

I endeavoured to thank him, but he would not listen to me; on the contrary, he insisted on my listening to *him*.

"I must tell you that I do not approve of this step you are taking—no more does Lucy. Of course old Jane de Castro will look after you, but you will find her a dull companion, and I do not see how you can possibly hold on with her for more than a few months. I can enter into your feelings in wishing to be near your brother, but I am sure you ought to think a little of yourself, and after you have seen him and cheered him up a bit, you really should go home."

I listened to his advice with profound respect, but I was sensible that nothing would induce me to accept it. Mrs. Lakin, too, had provided me with a generous supply of admonition and warnings; and also endowed me with a basket of provisions that would have kept a hungry family for a week. She exhorted me to write to her continually, and actually threatened to come down to Bangalore in order to see with her own eyes how I was getting on.

In the midst of our leave-taking talk and Mrs. Lakin's last instructions, Zora's big motor glided into the compound. My boxes were placed upon the roof—a tiffin basket also—and Zora herself accompanied me down to Wadi, closely veiled. She gave me much sweet sympathy and many wise injunctions, saw me into a comfortable carriage in the Madras mail, and behold me launched into a new world!

Before my departure I had written to Mrs. Soames, Mrs. Mills, and other friends, bidding them farewell, thanking them for all their kindness. To poor Mrs. Lakin I deputed the heavy and thankless task of explaining my flight. In answer to numerous inquiries she assured her questioners that

I had insisted on leaving, in spite of all that she could urge or do, but the truth was, I could not endure to remain in Secunderabad. I had been very mysterious about my destination and address; my desire was, if possible, to be absolutely forgotten. For all these stories may my good kind friend be absolved.

It was naturally assumed that I had taken flight to England, until Mrs. Potter announced in the *morghi khana* that I had been seen on the road to Wadi in Balthasar's great grey motor with luggage on the top, *and not alone.* Moreover, it was an incriminating coincidence that Balthasar himself had disappeared from Chudderghat on the very same day!

CHAPTER XXV
AT BANGALORE

After changing at two junctions, and a tedious but eventless journey, Kipper and I arrived in Bangalore, and drove off in a dusty, shuttered gharry to 202 Infantry Lines, the abode of Mrs. de Castro.

Bangalore itself lies chiefly around a maidan or parade ground about a mile long, bordered with a ride and trees, and encircled and traversed by the principal roads in the station. Parallel to the maidan are the infantry lines; they lie behind what once were infantry barracks, and are now commissariat stores. Formerly the bungalows were occupied by officers, but these quarters—like the barracks—have passed into a different use, and are rented by clerks, shopkeepers and railway subordinates. Number 202 was large and old and gloomy, situated in a small compound with two entrances, flanked by imposing gate piers, but there were no gates. The front of the bungalow was completely veiled by an enormous lattice-work porch, covered with flowering creepers—wine-coloured bougainvillea and blue masses of "morning glory." The little drive was full of ruts, the steps up to the veranda were lined with many pots of caladiums and maidenhair; evidently these had been recently watered, for the first sensation I received, with respect to my new residence, was an all-pervading smell of wet earth.

As we rumbled up and came to a noisy halt a little old woman shuffled out of the doorway directly facing the steps; and as I descended from the gharry she exclaimed in a shrill, querulous voice:

"So you have brought a *dog!*"

I hastened to assure her that I could vouch for Kip's good conduct, and that he would be no trouble whatever to her.

"But what about my cats?" she snapped. "By the look of him I should say he would trouble *them*."

Again I declared that I would be guarantee for his behaviour.

"And you're a lady!" she continued in the same complaining key. "Miss Lucy never told me that."

"I hope it is no drawback?"

"Well, it is in a way," was her unexpected reply. "I'm not a lady myself. I was a lady's maid, and I've been looking for a nice homely girl who would read to me, and run to the bazaar, and be a sort of companion."

"I think I can manage all that," I replied, and turned to pay off the *gharriwan*.

The small amount of my luggage undoubtedly mollified my landlady, and having assured me that I had given the *gharriwan* double his fare, with considerable pomp and circumstance she preceded me into the drawing-room, which, as in most old bungalows, opened directly upon the veranda. Her air implied that she was now about to exhibit something superior and out of the common. What a room! The middle of it was occupied by a vast round ottoman, hard—I subsequently learned—as stone, covered with the most hideous black and green cretonne I had ever beheld. The floor had recently been matted with cheap and odoriferous matting. The walls were coloured a blinding blue and hung with fearful chromos. Between the walls, the matting, and the new cretonne, I gathered that this terrible apartment had been recently, as it is called, "done up." There were a few cane chairs, a blackwood table, and an old cottage piano with a faded red silk front.

In order to reach my quarters we passed through a network of small empty chambers to a room which was large and very bare. A little bed was as an island in space, the dressing-table was also small, a camp chest of drawers the sole accommodation for my wardrobe. As I glanced around this desert of an apartment, I resolved to supply myself immediately with a writing-table and an arm-chair.

I soon discovered that Mrs. de Castro kept but few servants. The so-called "boy," a man of forty, combined the offices of cook and waiter. To me the food was unfamiliar, and consisted of peculiar pillau, tank fish, and curries of the most startling varieties; our fruit was pomegranates and custard-apples.

Everything, however, was beautifully neat and clean, and as soon as Mrs. de Castro had resigned herself to her disappointment in finding me a *lady* we settled down together on the most amicable terms.

My hostess must have been about seventy. Her sight was rather bad, but otherwise she was by no means decrepit—in fact, was surprisingly active for her age. I let her see at once that I was resolved to be independent—to go out and come in precisely as I pleased; at the same time, I was willing to read aloud the *Bangalore Herald*, to write a chit, or even to carry a message into the bazaar—which lay at the end of our road. She quite took to Kip, who soon established himself in a very secure position in the house, and we three got on together so well that at the end of a week I do not think a casual visitor would have discovered that I had not been living in Infantry Lines for years. My landlady seldom went out, save on Sunday across the maidan to St. Mark's Church, but she gave me ample directions, and I soon found my way about our immediate neighbourhood.

My first distant expedition was to see at least the exterior of the jail. I think Mrs. de Castro was not a little astonished at my anxiety to know its whereabouts.

"The jail is nothing to look at," she said. "You go into the Cubbon Park—there's a sight for you! Some day I'll hire a gharry and take you down to the Lal Bagh gardens."

I had been debating in my own mind whether I would tell this good woman the whole truth and nothing but the truth. As a friend of "Miss Lucy's," in other words Mrs. Lakin (to whose mother she had been maid), I had some claim upon her interest and loyalty. She entertained a number of visitors, chiefly women, the wives of shopkeepers, clerks, railway guards and sergeants—a particular set of her own. These swarmed in of an afternoon to have a cup of coffee in the veranda and enjoy a bit of a talk, importing all the latest and raciest bazaar gossip, in which Mrs. de Castro took the most eager interest. Naturally to such people I was an object of the liveliest curiosity; with respect to me, I believe these poor puzzled women floundered about in a very quagmire of conjecture. I avoided them as far as possible, but nevertheless I could not wholly evade them, and their questions and hints were exceedingly sharp. With Mrs. de Castro sharing my secret I was convinced that I could hold them at bay, and accordingly made up my mind to speak. One morning as we sat at breakfast, I began abruptly:

"Mrs. de Castro, I am sure you wonder what I am doing here, a stranger to the place. There is not a soul that I know in the whole of Mysore, save one. You will also be wondering why I am often asking questions about the jail? Now I will tell you the reason—my brother is there."

"What!" she cried, "the new superintendent?"

"No, I am sorry to say he is undergoing a two years' sentence—his name is Captain Lingard."

"Oh lor!" she cried, lifting up her withered hands, "do you tell me so? I heard about the officer from my husband's nephew, who is head warder.

And so that's what's brought you to the station. Dear, dear, dear! What's he been a-doin' of?"

"It was about money," I replied.

"Ay," she answered sagely, "it is always money or women."

"My brother took funds belonging to the regiment, intending to repay them, but before he could do so they were missed."

"Ah," she exclaimed, "and then the fat was in the fire! Jail," she continued, "is a terrible place for a young gentleman—indeed, it's not very what you may call homey for anyone."

"I believe it will break my brother's heart," I said. "I have told you this, Mrs. de Castro, because I think you feel kindly towards me."

"To be sure, to be sure," she mumbled.

"And I want you to keep this dreadful thing a dead secret?"

"I'll do my best, and I'll do anything for Miss Lucy's friend; but the women who come here are just chock full of curiosity. They can see what you are, and they think it mighty queer your living in this small humble way. Well, I must compose some sort of a fairy tale to tell them."

"Tell them that I'm eccentric," I suggested; "that I come to you to be very, very quiet—tell them that I'm writing a book."

"Yes, yes, that'll do splendidly, and you can have your writing-table put in one of the little rooms, and keep yourself as much to yourself as you please, whilst I throw dust in their eyes."

"I think I shall go up to the jail this evening," I said. "I've been here a fortnight, and have never made it out yet."

"No, no, early to-morrow would be your best time. Not that you would *see* him—don't you run away with that notion; but you might chance on Mr. Hodson, the superintendent, about nine o'clock, and get a few words with him, and as you're so nice spoken—and so nice looking—perhaps he might make things a bit easy."

The next morning after I had had my early tea—at Mrs. de Castro's it was not tea but excellent Mysore coffee—I tied up the reproachful Kipper in the veranda, and received instructions as to the route from my hostess, who escorted me to the entrance, still wearing a bed jacket and red felt slippers.

"You'll just go round this corner"—(ours was a corner house)—"up on to the Cubbon Road, past the magazine, and then turn into the Petta Road; walk along that till you come to Government Offices, the D.P.W.—my husband was a clerk in them—go round that corner, and you'll find yourself on the way that leads to the racecourse—the jail is on your left. The whole distance isn't more than a mile and a quarter. I expect people will think it strange to see a nice-looking young lady like you tramping about in the dust all by herself; they'll be wondering who you are, and what's your business. I'm sure Mrs. Cotton and Mrs. Dicks, my neighbours, will do their dead best to dig it out of me, but I can be as close as a snail. Well, well," she concluded, "mind you don't stay out too long in the sun." And with this adjuration she left me.

CHAPTER XXVI
WITHIN THE PRECINCTS

I had resolved on, yet dreaded, this expedition, knowing that to see even the outside of the place where Ronnie was imprisoned would fill me with sickening horror; but the longer I deferred the excursion the more reluctant I should be to face it. I reasoned down my antipathy and shrinking, and urged myself not to be a fool. Was I not living in Bangalore solely to be near Ronnie? And I wished him to know what would surely comfort him: that I was within reach.

It was a delightfully fresh morning as I started forth and took a short cut over the maidan. In the distance I noticed a regiment on parade and a number of people riding. As I made my way across the track a girl passed me, galloping along with a radiant face. How she was enjoying herself! Six weeks ago and I had been as she! but now, I seemed to have lost my identity.

Leaving the maidan behind me, I turned into the Petta Road and, at the end of a short walk, found myself outside the precincts of the jail. After considerable delay I was admitted by a warder, ushered into a large, bare, whitewashed room, and invited to state my business.

"I wish to see the superintendent," I murmured.

"The superintendent is engaged, but perhaps the deputy will give you an interview."

"Very well," I assented, "but if it were possible I should feel obliged if the superintendent could see me even for a moment."

After waiting for about half an hour I was escorted to an office, in the middle of which was a large table, and sitting at it a stout, elderly, dark man in a sort of blue serge undress, with letters on his collar. He looked up interrogatively as I entered, and said:

"About the vegetables, I presume, madam?" (All Indian jails supply these.)

"No," I replied in a faint and tremulous key. "I have called to inquire about my brother, Captain Lingard?"

The superintendent hastily pushed back his chair and rose; he appeared too astonished to articulate, and gazed at me in a sort of dull amazement.

"I am staying in Bangalore in order to be near him," I continued.

"With friends?" he asked at last.

"Oh no, just lodging with a woman in the Infantry Lines, Mrs. de Castro."

"Yes, I know, her nephew has a post here. You are not staying for any time, I presume?"

"Yes, I am."

"But what about your relatives in England—will they think it suitable?"

I made no reply. I had come to ask questions, not to supply information.

"About my brother—how is he?"

"Ah, it's a sad business—such a nice young fellow!"

"Is he at all—at all—reconciled?" I faltered.

"No, he is taking it terribly hard—does not eat, does not speak, and they say he does not sleep. He has lost seven pounds in weight; if he goes on like this we must put him in hospital."

"What does he have to eat?" I inquired.

The official turned about, took down a card from the wall and, without a word, handed it to me for reference. Glancing over it I read: "Every European prisoner is provided with a tin plate, mug and spoon. The following is the daily dietary, prescribed for a European prisoner on hard labour."

"*Hard labour!*" I read aloud, and looked at the official interrogatively, who nodded in reply.

The list further continued: "Bread 24 oz., rice 8 oz., beef or fish 10 oz., vegetables 8 oz., tea 1/4 oz., sugar 1/2 oz., salt 3/4 oz., condiments ditto, milk 4 oz."

"Quite a liberal diet," remarked the superintendent, as I returned the card.

"And is my brother really doing hard labour?"

"Oh, yes; he is a fine muscular young fellow, the exercise will be good for him. Just at the moment he is pounding coco-nuts with a wooden mallet. After a time, if he conducts himself well, he will be made a convict warder."

"What is that?"

"He is given authority over the other prisoners, and does no work himself. He preserves discipline, is among the convicts day and night, and has charge of his own ward. Of course he receives no pay and wears the prison dress; eats the same food, and is subject to discipline himself. Being an educated man, your brother, if he behaves well, is bound to get a billet either as warder, or to keep the jail books, or superintend the carpenters' shops."

"How soon will he get one of these posts?" I inquired.

"Not for some time, I'm afraid."

"When may I see him?"

"In about ten weeks. Every three months prisoners are allowed to receive visitors."

"Ten weeks!" I repeated. "Oh, do let me have one word with him *now*; do, I implore you."

"My dear young lady, I dare not break the rules," he protested, "though I pity you from the bottom of my heart."

"But think of him, cut off from everything—everything he has been used to, absolutely friendless, and cast among natives and criminals. He has no idea that I am in Bangalore. Surely I may send him one line to comfort him?"

"No, no, no, that would be against all rules."

"It's like beating with bare hands on a stone wall," I cried in despair. "It makes me frantic to realise that I am within a few yards of my brother, and may not see him!"

"Well, if it comes to that, I might stretch a point," said the superintendent. "He may not see you, but if you think you can bear it, I might let you have a peep at *him*."

"Oh, thank you, thank you a thousand times."

"All right then, if you will not be upset, I'll take you up to a place where you can get a glimpse of the yard."

As he concluded, the kindly superintendent rose, opened a door, and ushered me along some bare stone passages. Then we passed through a large room, where convicts were working at hand looms, weaving various beautiful Indian carpets. They seemed to be really interested and engrossed in their work, which looked exceedingly intricate and tedious. My escort halted before one loom where two men were working, and pointed out a lovely blue and cream carpet, about half completed.

"This has been commissioned by an English countess," he explained. "It has taken six months' work, so far; most of the carpets on the looms are already sold; this is a particularly fine specimen, and we are very proud of it."

He said something to the workers in their own language, and they received his comments with wide and appreciative grins.

But I had come to see Ronnie—not carpets—and I think my companion instinctively felt that I had no wish to linger; so he soon escorted me out of the department into another section. As we proceeded, he informed me that at the moment they had five hundred inmates in the prison, mostly men, who did all the domestic and garden work, besides weaving carpets and making tents and gunny bags.

"This is the central jail," he added, "the only one in the province; the rest are merely district jails and lock-ups. You would be surprised at the number of old people that are confined in India. They are sworn in by their families, in place of younger men, who are the real criminals, and they are fairly well provided for for the rest of their lives."

To which statement—mentioned in the most casual manner—I listened with indignant horror.

I was also not a little moved by the number of convicts we encountered as we went along the stone passages. Every one of them wore irons on his legs, which clanked as he walked. Both prisoners and warders glanced at me furtively as I passed. Lady customers were no doubt occasionally to be seen in the carpet department, but I was in the division reserved for hard labour criminals and the most desperate characters. At last we reached a flight of steep steps, and climbed into a little room overlooking a yard, which was enclosed with high spiked walls. Here a number of prisoners were thumping coco-nuts with wooden mallets, "to make coir," as my companion explained to me. They wore cotton coats, drawers, and caps stamped with that significant mark the broad arrow, and every man was fettered from ankle to knee. As my eyes roved anxiously among the crowd I realised that they were all natives of the country except one—one with a rigid white face, who was pounding away with a sort of mechanical ferocity.

At first I did not recognise him, and thought with a little dart of relief, "Here at least is a companion for Ronnie;" and then I realised that it was Ronnie himself! Changed, oh, incredibly changed, in two short weeks! I was so horrified and so suddenly unstrung that, almost in spite of myself, I screamed out "Ronnie!" I saw him look up, but I think the steady thumping of the wooden mallets had deadened my cry. My companion, who was extremely angry, seized me by the arm and drew me forcibly out of the room.

"There you see, that is what I get for my kindness!" he said indignantly. "It will be a lesson."

"Oh, forgive me, *do* forgive me," I sobbed. "I couldn't help it." And then I leant against the wall and wept. I think this was almost the bitterest moment of my whole life. There was my brother, the image of despair, working out his sentence within those tall ugly walls, cut off from everything he had ever cared for. I believe my tears somewhat appeased the superintendent.

"Don't take on, don't take on. Come away down to my room," he said, "and pull yourself together a bit."

As soon as we had reached this haven, he offered me a chair and sent for a glass of water, and when I was more composed he said:

"I was afraid you might be upset."

"Of course I am, my brother looks as if he were dying."

"He looks badly, I grant you—they all do at first—I mean the Europeans. It isn't often we have them—not for years. A private was hanged ages ago, for shooting his comrade in the barrack room. I remember as if it was yesterday, the escort marching him up from cells just after daybreak one December morning, and the band playing the Dead March in 'Saul.'"

I shuddered involuntarily.

"This is only a second class jail," he resumed. "Serious cases are sent elsewhere. Your brother was moved down here for two reasons; the authorities did not wish to have him so near the regimental lines as Secunderabad jail. Every time a Tommy went by 'Windsor Castle' he would think 'One of our captains is lying in there.' Another thing, the Bangalore climate is less trying; we have no real hot weather, and of course there are no punkahs in jails. It's just a year ago since I saw Captain Lingard playing here in the polo tournament. There wasn't one to touch him! He seemed to have complete command of his ponies, and his strokes were a wonder. I little thought that his next visit to the station would be to *me*."

"No; who could have dreamt of such a thing? It all seems like a hideous nightmare."

"Look here, Miss Lingard, as far as I can I will help your brother, but to show partiality to one man because he is of my own race would upset all discipline, and lose me influence and authority. As it is, I have an unruly crowd to deal with; we've had more than one unpleasant outbreak. I believe there is one thing I can do for you—I will overstep my rules for once, and will give your brother a message."

"Will you? That really *is* kind."

"Well, what shall I say?"

"Give him my love, and tell him that I am in Bangalore, and hope to see him on the first visiting day. Tell him that I am living with a respectable old widow, and that he is never, never out of my thoughts. Ask him to try and look at the bright side of things and to think of the future, when we shall be together, and all this trouble will have passed over like a thunderstorm. May I send him books?"

"No, but he can have the use of the prison library, such as it is."

"Should I be allowed to present books to the prison library? As you so seldom have a European here, your stock must be rather low."

"That is so," he admitted. "I don't do much reading myself, but I think the books there are nearly all missionary stuff, sent in from somebody's sale. You might be allowed to present a few, and you could forward them through me. You must cheer up a bit," he added; "after all, the two years will soon run round."

"Two years of a living death," I protested; "what an awful punishment for a momentary madness! My brother was dreadfully in debt, the money tempted him; he meant of course to replace it, but there was no time. It has been paid back now."

"Yes; I understand that it was gambling brought Captain Lingard to this. It has landed a good many natives here—chiefly Burmese and Malays. The Burman is an inveterate gambler, so are Chinamen. Most of our local cases are village brawls, theft and murder. Well now," he said, rising, "I must ask you to excuse me; this is my very busy time. Would you like me to send for a gharry?"

I had intended to walk back, but I now felt so utterly shattered that this feat would be impossible, so I thankfully accepted the superintendent's offer, and was presently being bowled away to Infantry Lines.

All that day I lay on my bed prostrate, for I now acutely realised the weight of Ronnie's sentence. Would he ever survive to complete it? Could that convict with the fixed white face and the sunken staring eyes be my handsome, cheery brother?

I think Mrs. de Castro understood that I had recently received a terrible shock. She brought me her recipe for all trouble—a cup of the most excellent coffee—as well as a bottle of eau-de-Cologne with which to bathe my throbbing head. Kip also was tenderly attentive. He knew that I was in some sore grief; his eloquent eyes spoke volumes, and he licked my hand from time to time, doing all in his power to offer me his dumb sympathy.

No doubt it was the reaction from all I had gone through, culminating in my visit to the jail and sight of Ronnie as a convict, but after this expedition I broke down. I did not actually become a bedridden invalid, but I seemed to have lost all energy. I could not eat, I slept badly, and I was subject to exhaustive fits of crying. Mrs. de Castro was seriously concerned, and endeavoured to feed me, dose me, and scold me into a more cheerful frame of mind. She explained, with much wisdom, that I could do no good to my brother by starving and fretting and ruining my health.

One morning she threw two letters on my writing-table and said:

"These have just come by the dâk, and I expect *they'll* cheer you a bit!"

I glanced at them, and saw they had been readdressed by Mrs. Lakin. The first I seized upon and opened was from Brian, which said:

"My darling Eva,—By bad luck I missed writing to you last week, but it happened to be the day of my father's operation; my mother was dreadfully anxious and upset, and I forgot the Indian mail. My poor little girl, all this trouble about your brother has been a terrible affair for you, but I do not see why it should be the means of breaking off our engagement, nor will *I* ever consent to it. As Mrs. Falkland you will have done with the name and association of Lingard, and even if people remembered that your brother had been tried and convicted, instead of being censorious they would be sincerely sorry for you. I am, as you expected, also sorry for your brother. When I was out at Secunderabad I could not help seeing the way things were going, and once or twice I tried to give him a hint, but it was no use. I also had an idea of talking to you on the subject, but on second thoughts I decided it was better not to disturb you, and I did not expect matters would have come to a crisis so soon. I also consoled myself with the saying that 'half the troubles in this world are those that never happen.' This trouble unfortunately *has* come off! I think you are foolish in remaining out in India— whereabouts you do not say. Just at first I know that your brother will not be allowed to see a visitor, so your presence in the country won't be much good to him. No doubt he will be promoted into a post where he need not mix with the worst class of criminals. I wish it were in my power to do something to alleviate his horrible condition, or to reduce the term, but no doubt his own conduct and character will effect that. My poor little girl, I cannot tell you how acutely I feel for you; I know that this trouble is heart-breaking. I will write next mail, and I implore you when you receive this to cable your address, and send me a letter to say that second thoughts are best, and you are returning home to

"Your always devoted,
"Brian."

This letter I read over three times before I opened the next. It gave me courage and a momentary gleam of happiness; nevertheless, I was determined to remain in Bangalore and stick to Ronnie. Supposing I were to go home as Brian suggested, and abandon Ronnie to his fate; in spite of my fiancé's comforting words I believed that all my acquaintances would look upon me coldly and obviously strive to keep the subjects of brothers, convicts and jail out of their conversation.

My next letter was from Aunt Mina:

"Dear Eva,—Your uncle has deputed me to answer your letter, and I commence it by saying that although we have a knave in the family, we see no reason to tolerate a *fool*. Your brother, who has blackened the Lingard name, disgraced us and you, is the knave, but you, who have rushed after him, leaving the shelter of your friends at Secunderabad, are acting like a fool. You must return home *at once*. Your uncle, who stands in the place of a parent to you, desires me to say that there is to be no question of this. We expect you to start within a week from the date on which you receive this letter. You will, of course, come to Torrington and make your home here. We understand that you have paid up the money of the canteen fund. Your uncle had intended to do this. He desires me to say that a cheque for your passage home will be lodged; you are to return by the P. & O., and will be met at Southampton. Should you refuse to obey, and set your face against our plans, the hundred a year allowance will cease; not only this, but your future proceedings will be of no further interest to this family and we shall look upon you as much dead to us as is your brother. I know you are always inclined to be headstrong, and to wild and impulsive actions, but on this occasion I sincerely hope your recent experience will have taught you *humility* and common sense. We are inclined to fear that *you* may have contributed to Ronnie's disaster. A girl of your age, with no experience of India, possibly spent extravagantly and incurred large bills. Apparently it is only since *you* have lived with Ronnie that he has come to grief. Of course our conjectures may be mistaken—I am sure I hope so. This terrible family scandal has tried us greatly. The case was in every newspaper, with a *portrait*; and at present—speaking for myself—I do not care to go about and meet my neighbours. However, dear Mrs. Paget-Taylor is, as usual, a wonderful consoler and a tower of strength. By this day month, at the latest, we shall look for your arrival. I see that the *Malwa* sails on the 27th.

"Your affectionate aunt,
"Wilhelmina Lingard."

I did not read *this* letter over three times, but giving way to one of my childish passions I tore it into little bits, and then, while the fit was still upon me, sat down and dashed off what I have no doubt was considered a most intemperate reply. I refused absolutely to return to England, and said that I was satisfied to take my place beside Ronnie and be repudiated by the family; their money I did not want—and I remained faithfully, Eva Lingard.

Thus I was now cut off from my few relations, and had, with my own hands, barred the doors of Torrington.

CHAPTER XXVII
DARK DAYS

Without a day's delay I sent down to Higginbotham's in Madras and ordered a large supply of books. When these arrived I scribbled in some of them in French, hoping that Ronnie might discover my messages. I implored him to make the best of everything (as I was doing), not to lose heart, but to look forward to better days when we would be always together. I assured him that as soon as permitted I would go to see him, and that I was "keeping up," and he must do the same. Then I packed up the parcel and dispatched it to the jail by a coolie, with a note to the superintendent reminding him of his promise to allow me to add to the library. I had written as cheerfully as I could, but though I assured Ronnie that I was "keeping up," I regret to say this was not the truth. In spite of the consolations offered by Kip and Mrs. de Castro, I was abjectly miserable, a wraith of my former self. My face looked small and pinched and my eyes were sore from secret weeping, for always in my mind I saw Ronnie's expression of absolute despair, and ever in my ears sounded the "chink, chink, chink" of the convicts' irons.

Such was my depression that Mrs. de Castro was roused to what were, for her, desperate and expensive remedies. Almost every afternoon she hired a second-class gharry from the bazaar, and carried me out to "eat the air." Once we drove down to the celebrated Lal Bagh, those beautiful gardens, said to have been laid out by Hyder Ali. I confess that I enjoyed this excursion, although I skulked in out-of-the-way paths, for fear of meeting some of the fashionable European community. Mrs. de Castro understood this attitude; her sympathy was full of insight, and our future drives were in directions where one was not likely to come across any of the gay world from the cantonments. We went expeditions to Cleveland Town and round the Ulsoor Tank, but the cantonment bazaar and shops were a magnet that proved irresistible to my companion. Many a half-hour I would sit in the gharry, whilst she bargained over a couple of yards of calico, a bar of soap, or a tin of biscuits—speaking Tamil as her native tongue.

If she came off best these proceedings afforded her as much pleasure as if she had been to a play or a concert, possibly more. Her haunts were not the modern European emporium, but out-of-the-way streets and alleys near the grain market, and the Arale-Petta—both busy scenes of bartering and traffic.

Occasionally I accompanied her into these places, and whilst she chaffered, what strange discoveries I made, as I poked round in the dim interiors! Sometimes it was piles of ancient "tinned" soups and vegetables, that may have been on the premises for half a century; sometimes it was dusty piles of old books, broken furniture, spotted prints, chairs with the stuffing coming out, the remains of chandeliers (so dear to the Oriental heart), and now and then a really good piece of furniture, such as a Chippendale seat, or a French mirror, covered with dust and cobwebs—possibly wondering what *they* were doing in *cette galère*.

These expeditions were no doubt undertaken for my health and with a view to raising my spirits, but I cannot say that they accomplished their object. Now and then we walked in the Cubbon Park, and every Sunday I accompanied my landlady to church. In the mornings, as I exercised Kipper along the least frequented roads, although I was plainly and even shabbily dressed, I noticed that people stared hard at me. In India, stray and solitary females are exceptional. There one belongs to a family and household, and is bound to have some *raison d'être* for residing in the country. To meet a strange English girl, whose appearance was unfamiliar, at bandstand or social gatherings, and who had apparently no other companion than a fox-terrier, gave those who encountered me legitimate reason to stare and to wonder.

Many inquiries were made by Mrs. de Castro's circle. It was evident from her disclosures that they were not entirely satisfied with her tales of my eccentricity and book writing. I promptly realised that the less mystery about me in our household the better. I had no objection to associating with Mrs. de Castro's neighbours and set, and made it my business of an afternoon to come into the veranda and help to make coffee and conversation, and to hand about "hoppers" and rock cakes. After all, it was the least I could do in acknowledgment of my hostess's well-meant kindnesses, such as the drives to the bazaar, and the packets of peppermint, the little bunches of monthly roses and oleanders with which she endowed me. I could not take an active part in discussing bazaar prices, nor enjoy succulent particulars of the whims and shortcomings of other ladies and their families in Infantry Lines and St. John's Hill. It was a matter of indifference to me, nor was I in the least excited to learn that "Mrs. Captain Watson had had five ayahs in a fortnight," but on the subject of dress my foot was more or less upon my native heath, and I was in a position to offer Mrs. Sergeant Mullins and Mrs. Conductor Cooper some really useful information; I was also prepared to lend them a pattern blouse and "the new skirt." By this generosity I captured their hearts!

"You're not very dressy, and you don't go out much yourself," remarked Mrs. Batt, the wife of a retired sapper—a nice-looking elderly woman, with sharp grey eyes and an assertive manner—to me, one of the most formidable of the company.

"No," I replied, returning her challenge, and looking her straight in the face; "Mrs. de Castro may possibly have told you that I have come to Bangalore for complete quiet and retirement. I know no one here, which under the circumstances is the greatest advantage. I have lately experienced an overwhelming sorrow."

Mrs. Batt coolly inspected me up and down; no, I was not wearing mourning.

"And," I continued, "I am not disposed to return to England—at present."

I believe this statement satisfied the company. With one consent they very naturally attributed my melancholy and reserve to a love affair that had gone wrong, which idea after all had a substantial basis—my love affair *had* gone wrong—but, unfortunately, that was only a part of my trouble. It is an undeniable fact that all womenkind are interested in affairs of the heart, and my new acquaintances accorded me their unspoken sympathy. For this I had no doubt to thank their natural kind-heartedness, but perhaps my generosity in the matter of advice and patterns may have had a little weight. In future, however, Mrs. de Castro was no longer submitted to the "question torture." I was received as an acknowledged member of her set, and she was left in peace. I made myself as useful to my landlady as possible; read her the *Bangalore Herald* from end to end, wrote her notes, played draughts and trimmed her Sunday toque. Considering our respective ages, education and station, we really got on together amazingly well. She had been most loyal to me. I can never forget how once, when Mrs. Cotton touched upon my tragedy, and began: "They *do* say there's an English officer in the jail—such a handsome fellow too——" she cleverly turned the subject with a fresh and startling scandal. I had impressed upon her that if any of the military people—who of course were aware of my brother's fate—came to dream of my presence in Bangalore I would depart within the hour. I was quite sure, I added, that if they *did* know they would be only too kind to me, but their kindness, however well meant, I should not yet be able to endure. My wound was still so raw that I shrank from even a touch of sympathy.

The *dâk-wallah's* arrival with his big brown wallet invariably excited my interest. From time to time he brought me letters from Mrs. Lakin. On one occasion her dispatch was so heavy as to require five annas postage, as it enclosed others. One was from Captain Hayes-Billington, to tell me that his wife had passed away. It was apparently written in great distress, the thin cheap paper blistered with tears:

> "She asked me to be sure and let *you* know; Dulcie was always fond of you. Ever since she came down here she has been failing, and by degrees just faded away out of life. She was glad to go—but *I* am heart-broken."

Mrs. Lakin, who was my constant correspondent, announced in her letter that they were leaving Secunderabad immediately:

> "My dear, such an uprooting after thirty years in India! I cannot bear to think of how our poor household gods will be scattered. Some, such as the Deschamps furniture, I intend to take home; some I shall send to the girls. One of them will give the old chestnut horse a stall and a feed. I have endowed my ayah and butler with a cow apiece, and distributed my poultry among the women in the lines—but what am I to do about your letters? I enclose two. How are your correspondents to find you? Here it is generally believed that you have returned to London; even Mrs. Soames is off the scent. She intends when the regiment does go home to look up your relatives and discover your whereabouts."

Mrs. de Castro was always gratified when I had a letter from "Miss Lucy," as she still called her. The letter invariably contained kind messages to "Jane."

"It seems only the other day since she came out to India," she remarked (when I told her the news), "and now she's going home for good. I remember her, such a slim young lady with lovely blue eyes and curly hair. It was not long before Mr. Lakin fell in love with her. He was only a lieutenant in a Madras Native Infantry regiment, but in spite of all her father and mother could say (and they said a *lot*) she would have him; and they took a little bungalow at thirty rupees a month at St. John's Hill. Well, the match didn't turn out so badly after all. Colonel Lakin will have a good pension, and after their long spell out here they'll enjoy themselves in England."

Before Mrs. Lakin returned to "enjoy herself in England" she enclosed me another letter, which was from Brian. It said:

> "My darling Eva,—You are making me miserable. I cannot understand why you do not write to me, and I have no idea where you are, so send this to care of your good friend Mrs.

Lakin. Probably you are hiding in some little hill station, for the hot weather will by this time be upon you. But why hide from *me*? Why not trust me as I trust you? I had an anonymous epistle from Secunderabad recently, announcing that you had been seen driving all over the place in Balthasar's motor, and that it was well known that you had actually left the place in his company. I need not tell you that I didn't believe one word of this. I put the poisonous letter in the fire and would have liked to do the same with the writer! You will probably have seen the announcement of my father's death in the papers; he passed away a fortnight ago; to the last we had hopes. My mother is completely broken down, and I have no end of family matters to get through. Only for my mother's health, and most urgent business, I would go out to India in the place of this letter. Last week I motored over to Torrington, thinking that I might glean news of you, but I was astonished to find that you were as much in their black books as your brother. I wonder what you have been doing, Eva? I asked the question point blank, but as our engagement has never been given out, they evidently thought me guilty of unpardonable cheek, and implied that their family affairs were no business of mine—they let me see it too! They are taking the court martial, etc., terribly to heart, and are going abroad for six months with the idea of living the whole thing down. If they didn't make so much of it themselves, other people would soon let it drop. I hear from Secunderabad from time to time; the general impression there seems to be that you are in England. I am told that the Lakins are coming home, so that I can no longer write to you to their address. Surely you will answer *this*!

"Your, as always, devoted and faithful
"Brian."

I was much surprised one afternoon to see a carriage and pair drive under our porch—Mrs. de Castro's visitors came in gharries or on foot. She rushed to me with a scared face, waving a visiting card in her hand.

"It's Mrs. Hodson, the wife of the superintendent of the jail; she's asking to see you!"

All sorts of dreadful visions passed through my mind. Could Ronnie be dead, and had she come to break the news?

"Show her into my little room," I said—one of the bare apartments I had fixed up with a writing-table, a few cheap chairs and a couple of rugs. Here I sat, read, and worked—nothing would induce me to frequent the dismal drawing-room.

Presently Mrs. Hodson was ushered in; a plain pale woman, with a long thoughtful face and a pleasant smile.

"I hope you won't think that I have taken a liberty," she said, "but my husband thought that perhaps you might like to make my acquaintance."

"It is most kind of you," I murmured; "won't you sit down?"

"You do not know anyone here, nor wish to know them, I understand, but still perhaps you will make an exception of me. You might like to come up and sit in our lovely garden and feel that you are near him, and that we are always ready to befriend you both."

"You are *very* kind," I repeated. "Can you tell me how he is?"

"Yes, he is more resigned. Since he has had your message and those books you sent to the library he seems more cheerful, and is no longer losing weight. As he is steady they have made him a convict warder, so now the rules are relaxed. You will be able to see him to-morrow afternoon, and I will send the carriage for you."

I was so overpowered by this unexpected news that for a moment I could not speak.

"There was a fortnight yet," I stammered at last.

"That is true, but a convict warder has privileges, and sees his friends oftener than once in three months. You look so white and sad, I wonder if you would care to come for a drive with me? Yes, and we will take your dog, and go up past the racecourse along the Nundy Droog Road, where you will get plenty of air, and scarcely meet a soul."

"I should like it immensely," I said, springing up, "and I'll fetch my hat."

As I left the room, I nearly collided with Mrs. de Castro, who was bearing in with her own hands a tray of cakes and coffee. There was no avoiding this refreshment, and I could see that she was extremely proud of entertaining the wife of the jail superintendent in her own house.

I enjoyed that drive more than anything for a very long time. The fresh air and the swift motion revived me. How different from rumbling along in a gharry with my landlady, who preferred excursions into the bazaar, or down St. John's Hill, and had no taste whatever for the open country! We passed cheery parties of riders coming from the racecourse; among them I recognised a man I had seen at Silliram, and hastily turned away my face. Mrs. Hodson was not a steady talker like Mrs. Soames, or my former self, but she opened her mind to me and took me into her confidence.

"In one way you and I are both in the same boat," she said. "You shrink from society because of your brother's trouble—society shrinks from me because I, an Englishwoman, and well born, have married a Eurasian or Anglo-Indian, as they are now called. I have never, never regretted the step, excepting that it cuts me off from women of my own class. They will talk to me, and even come to my house, and admire my garden, but between us all the time a great gulf is fixed. I was a governess out here; my health broke down, and I was almost penniless when Richard Hodson came to my rescue—or rather his sister did. Ultimately we were married, and in my way I am happy. If I had one or two real women friends I'd have nothing left to wish for. At first the jail and the convicts depressed me. The 'chink, chink, chink' of the irons moving to and fro about the garden got on my nerves, but now I do not seem to hear them! To-morrow you must come and see my garden. I wanted so much to have your brother to work in it; it's healthier and more interesting than making gunny bags, but when my husband spoke to him he said that nothing would induce him to show himself out of doors."

The next afternoon Mrs. Hodson's pretty victoria arrived to carry me to the jail. My heart was thumping hard as we drove along, and when I got out and was received by the superintendent I was trembling so much that I could scarcely walk. However, I managed to crawl to the room where prisoners received their friends and there I found Ronnie awaiting me.

At first he bore up wonderfully, but for my part I was so overcome that I could only weep and murmur, "Ronnie! Ronnie!" At last he too broke down. The spectacle of a man crying is inexpressibly tragic. I thrust my own miseries aside and did my utmost to console him. I felt something like a nurse comforting a child that has hurt itself. "What was the use of anything?" he murmured, why look forward? He was branded for life; wherever he went the horror would follow; no nice girl would ever marry *him*! After a time, when we were more collected, he said in his old peremptory style:

"Now you know, Eva, it's all wrong your being out here. I won't allow you to sacrifice yourself for me. You really must and shall go home."

"But I can't go home," I replied, "I've cut myself adrift from Torrington. They said if I remained in India they would drop me altogether, so you see I've burned my boats! Even if I were to humble myself, they would never, never receive me."

"Falkland will receive you," declared my brother, "you have not sent him one of your fiery letters?"

"I have never sent him any letter at all."

"How's that? You have done one mad thing in pitching your tent at Bangalore, although I know it has been for my sake. You will be still madder if you break off with Falkland, who honestly is a rattling good fellow. If only I'd taken his hints and pulled up a bit I wouldn't be here now, a disgrace to myself and to you."

"Never mind me," I protested, "but tell me how you are getting on?"

"How can I get on until I get out?" he replied with a touch of his former manner. "I still have to serve one year eight months and two days. I must say the superintendent is a white man, although his colour *is* a bit dusky. He keeps me as much apart from the rabble as he can, and now I've promotion I am a sort of official myself. When I first came here, Sis, if I'd seen any means of committing suicide I'd have taken my own life. I was so hopelessly, abjectly miserable; the more I thought, the worse I felt; but do you know, one day, when I was in the very deepest depths of black despair in the labour yard, I distinctly heard your voice calling me, and that gave me a wonderful 'buck up,' and reminded me that I wasn't altogether alone in the world."

I debated in my own mind whether I would tell him that he had really heard me or not, and I decided against it. Somehow I instinctively felt that he would hate to know that I had witnessed him doing hard labour in company with thieves and murderers.

"Did you find my little notes in the books?" I asked. "Writing in that way was, I know, deceitful, but I hoped you would come across some of my scribbling."

"Yes, I did, rather—and that cheered me no end. Knowing that you were in the station, and that I would see you, raised me out of the Slough of Despond."

"There," I exclaimed, "so I *was* right to come after all!"

"Do you know anybody in the station?" he inquired.

"No, not a soul! I lie low all the time. I associate with Mrs. de Castro's friends—sergeants' wives and the wives of telegraph clerks, and so on."

"Mrs. de Castro's friends!" he exclaimed.

"Yes, and I like them," I said, "they know that I have some trouble and are most truly kind and sympathetic. It's a very good thing to see another side of life."

"By Jove, Eva, you have seen a good many sides of life, what with Beke, the old professor, and Mrs. Hayes-Billington, and now *my* crash—your experience has been extraordinarily varied."

"I said that I know nobody here, and no one knows me, but the other Sunday in church I thought I caught a glimpse of Sally Payne. I don't think she recognised me, and I sneaked out before the sermon. She *has* been here, because in reading the *Bangalore Herald* I saw among the list of guests at the West End Hotel, 'Miss Payne and maid.' I was always fond of Sally," I added, "and I think she liked me. Do you remember we arrived in Secunderabad on the very same day?"

"I wish she could take you out of Bangalore," said Ronnie. "Because my life is spoiled there is no reason that yours should be. You have helped me over the first bad bit, and I shall rub along all right now. If I have any luck I might get something taken off my sentence. The superintendent talked about putting me in the office to do the jail accounts, but I'd rather have my present job. I'm more independent, and I'd hate having to sit and write all day long."

"Are they troublesome, your ward?" I asked.

"No, not with me. You see, I understand order and discipline from being in the Service. I stand no nonsense, and soon wheel them into line, but they *are* a rough lot. Some such powerful murderous-looking brutes."

I was telling Ronnie about the superintendent's wife, how she had taken me out to drive, and invited me to sit in her garden as often as I liked, when a warder entered, salaamed, and said:

"Sorry, Miss Sahib—the time is up."

CHAPTER XXVIII
HYDER ALI'S GARDEN

My new acquaintances, Mr. and Mrs. Hodson, were both very kind to me; she frequently called to take me for a drive into the country (Hibbal way). Afterwards we sat in her delightful garden with its spreading grass plots, clumps of bamboo and loquat trees, and profusion of English flowers. The sole drawback to this Elysium was the presence of convicts, clanking to and fro, as they watered and worked among the vegetables; but I suppose in time one grows accustomed to anything—as it is said of poor eels, with respect to their skins!

Thanks to Mr. Hodson, I had several private interviews with Ronnie. I was permitted to give him cigarettes, and to supply him with papers. He no longer gave way to an unreasoning frenzy of despair, but was more like his former self; his eyes had their old boyish look, and had lost their dull, glazed appearance. I had now been four months at Bangalore; the time had crawled like centuries, and as I gazed into my glass I told myself that I was almost unrecognisable. Undoubtedly the shocks I had received since I left England had told upon my appearance. My face was white and very thin, and my hair, of which I had once been rather proud, looked lank and dead. After all, although I kept up a certain amount of cheerfulness with Mrs. de Castro and her friends, I sometimes wondered that I was still alive. No one but myself knew of the nights and nights when I lay awake for hours or paced about my room. The weather was hot and I would have much preferred to walk in the compound, but for my not unnatural fear of snakes and bandicoots. A want of sleep, want of appetite, and a want of hope were my three chief ailments. I had to bear up against not one, but *two* heavy troubles. The overwhelming disgrace of my brother and the collapse of our little home; the cruelty of relations who had closed their ears to our appeals. Sometimes, with a sort of rage, I told myself that had Uncle cabled out the money to Ronnie, he would have saved him in time. Here was surely a sufficient load for one pair of shoulders. But besides all this, a grief that affected me even more acutely was the loss of my lover; this was a personal ache that nothing could deaden or alleviate. It had been my own fault that our correspondence had lapsed, but to what could it have tended after all?

Brian and I could never be anything to one another. He was naturally the soul of generosity and chivalry, but we would have to face the Falkland family, public opinion and general discredit. How could Lady Louisa—said to be the incarnation of pride—receive a daughter-in-law whose brother was a convict, the subject of a notorious military scandal? Much as Brian might care for me, I could never be anything but a millstone round his neck.

Sometimes my feelings got the better of my convictions, and an intolerable longing surged up in my heart. At night I would sit down and pour out my soul in long letters. These letters gave me a wonderful amount of temporary relief, but when I read them over in the cool light of morning I invariably destroyed them. I had not had a line from Brian for more than six weeks, and such is the perversity of human nature, now that he had ceased to write to me I felt an almost irrepressible temptation to write to him! Nevertheless I did not yield to it, though I often debated the question—to write or not to write? Even if I wrote, and assured him, as before, that all was at an end between us, but that I was in Bangalore, and would be glad to hear from him occasionally—to what good would this tend? It was far better and wiser to drop entirely out of his life, but this resolve did not conduce to happiness or even consolation.

Kipper's spirits were undoubtedly affected by my own condition of hopeless depression—it may have been the effect of a brain wave—but at any rate whenever we took our walks abroad he no longer bounded exuberantly in front of me, barking from purest *joie de vivre*, and challenging all creation from lizards to camels. Now he kept sedately to heel like a sober elderly dog, obviously on duty and in sole charge of an elderly mistress. When indoors he lay motionless beside my chair or bed, following my movements with anxious and adoring eyes, and occasionally heaving tremendous sighs.

He found his simple relaxation in killing bandicoots (a rat-like creature with a blunt repulsive face) and in the visits of the tall yellow and white pariah, who lived next door. I must confess that this intimacy filled me with amazement. At Beke, Kipper had kept coldly aloof from the society of his own kind, and had cruelly and even painfully snubbed the advances of second-rate dogs. If these could but behold him now!—abandoned to the fascination and blandishments of a hideous spotted alien, resembling a low class overgrown lurcher; rolling with him luxuriously in the dust, running mad puppy circles, and playing hide and seek among the shrubs and oleander bushes in Mrs. de Castro's compound! I will say this for Kipper, he never returned the visits of his playfellow, and had still some lingering sense of *les convenances* and etiquette for "Europe" terriers.

Once, when the "Pi" had the audacity to join us in our walk, and came prancing towards us with a "Hallo, well met!" expression on his cunning long face, Kipper realised that he must draw the line here, and after a word or two in nosy dog talk, the intruder accepted a hint, and disappeared.

One evening we had been for a constitutional far beyond the high ground and racecourse, and I returned to the de Castro bungalow dusty, thirsty and tired, looking forward, I confess, to a good cup of Neilgherry tea. As we entered the veranda, Kip stood for a second motionless, and then flew like a wild creature into the cave-like drawing-room, and I said to myself:

"The Pi is there, lying in wait for him! He must *not* be allowed into the house."

I was about to follow and eject the intruder, when Mrs. de Castro came forward in a state of unusual excitement and with much nodding and gesticulation informed me in a mysterious whisper:

"A lame gentleman has called to see you. He came in a motor. I told him that you were out, but he said he would wait; and he has been sitting in the drawing-room for more than an hour."

"Unfortunate wretch!" I thought to myself, "who can it be?"

Well, there was no use in speculating, I would soon see. Perhaps some friend of Ronnie's? As I entered the drawing-room—which was dim even at noonday—a tall man, leaning on a stick, came hobbling towards me, and as he approached the door I saw, to my stupefaction, that it was *Brian*!

"Eva," he exclaimed, "so I have found you!"

I was so overwhelmed with astonishment and joy that I was obliged to sit down, and then, like the poor, weak fool that I was, I immediately began to cry. Brian drew up a chair beside me, seated himself, and gripped my nearest hand.

"You did not suppose," he said, "that I was going to allow you to slip out of my life like that, did you? I told you once upon a time that I was tenacious. I did not tell you then, but I say to you now, that the day we met on Slackland's Flats—looking into your eyes, I beheld my destiny—and to my destiny I hold fast. I would have been here six weeks ago or less, but I was smashed up in a motor accident—concussion and a broken leg—simple fracture—and so they kept me in a nursing home, whether I liked it or not. As soon as I could stand I escaped and came out by the mail—and here I am!"

"How did you find me?" I faltered.

"Tell me first, are you glad to see me—as glad as Kipper?"

"Yes," I answered, "so very, very glad—though your coming can make no difference in one way. Do tell me how you found that I was in Bangalore?"

"It was through that little brick, Sally Payne. She is as sharp as they make 'em, and she had an idea that, instead of burying yourself in a hill station, or going home, you had followed your brother down to Bangalore. She said it would be so like you—and she was right. Sally saw you on her way to the Neilgherries; she stayed here for a few days looking about. She heard from her maid, who heard from her ayah, who heard it in the bazaar, that 'a tall young English lady lodging in Infantry Lines had apparently no friends—and there was something mysterious about her.' Then one Sunday she caught sight of you in church, and cabled to me at once; and now, Eva, I suppose you understand that I have come out on purpose to take you home?"

"No, no!" I protested; "I cannot desert Ronnie. Think of it—how could I!"

"From what I know of Ronnie he will never agree to such an unnecessary sacrifice. How is he getting on?"

"At first he wanted to kill himself, but since he has seen me he has recovered a little. The superintendent is as lenient and thoughtful as he dare venture; and, after all, a European prisoner, especially if he is well behaved and gives no trouble, may have a little more margin than, say, a murderer from the West Coast. Ronnie is now a convict warder. I saw him three days ago, and he seemed to be in better spirits."

"I wonder if I may be allowed to visit him?"

"Oh, yes, I am sure you may."

"I am also sure, from what I know of your brother, that he has no wish for you to remain in this country. Come now, answer me—tell me the truth—what does he say?"

"He urges me to return to England, but I know I am a comfort to him. Even if I would go Torrington is closed to me. They gave me my choice of remaining here, or having a home with them. Aunt Mina wrote that if I stayed in India on Ronnie's account they washed their hands of me for ever and ever."

"But, my dear Eva, Torrington is not the *only* home that is open to you in England. What about mine?"

"And your people, and your mother?" I asked.

"My mother sees eye to eye with me in this. I have brought you a letter from her. She knows all about you, and admires your devotion, as you will see. Now, my dear Eva, I should like to see *you*. This room is nearly pitch dark, and, by Jove!—what a room it is! But apparently your old landlady thinks no end of it; she has been sitting here part of the time to keep me company, and has told me the price of every single piece of furniture. She also told me, what interests me far more, that she is very fond of you, and what was a shock—that she does not think you are long for this world! Now call a fellow to bring lamps; I should like to be able to judge for myself!"

In two or three minutes our factotum staggered in with a lamp in each hand. As soon as he had hung one on the wall, placed the other on the round table, and enjoyed a thoroughly exhaustive stare at Brian, he withdrew.

"Now," said my companion, "take off your hat."

As I removed it unquestioningly and faced him in silence, I saw his eyes open, his lips close tightly; there was not the slightest doubt that the awful change in my appearance had administered a shock! I was painfully conscious that of my former prettiness not a trace remained. Brian rose, stick in hand, turned his back upon me, and limped towards the door. Yes, I was a wreck—apparently the sight had been too overwhelming; but surely he was not about to leave me like *that*? I hurried after him, and discovered that it was merely a manœuvre to conceal his emotion.

"My poor little girl," he murmured in a broken voice, "every word of the whole terrible story is written in your face."

He gathered me into his arms, and for once I shed tears of happiness.

CHAPTER XXIX
THE ORDER OF RELEASE

Hospitable Mrs. de Castro gave Brian a pressing invitation to remain to dinner and share "pot luck," represented, as I happened to know, by brain cutlets and Bombay toast—no fare for an invalid. He was about to accept with effusion, when he caught my swift signal of unqualified horror and murmured a polite excuse. At half-past seven a motor brought his man-servant to escort him to the West End Hotel, and he departed with reluctance, assuring me that he "would be round first thing in the morning."

"My, but that gentleman do set store by you," announced Mrs. de Castro, as soon as he was out of sight. "All the questions he asked about your health! I told him as your hair was falling in handsful, enough to stuff a cushion, and you could not abide your food, and your dress bodies were taken in inches round the waist, and the skirts just a-slipping off you. My word, but he was in a way. He says he has come to take you home."

"Oh no, Mrs. de Castro," I protested with emphasis. "I shall stay here."

"How could you have the heart to say no to a fellow with such lovely eyes? I'm sure *I* never could—and he was just counting the weary time till you come back, looking at his watch every two minutes. Well, I'm thinking you have a hard heart. Your brother has had his turn—has the other no claim?"

The next morning Brian had a long interview with Ronnie—our good friend Mr. Hodson being present—and when in the early afternoon we went for a motor drive Brian told me the gist of their conference.

"Ronnie is anxious for you to return to England with me. On this point he and I are absolutely agreed," announced my companion. "I have assured him that I shall pull every string I can reach to get his sentence reduced. I may be mistaken, but I have an impression that three months' hard labour for a gentleman means as much as six to a working coolie, and I am sure the indignity bites in ten times more deeply. As soon as Ronnie is released we will give him a real good start in the colonies. Meanwhile the Hodsons will keep a kindly eye on him, and he will feel that you and I are working like niggers on his behalf."

This conversation took place as we sped into the open country, and Brian said:

"I am doing all the talking. What has happened to my prize chatterbox?"

"Neither a prize nor a chatterbox now," I replied.

"Well, I hope you will return to your old form. Already you look a shade better, and you have laughed once. Have you read my mother's letter?"

"I have indeed. It is too, too kind—I shall treasure it always."

"She *is* a dear old Mum, I must say! Well now, shall we turn round and go to the Lal Bagh?"

"Yes, if you like, but why the Lal Bagh?"

"My father often talked of it when he had a reminiscent fit. He was quartered here forty-three years ago. His regiment was the Blue Hussars; their band played at the Lal Bagh, and all the beauty and fashion processed about like peacocks."

"No beauty and fashion are to be seen there now, only nurses and soldiers and Eurasians—except on show days, at long intervals. Polo and golf and the club have combined to write 'Ichabod' over the Lal Bagh."

"Well, let us go and see it all the same. I'd like to walk, or rather hobble, round in the pater's footsteps."

The Lal Bagh, or Red Garden, said to have been laid out by Hyder Ali, is an immense straggling enclosure, full of wonderful exotic plants and great trees shading long walks; it also contains many cages of wild animals.

This exhibition never appealed to me. I always felt so sorry for the animals; they looked, as a rule, hungry and miserable. We turned, therefore, in another direction and I gave my arm to Brian, who leant on me and his stick. Presently we found our way to the terrace and a seat. Here there was no one to disturb our *tête-à-tête*. We were entirely surrounded by the beauties of Nature; a wonderful profusion of sweet-scented flowering creepers, these and the palms, ferns, and forest trees in Hyder Ali's old garden seemed to envelop us in an atmosphere of enchantment and peace.

There was the blazing "Sally Bindon," the "Flame of the Jungle," the yellow Burmese forest flower, and the rose-pink "Antigone," with its clusters of blossoms, each and all draping trees and walls in our immediate vicinity. The cloudless sky was of a deep turquoise blue, the air soft and balmy, bulbuls sang in the rose bushes, brilliant butterflies and dragon-flies darted to and fro; the silence was languorous with serenity and ecstasy. We were in another world, far, far away from shame, disgrace and misery. As I

When we drove under the lattice-work porch I was amazed to find Mrs. Hodson on the steps. At a second glance I saw that she looked paler than ever and was evidently unnerved.

"There has been an accident to your brother," she began the instant the car stopped, "and I have come to fetch you," pointing to where her victoria was drawn up at the side of the bungalow.

"We can all go up in the motor," said Brian promptly, "it will take us there in five minutes. Please get in, Mrs. Hodson," and he made room for her.

Without a second's hesitation she accepted his offer, sat down beside me, and seized my hand. Then I knew for certain that the matter was serious; people invariably took me by the hand when tragedy was approaching.

"Tell me," I whispered with dry lips.

"We have been searching for you since three o'clock. There was a bad outbreak this afternoon in your brother's ward. Several notorious characters fell upon others with whom they had a blood feud; they fought with their spades and mallets, and one powerful brute, a Moplah, wrenched off his irons and battered a warder to death. Your brother fought like ten heroes — so much for an English gentleman! Finally he overpowered the ringleader, but a cowardly blow on the back of his head struck him to the ground at the very moment when the riot was quelled. I am afraid Captain Lingard is badly hurt; he is in the infirmary, and besides the jail doctor we have sent for the civil surgeon. All that is possible has been done. He has a fine constitution and may recover — while there is life, there is hope." She paused for breath and added, inconsequently: "I am thankful that Captain Falkland is here."

For my own part I felt so utterly crushed that I was speechless. A five minutes' run had brought us to the jail, and at the entrance we were met by Mr. Hodson. We followed him in dead silence into the infirmary, and there, on a low cot behind a screen, we found Ronnie. One glance was sufficient to tell me that he had received his death blow. He would very soon be *free*!

Two doctors were with him, a half-caste nurse was hovering about, and the chaplain had been summoned. Yes, these good kind people had done all that was possible. I could see by his eyes that Ronnie recognised me; with an effort he said, in a strange, far-away voice: "It's the order of release, Sis — and the best way out of it."

"No, no, Ronnie, *don't* say that," I protested as I sank on my knees beside him.